VOLUME 1

INVASION OF THE GILFREEM

Story by **Aubrey Sitterson**

Art by **Write Height Media** & **Zack Turner**

Bonus Story
HOME, KAIRU, HOME

Story by **Mike Raicht**

Art by **Dan Ciurczak**

REDAKAI

Volume 1
Invasion of the Gilfreem

Invasion of the Gilfreem
Story by Aubrey Sitterson
Art by Write Height Media & Zack Turner

Home, Kairu, Home
Story by Mike Raicht
Art by Dan Ciurczak
Colors by Chad Walker

Design/Sam Elzway
Editor/Joel Enos

Printed in China

Published by VIZ Media, LLC
P.O. Box 77010
San Francisco, CA 94107

10 9 8 7 6 5 4 3 2 1
First printing, October 2012

www.vizkids.com

PARENTAL ADVISORY
RATED
A
FOR
ALL AGES
REDAKAI is rated A and is
suitable for readers of all ages.
ratings.viz.com

mEDIA
www.viz.com

VOLUME 1
INVASION OF THE GILFREEM

TABLE OF CONTENTS

Gilfreem Space Cruisers

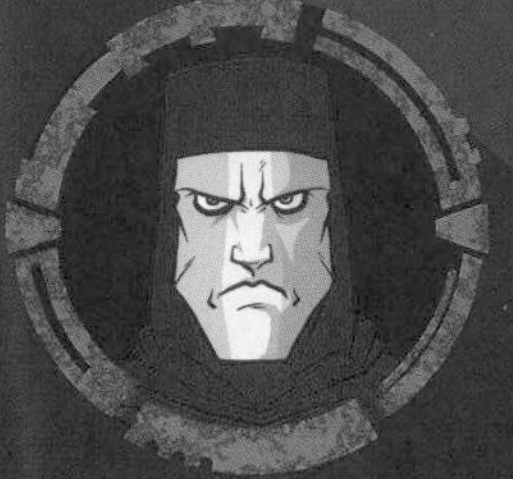

LOKAR

Lokar is the enemy of all Redakai and especially Team Stax. He and Boaddai were friends when they were young warriors, but while Master Boaddai uses his powers for good, Lokar is all evil.

E-TEENS

Lokar has gathered bullies and bad guys from all over the universe to do his bidding and search for more kairu. Though some have been tricked into helping Lokar, most E-Teens strive to be just as evil as Lokar himself. Team Stax has encountered many, and as long as Lokar wants to rule the universe, they'll be meeting even more!

TEAM HIVERAX

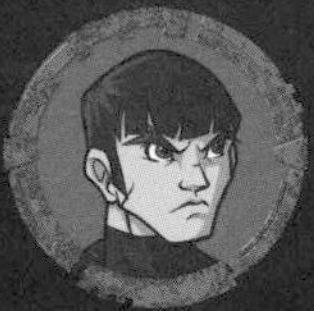

NEXUS

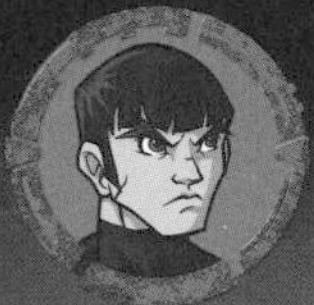

VEXUS

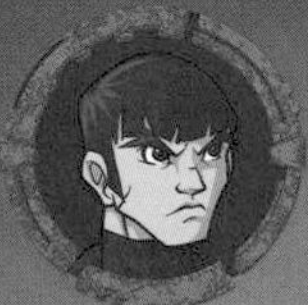

HEXUS

TEAM RADIKOR

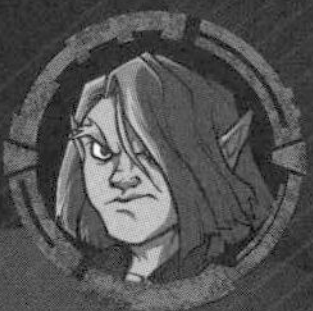

ZANE

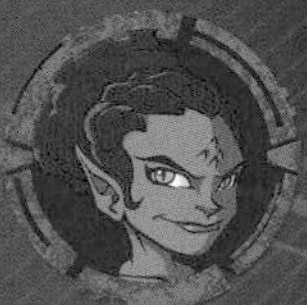

ZAIR

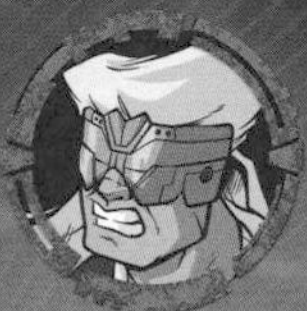

TECHRIS

The Story of Redakai

In the hands of good, the energy known as kairu is a living force that guides the universe. But in the hands of evil, kairu is the most dangerous power you could imagine. Those who learn to wield kairu become kairu warriors.

They can control kairu and harness elemental energies to attack, defend, and even transform into monsters of unimaginable power.

Using an X-Drive to store their kairu energy, and an X-Reader to activate it, both good and bad kairu warriors and masters travel the world in search of more kairu to become powerful enough to join the ranks of the most esteemed of all kairu masters: the Redakai.

CHARACTERS

TEAM STAX

KY

Ky trained with Master Boaddai to become the best warrior he can be. He is now the leader of Team Stax. Ky's father Connor was also a kairu warrior. Ky's signature monster is the plasma powered Metanoid.

MAYA

Maya is the voice of reason and the most levelheaded member of Team Stax. She can sense when kairu is nearby. She's an orphan who was raised like a grand-daughter by Master Boaddai. Her signature monster is Harrier.

BOOMER

Boomer is the brawns and funny-bone of Team Stax. Ky's best friend since they were kids, Boomer left his parents' farm to travel the world with Ky and Maya to find more kairu. His signature monster is Froztok.

MOOKEE

Mookee's planet was destroyed by the evil Lokar during the Great Cataclysm. He's the mechanic and cook for Master Boaddai, though not all his dishes are edible! He's become an important honorary member of Team Stax!

MASTER BOADDAI

Master Boaddai is a wise and powerful Redakal and works hard to train Team Stax in the ways of the kairu warrior. He'll stop at nothing to keep Lokar from getting his hands on more kairu.

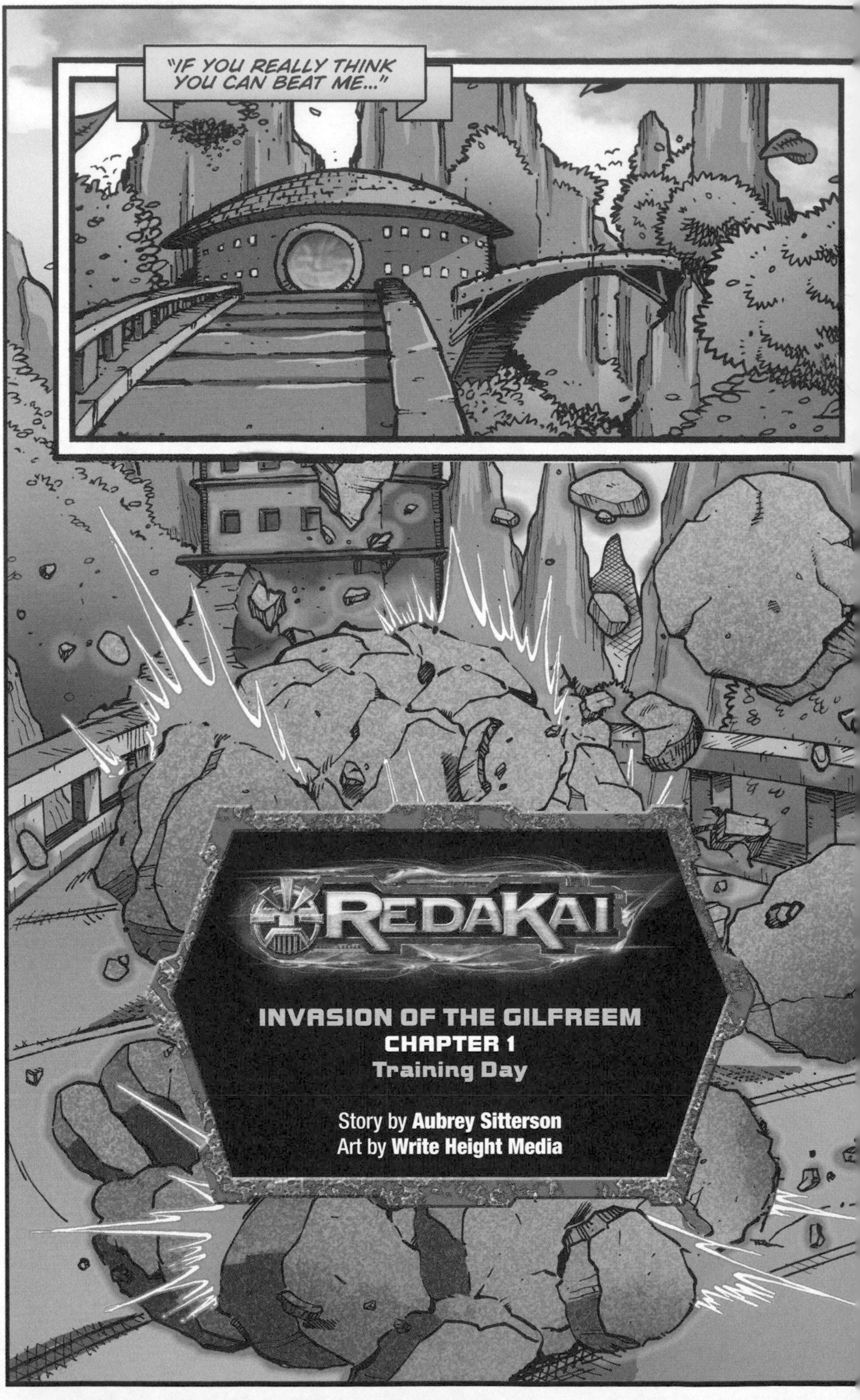
"IF YOU REALLY THINK YOU CAN BEAT ME..."
REDAKAI
INVASION OF THE GILFREEM
CHAPTER 1
Training Day
Story by Aubrey Sitterson
Art by Write Height Media

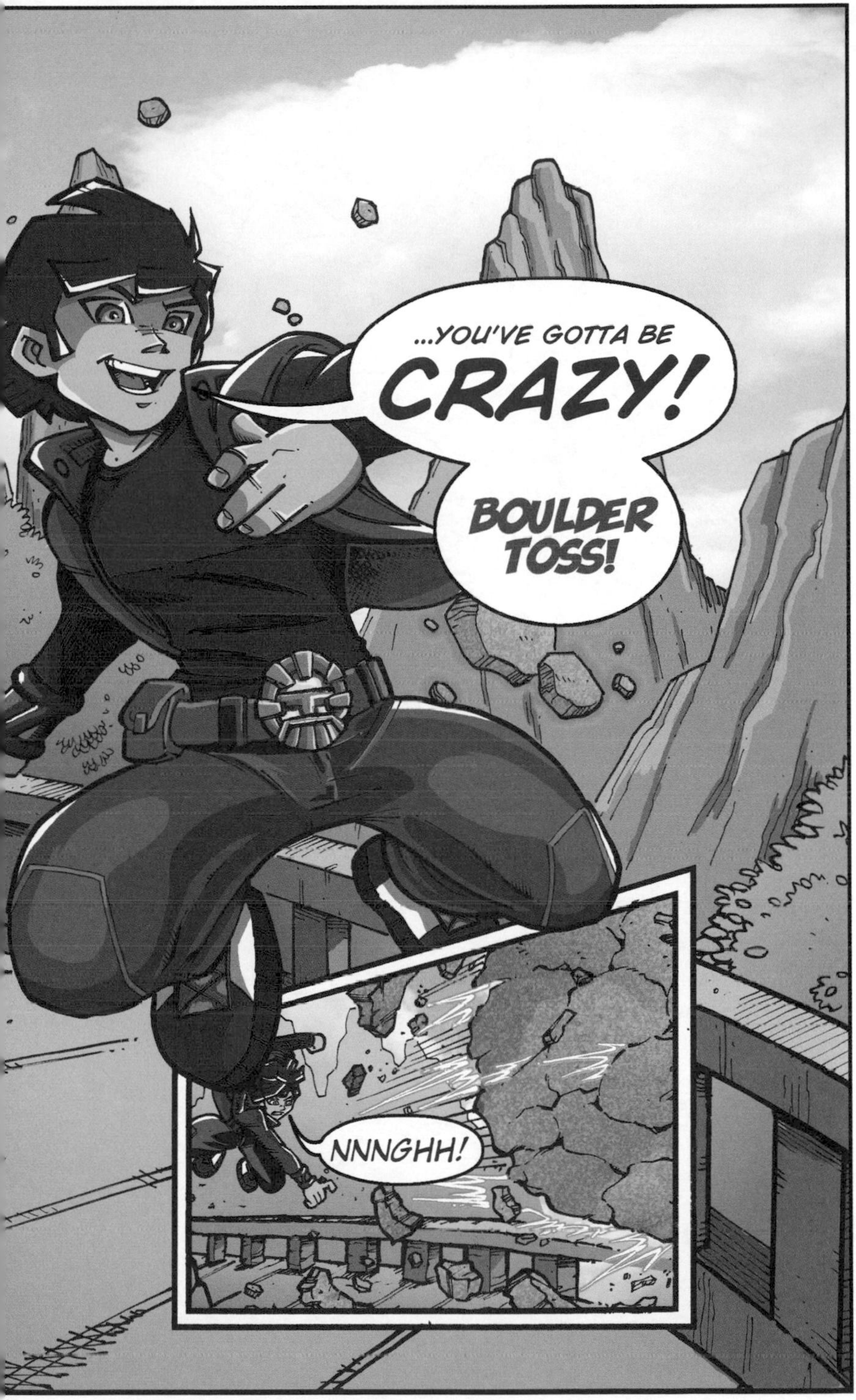
...YOU'VE GOTTA BE
CRAZY!
BOULDER TOSS!
NNNGHH!

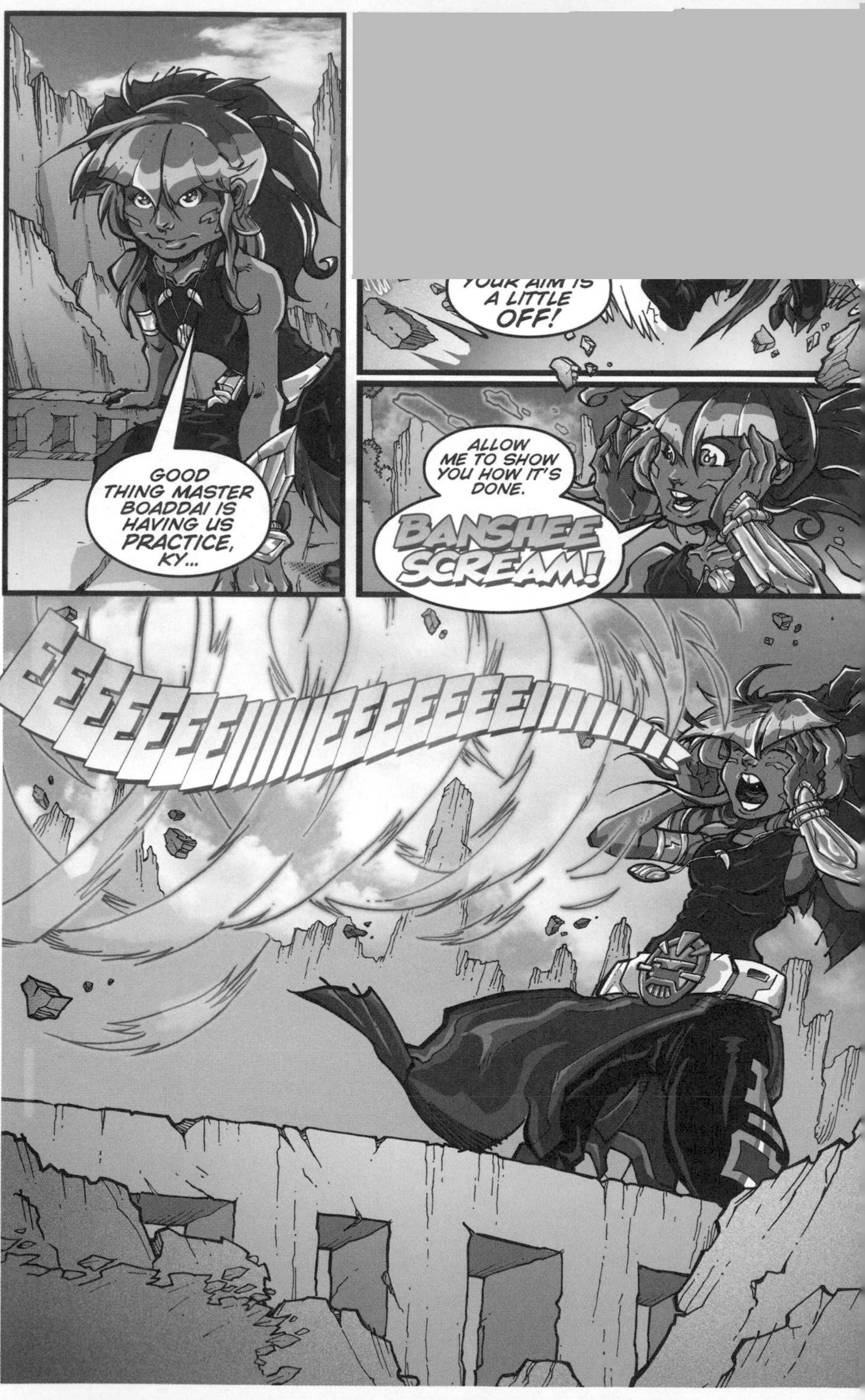
GOOD THING MASTER BOADDAI IS HAVING US PRACTICE, KY...
YOUR AIM IS A LITTLE OFF!
ALLOW ME TO SHOW YOU HOW IT'S DONE.
BANSHEE SCREAM!
EEEEEEIIIIEEEEEEEIIIIIIII

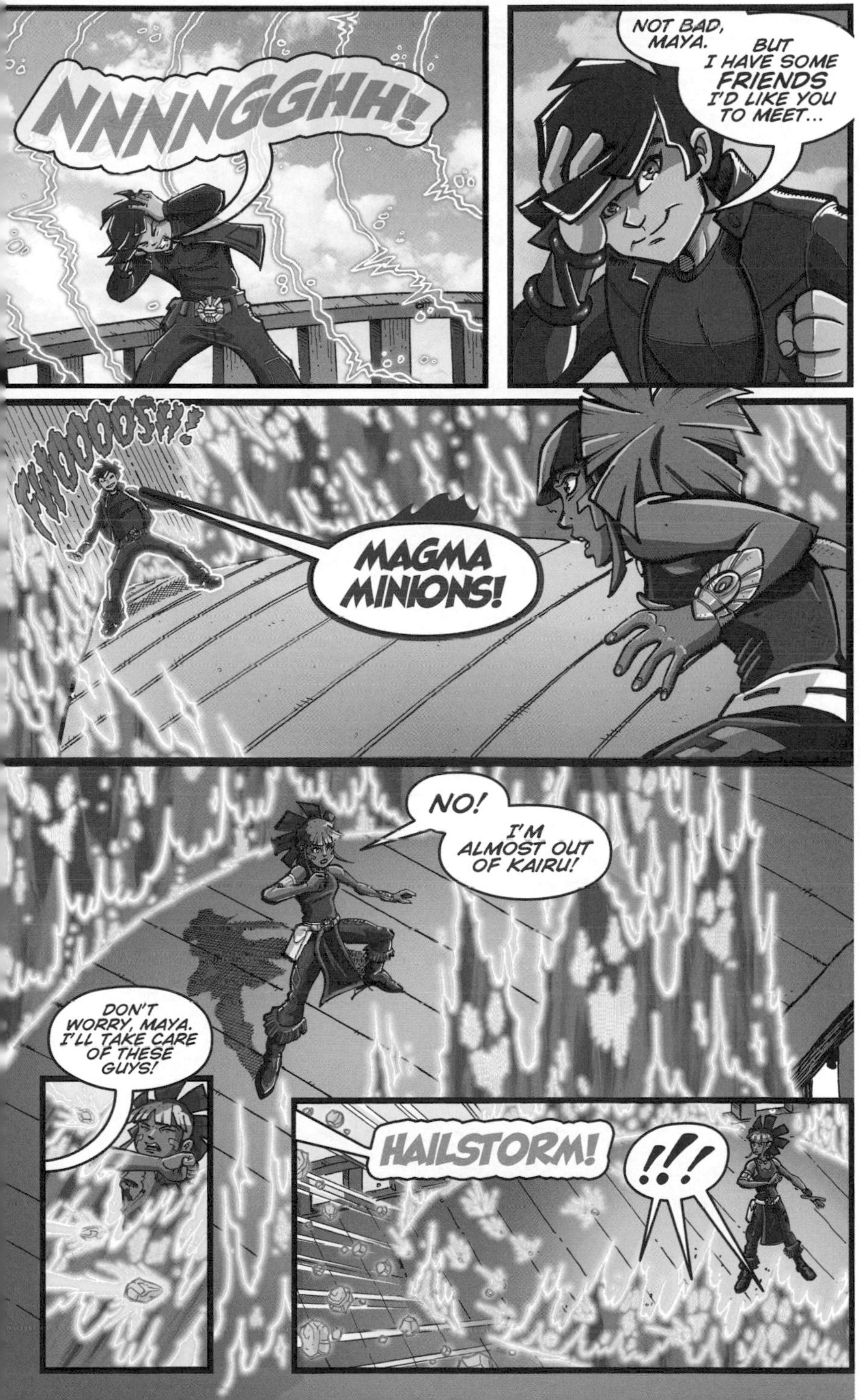
NNNNGGHH!
NOT BAD, MAYA.
BUT I HAVE SOME FRIENDS I'D LIKE YOU TO MEET...
FWOOOOSH!
MAGMA MINIONS!
NO!
I'M ALMOST OUT OF KAIRU!
DON'T WORRY, MAYA. I'LL TAKE CARE OF THESE GUYS!
HAILSTORM!
!!!

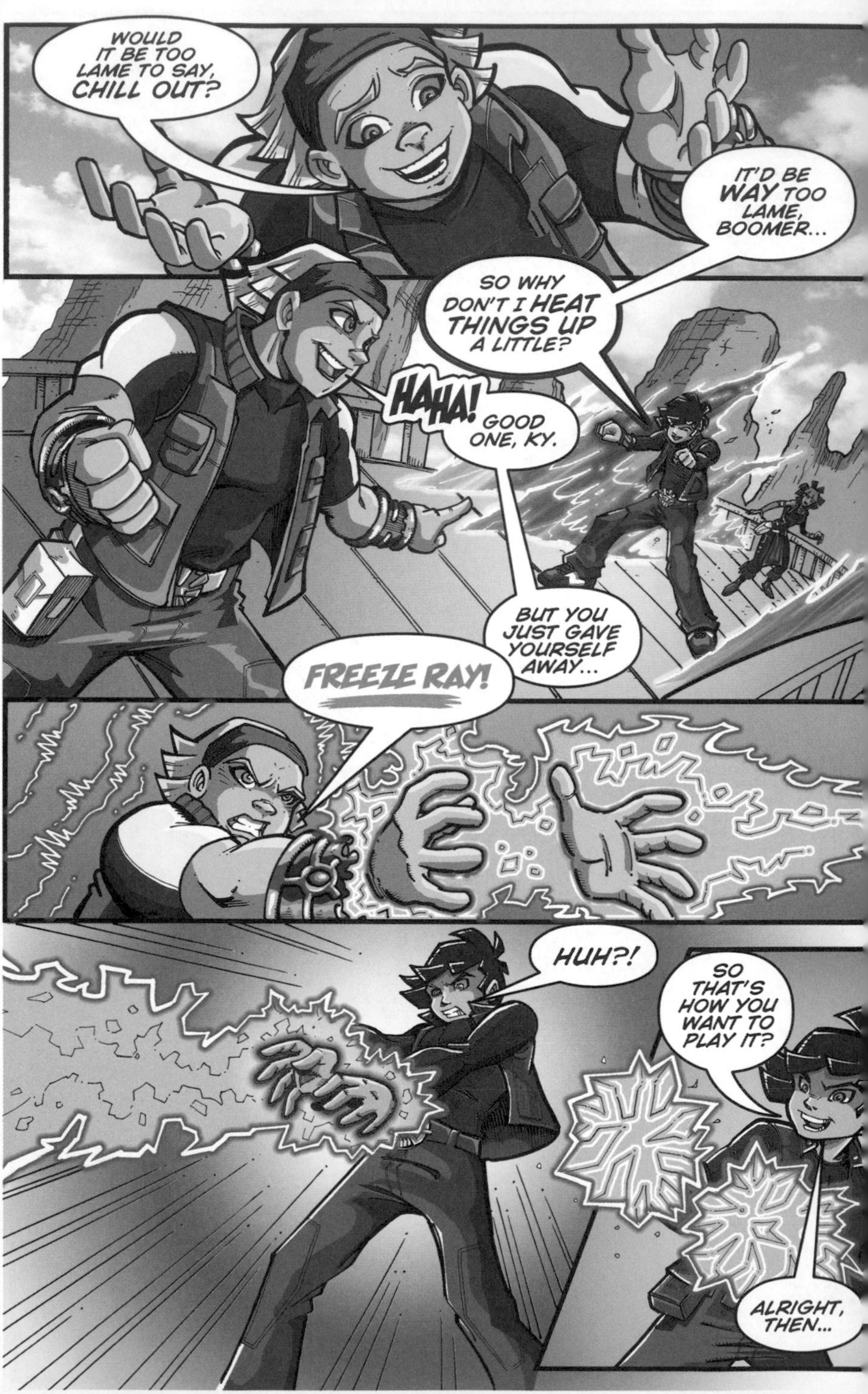
WOULD IT BE TOO LAME TO SAY, CHILL OUT?
IT'D BE WAY TOO LAME, BOOMER...
SO WHY DON'T I HEAT THINGS UP A LITTLE?
HAHA!
GOOD ONE, KY.
BUT YOU JUST GAVE YOURSELF AWAY...
FREEZE RAY!
HUH?!
SO THAT'S HOW YOU WANT TO PLAY IT?
ALRIGHT, THEN...

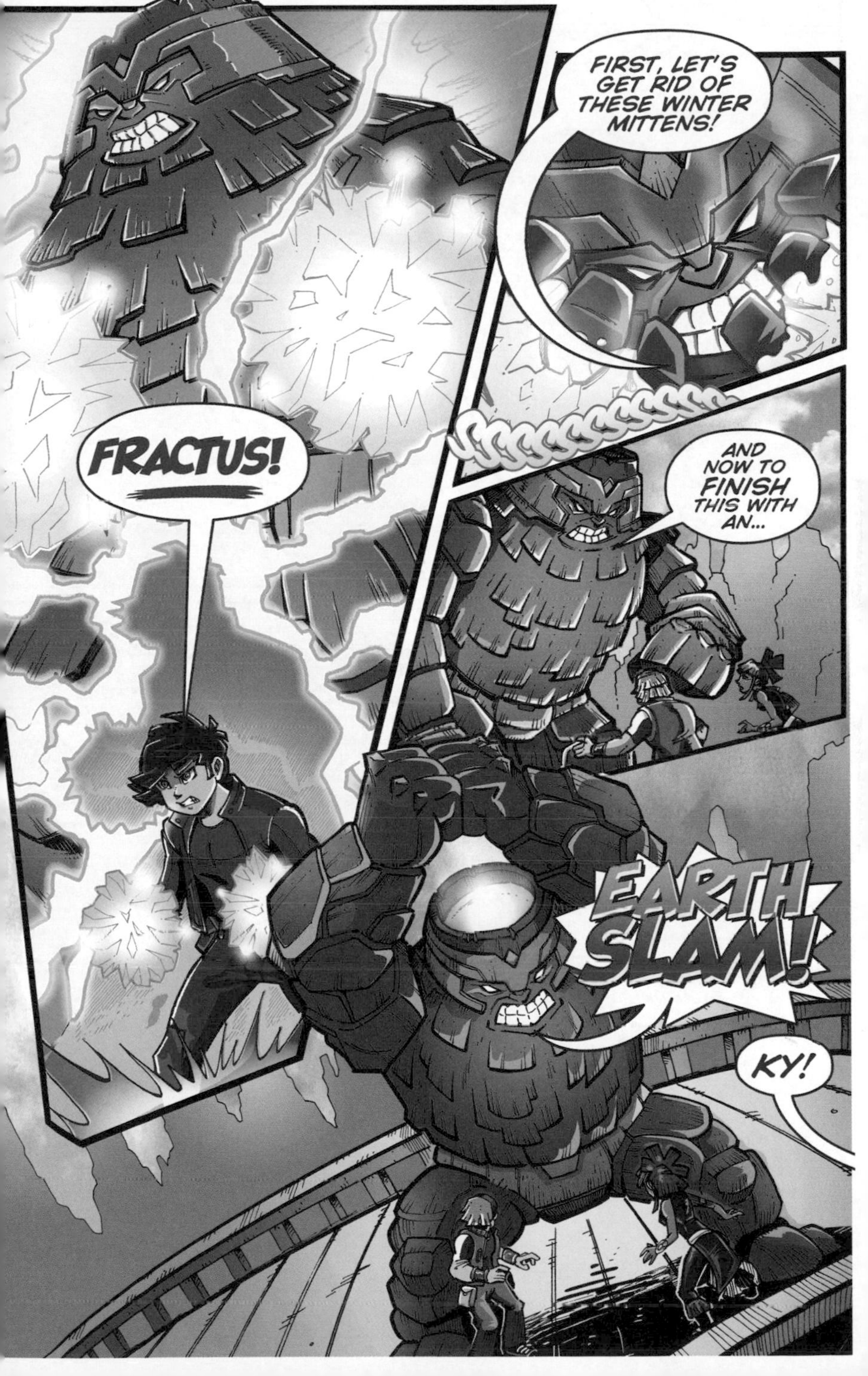
FRACTUS!
FIRST, LET'S GET RID OF THESE WINTER MITTENS!
SSSSSSSSSSSSS
AND NOW TO FINISH THIS WITH AN...
EARTH SLAM!
KY!

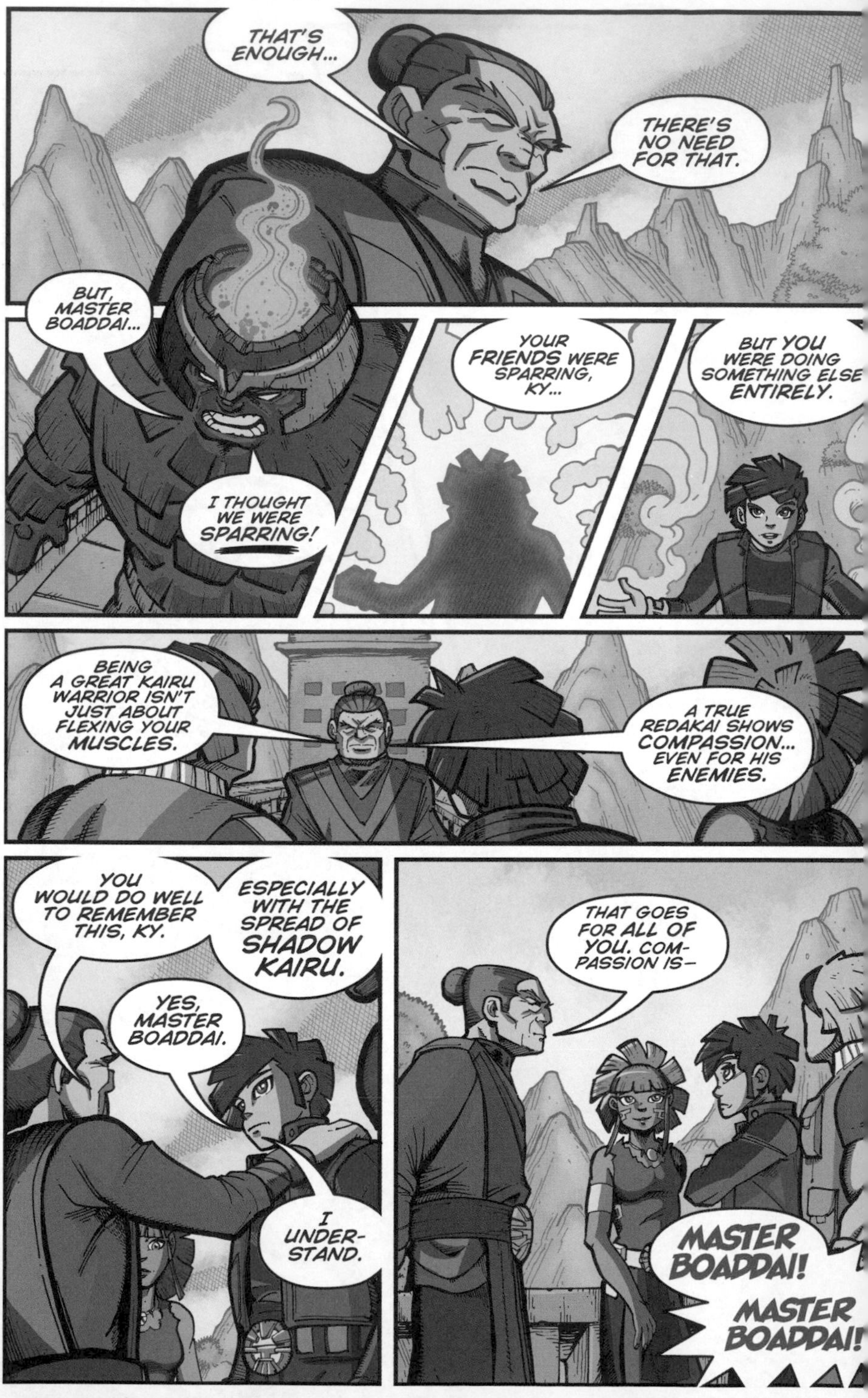
THAT'S ENOUGH...
THERE'S NO NEED FOR THAT.
BUT, MASTER BOADDAI...
I THOUGHT WE WERE SPARRING!
YOUR FRIENDS WERE SPARRING, KY...
BUT YOU WERE DOING SOMETHING ELSE ENTIRELY.
BEING A GREAT KAIRU WARRIOR ISN'T JUST ABOUT FLEXING YOUR MUSCLES.
A TRUE REDAKAI SHOWS COMPASSION... EVEN FOR HIS ENEMIES.
YOU WOULD DO WELL TO REMEMBER THIS, KY.
ESPECIALLY WITH THE SPREAD OF SHADOW KAIRU.
YES, MASTER BOADDAI.
I UNDER-STAND.
THAT GOES FOR ALL OF YOU. COM-PASSION IS—
MASTER BOADDAI!
MASTER BOADDAI!

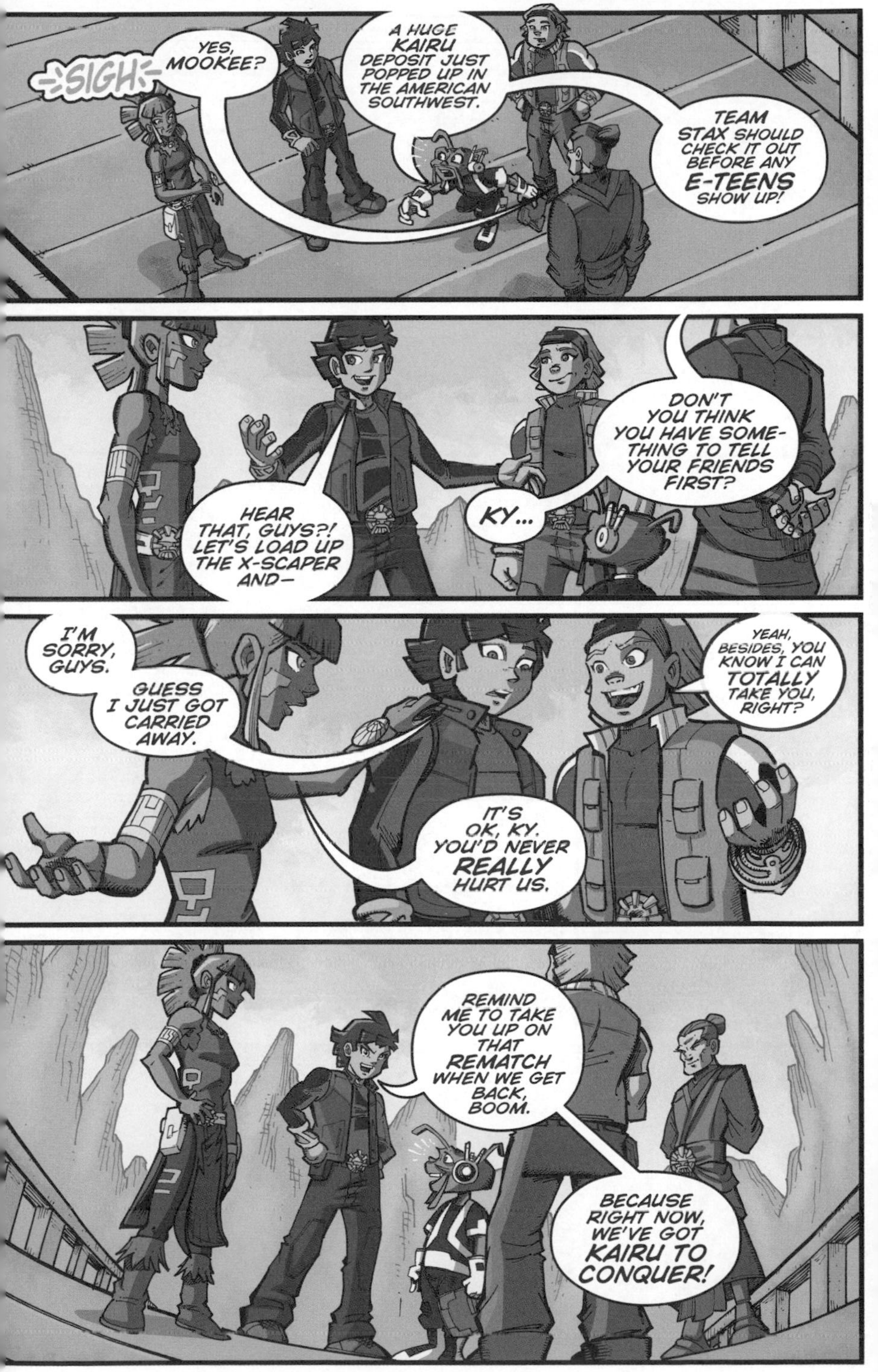

SIGH
YES, MOOKEE?
A HUGE KAIRU DEPOSIT JUST POPPED UP IN THE AMERICAN SOUTHWEST.
TEAM STAX SHOULD CHECK IT OUT BEFORE ANY E-TEENS SHOW UP!
HEAR THAT, GUYS?! LET'S LOAD UP THE X-SCAPER AND—
KY...
DON'T YOU THINK YOU HAVE SOME-THING TO TELL YOUR FRIENDS FIRST?
I'M SORRY, GUYS.
GUESS I JUST GOT CARRIED AWAY.
YEAH, BESIDES, YOU KNOW I CAN TOTALLY TAKE YOU, RIGHT?
IT'S OK, KY. YOU'D NEVER REALLY HURT US.
REMIND ME TO TAKE YOU UP ON THAT REMATCH WHEN WE GET BACK, BOOM.
BECAUSE RIGHT NOW, WE'VE GOT KAIRU TO CONQUER!

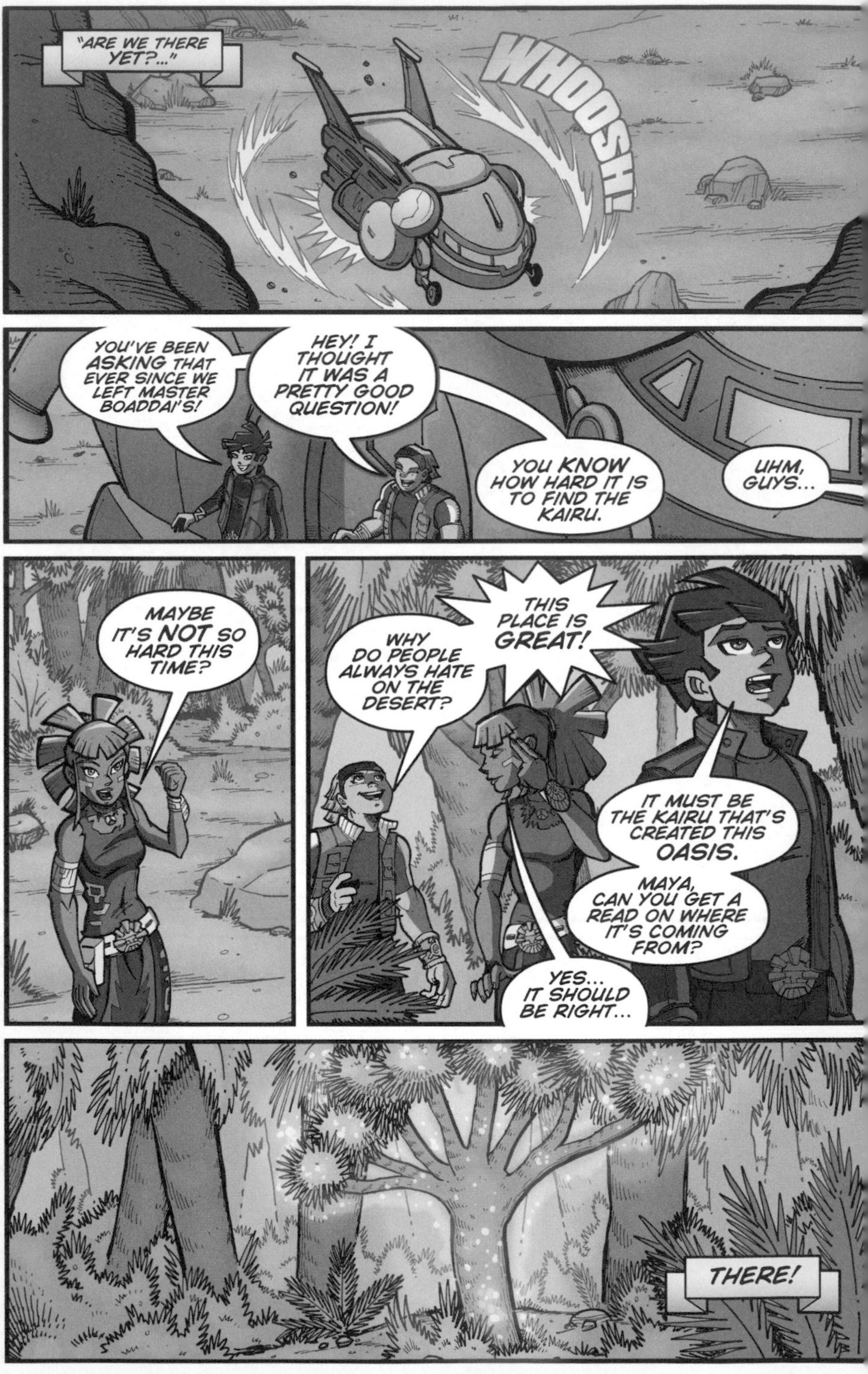
"ARE WE THERE YET?..."
WHOOSH!
YOU'VE BEEN ASKING THAT EVER SINCE WE LEFT MASTER BOADDAI'S!
HEY! I THOUGHT IT WAS A PRETTY GOOD QUESTION!
YOU KNOW HOW HARD IT IS TO FIND THE KAIRU.
UHM, GUYS...
MAYBE IT'S NOT SO HARD THIS TIME?
WHY DO PEOPLE ALWAYS HATE ON THE DESERT?
THIS PLACE IS GREAT!
IT MUST BE THE KAIRU THAT'S CREATED THIS OASIS.
MAYA, CAN YOU GET A READ ON WHERE IT'S COMING FROM?
YES... IT SHOULD BE RIGHT...
THERE!

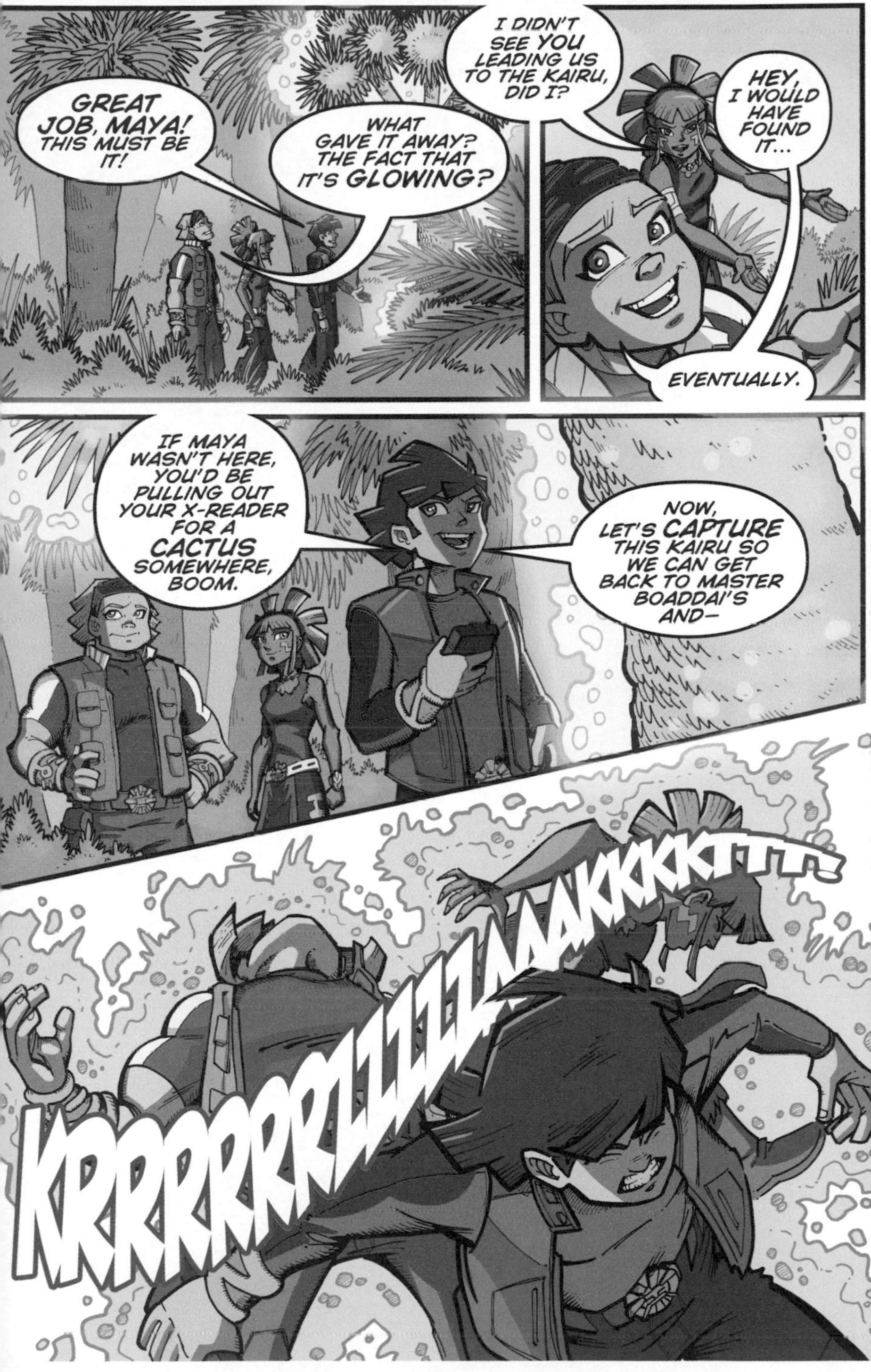
GREAT JOB, MAYA! THIS MUST BE IT!
WHAT GAVE IT AWAY? THE FACT THAT IT'S GLOWING?
I DIDN'T SEE YOU LEADING US TO THE KAIRU, DID I?
HEY, I WOULD HAVE FOUND IT...
EVENTUALLY.
IF MAYA WASN'T HERE, YOU'D BE PULLING OUT YOUR X-READER FOR A CACTUS SOMEWHERE, BOOM.
NOW, LET'S CAPTURE THIS KAIRU SO WE CAN GET BACK TO MASTER BOADDAI'S AND–
KRRRRRRZZZZZAAAKKKKKTTTT!

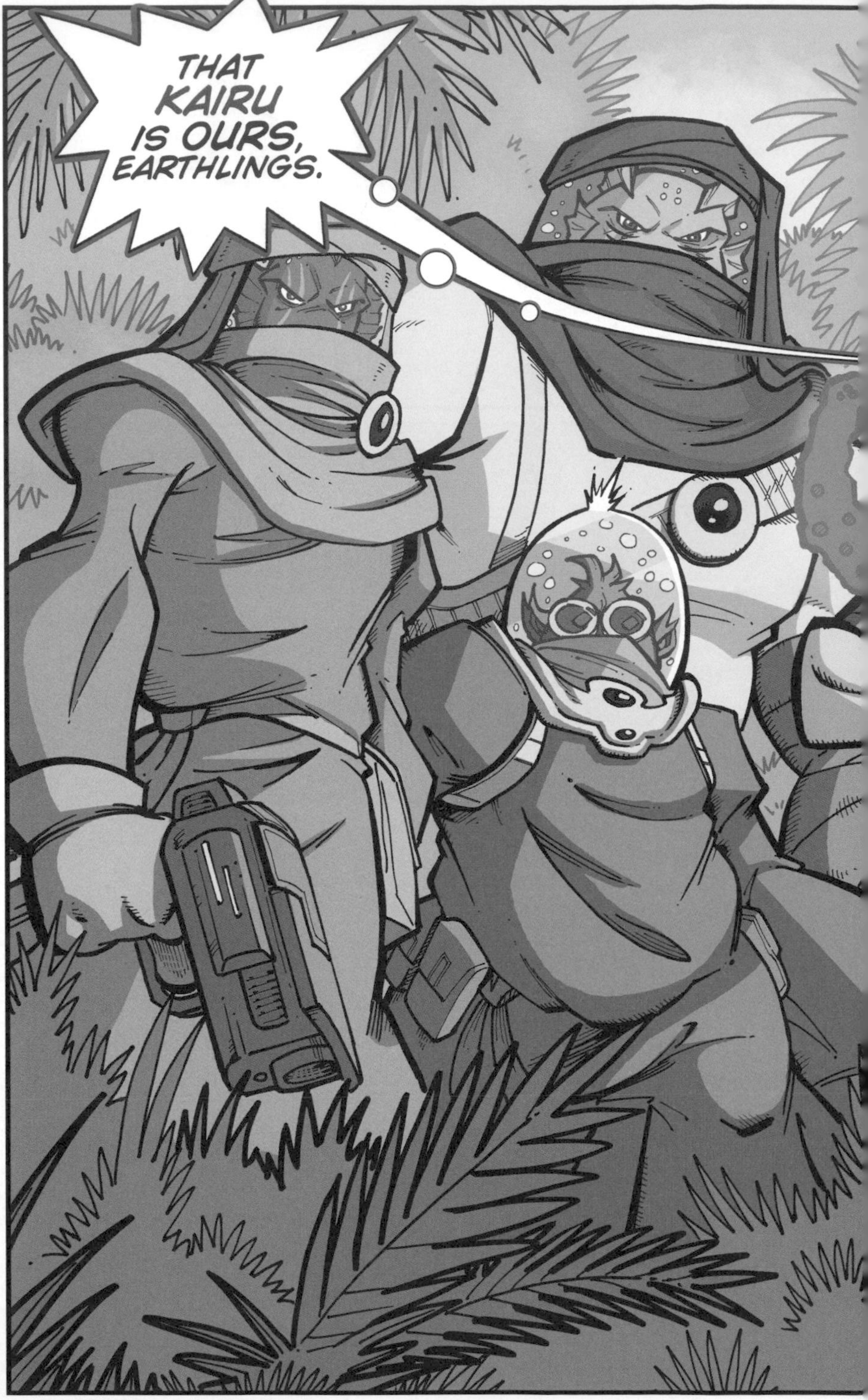
THAT KAIRU IS OURS, EARTHLINGS.

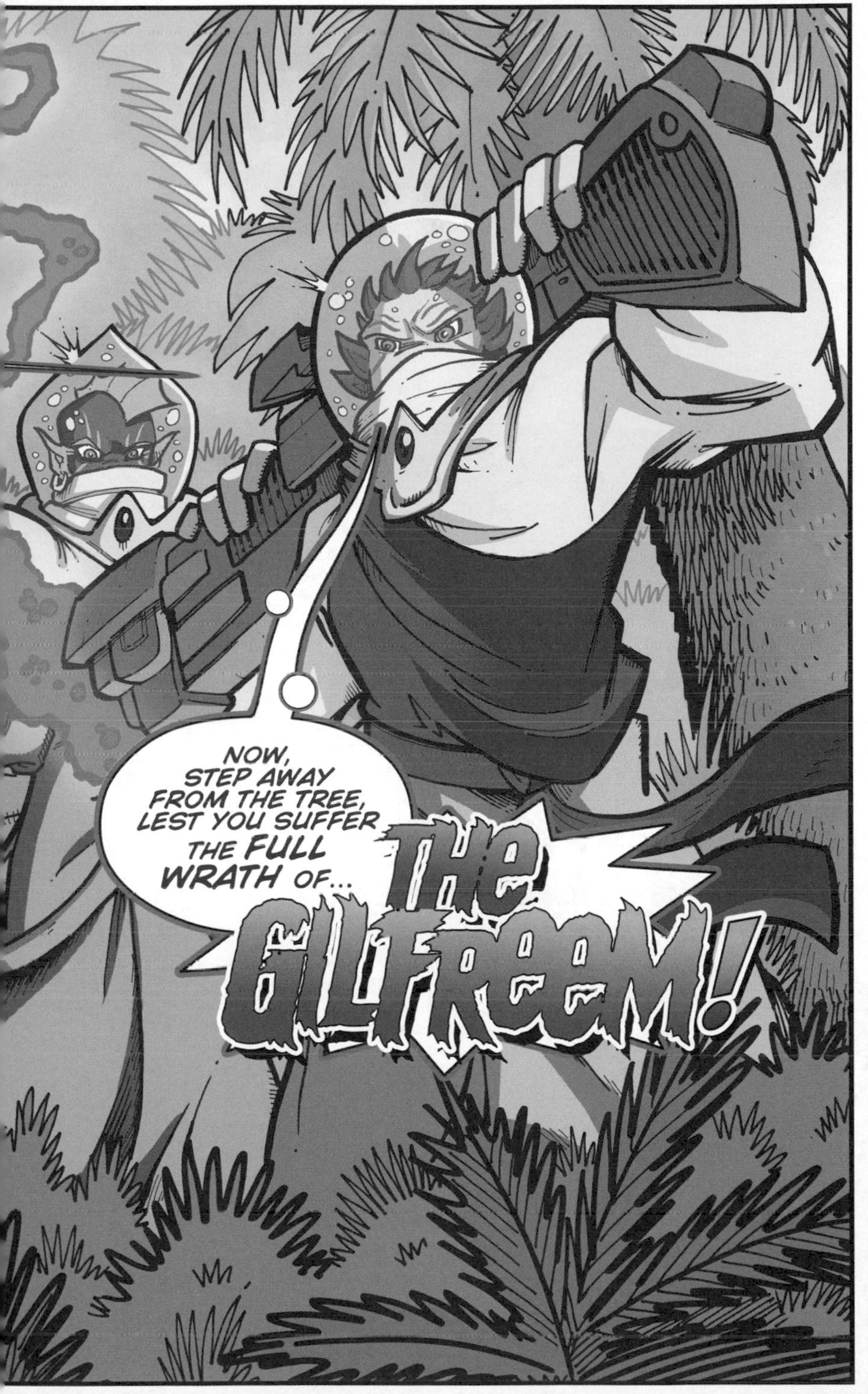
NOW, STEP AWAY FROM THE TREE, LEST YOU SUFFER THE FULL WRATH OF...
THE GILFREEM!

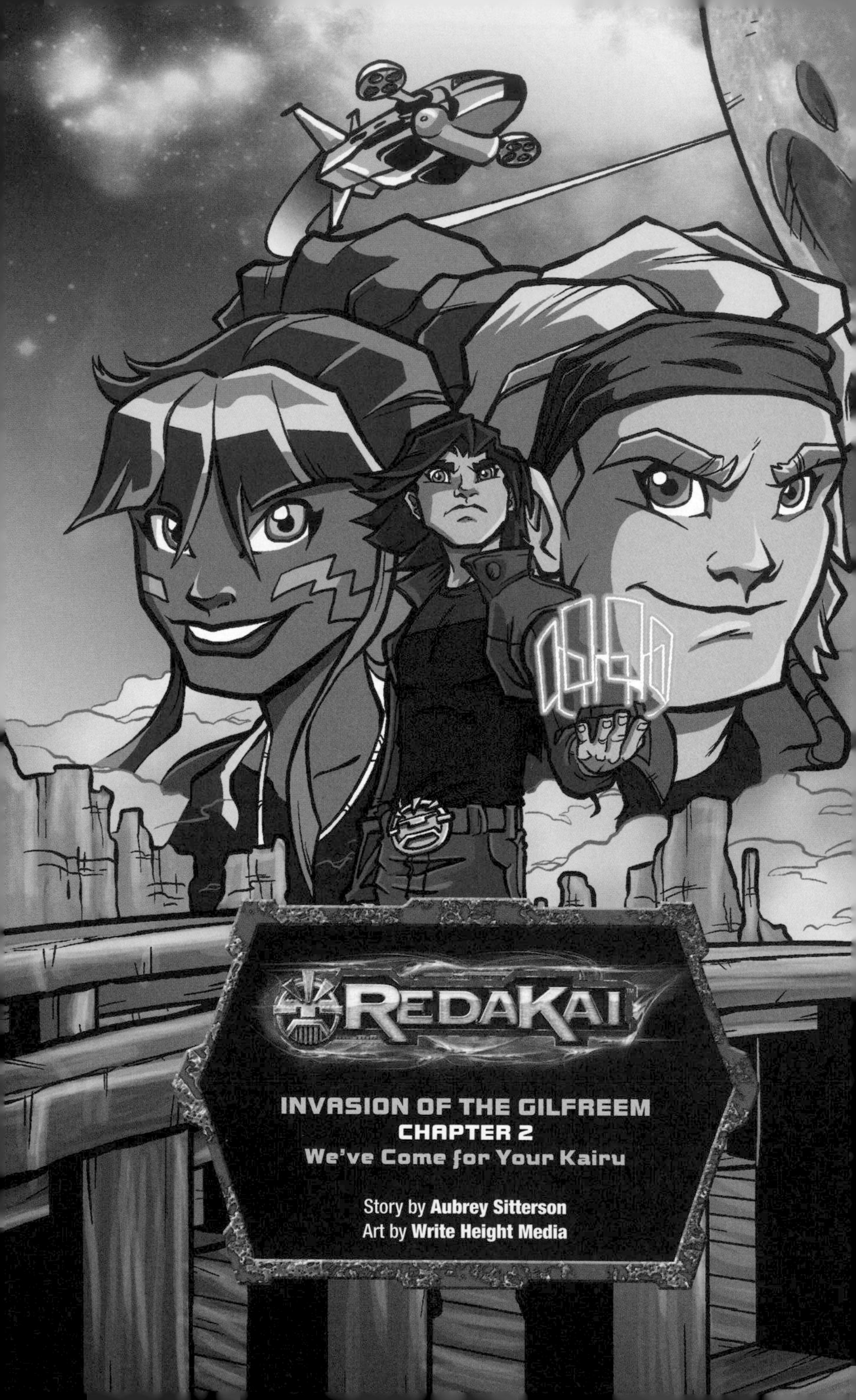
REDAKAI
INVASION OF THE GILFREEM
CHAPTER 2
We've Come for Your Kairu
Story by Aubrey Sitterson
Art by Write Height Media

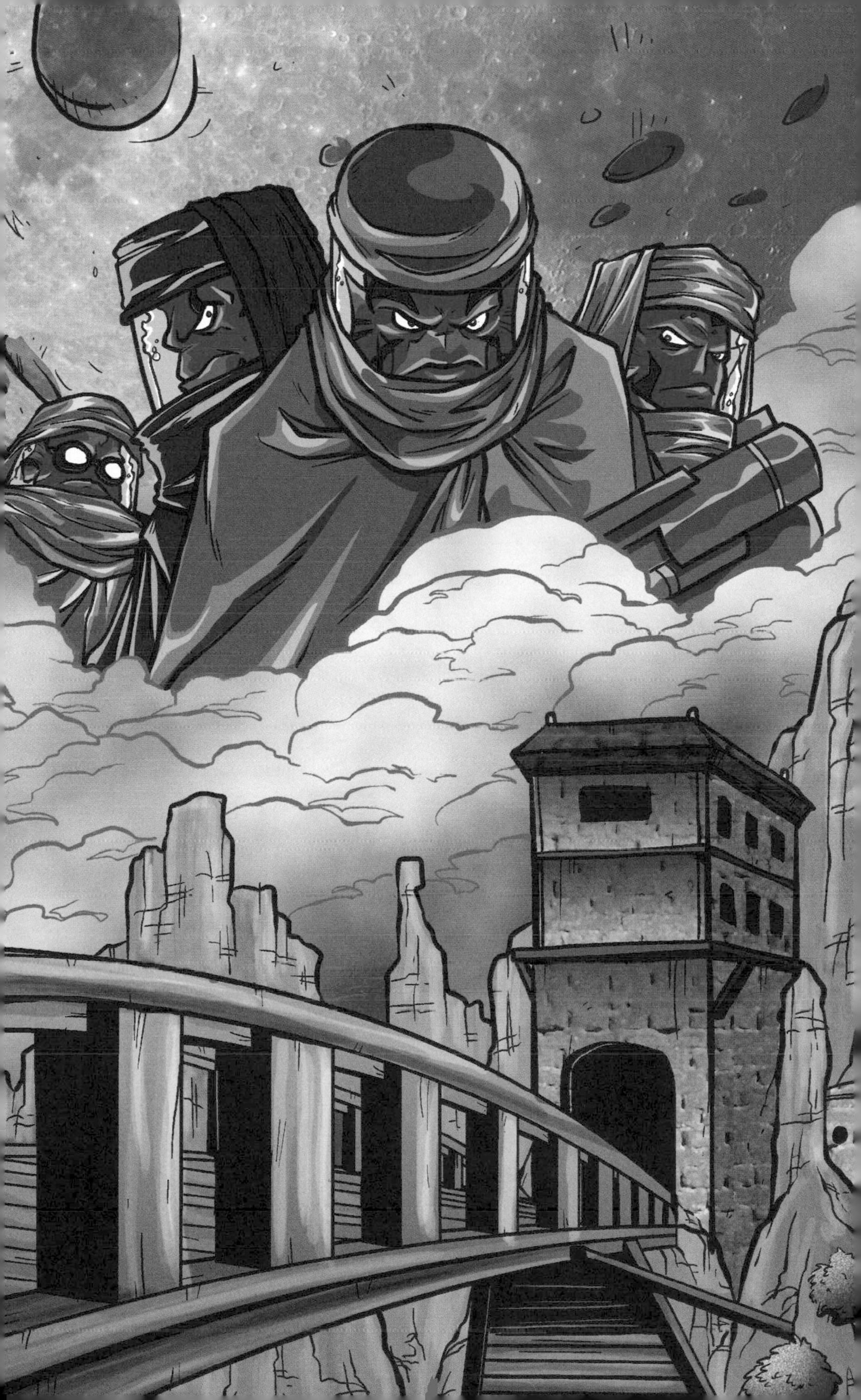

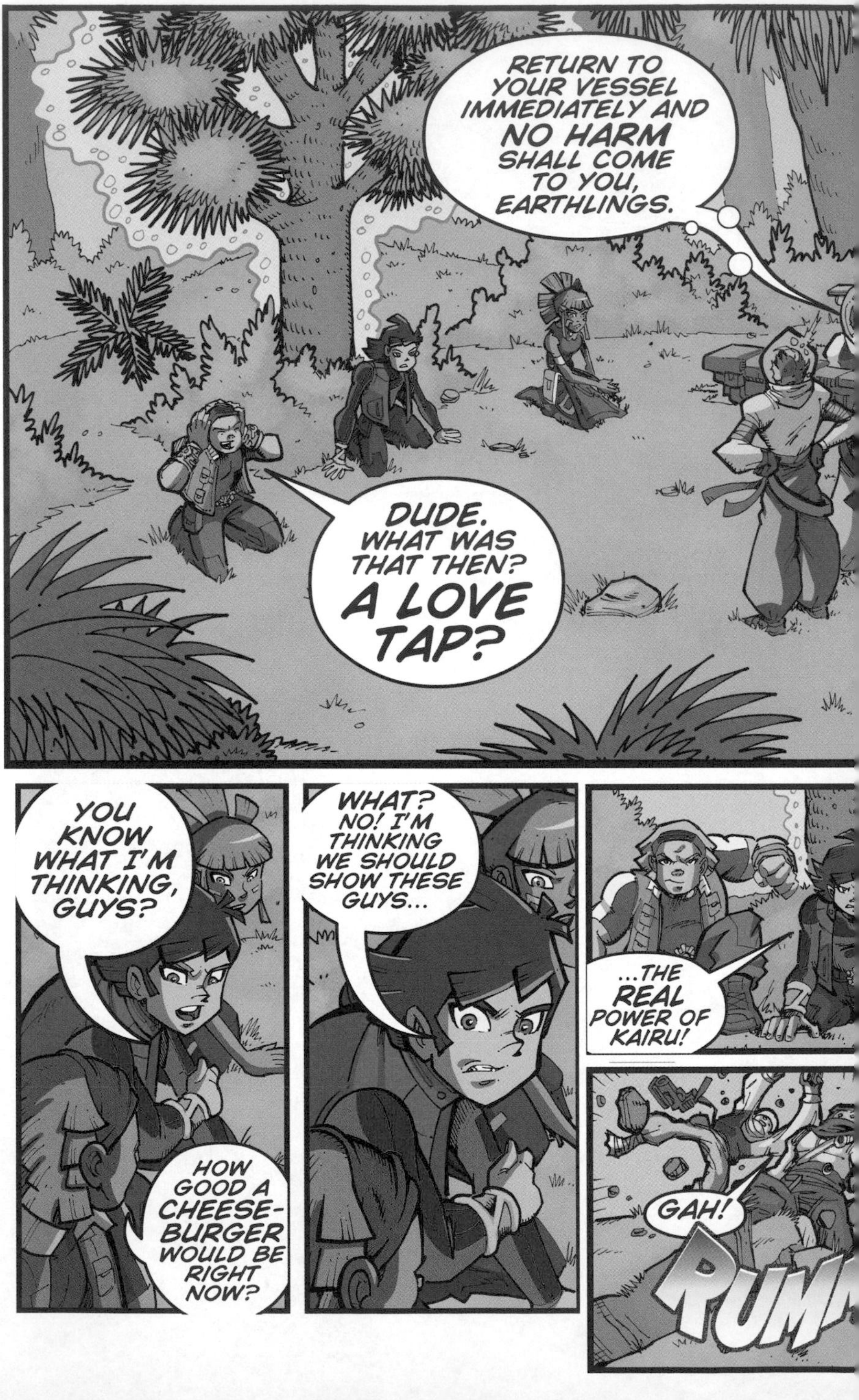
RETURN TO YOUR VESSEL IMMEDIATELY AND NO HARM SHALL COME TO YOU, EARTHLINGS.
DUDE. WHAT WAS THAT THEN? A LOVE TAP?
YOU KNOW WHAT I'M THINKING, GUYS?
HOW GOOD A CHEESE-BURGER WOULD BE RIGHT NOW?
WHAT? NO! I'M THINKING WE SHOULD SHOW THESE GUYS...
...THE REAL POWER OF KAIRU!
GAH!

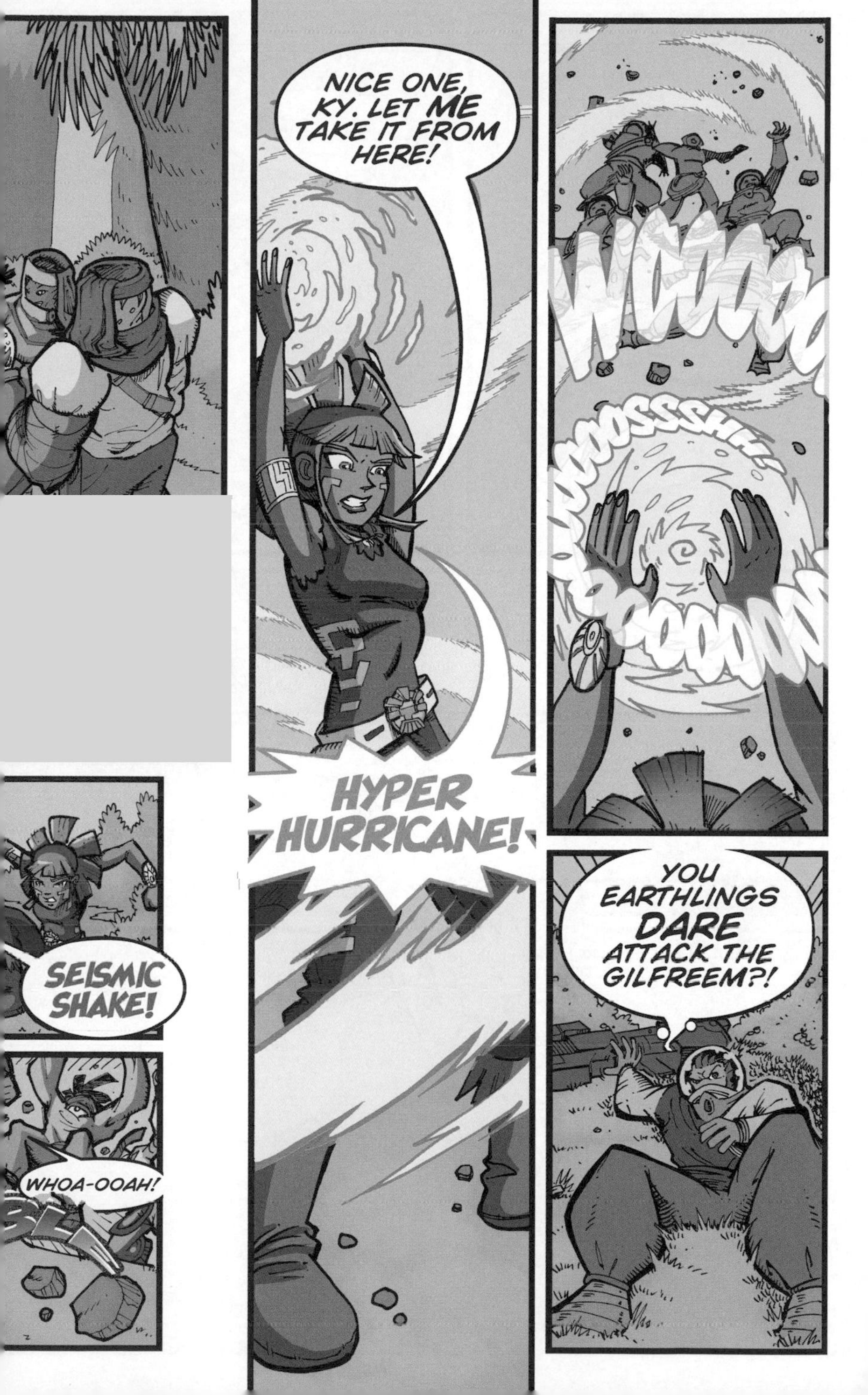
SEISMIC SHAKE!
WHOA-OOAH!
NICE ONE, KY. LET ME TAKE IT FROM HERE!
HYPER HURRICANE!
WOOSSSH!
YOU EARTHLINGS DARE ATTACK THE GILFREEM?!

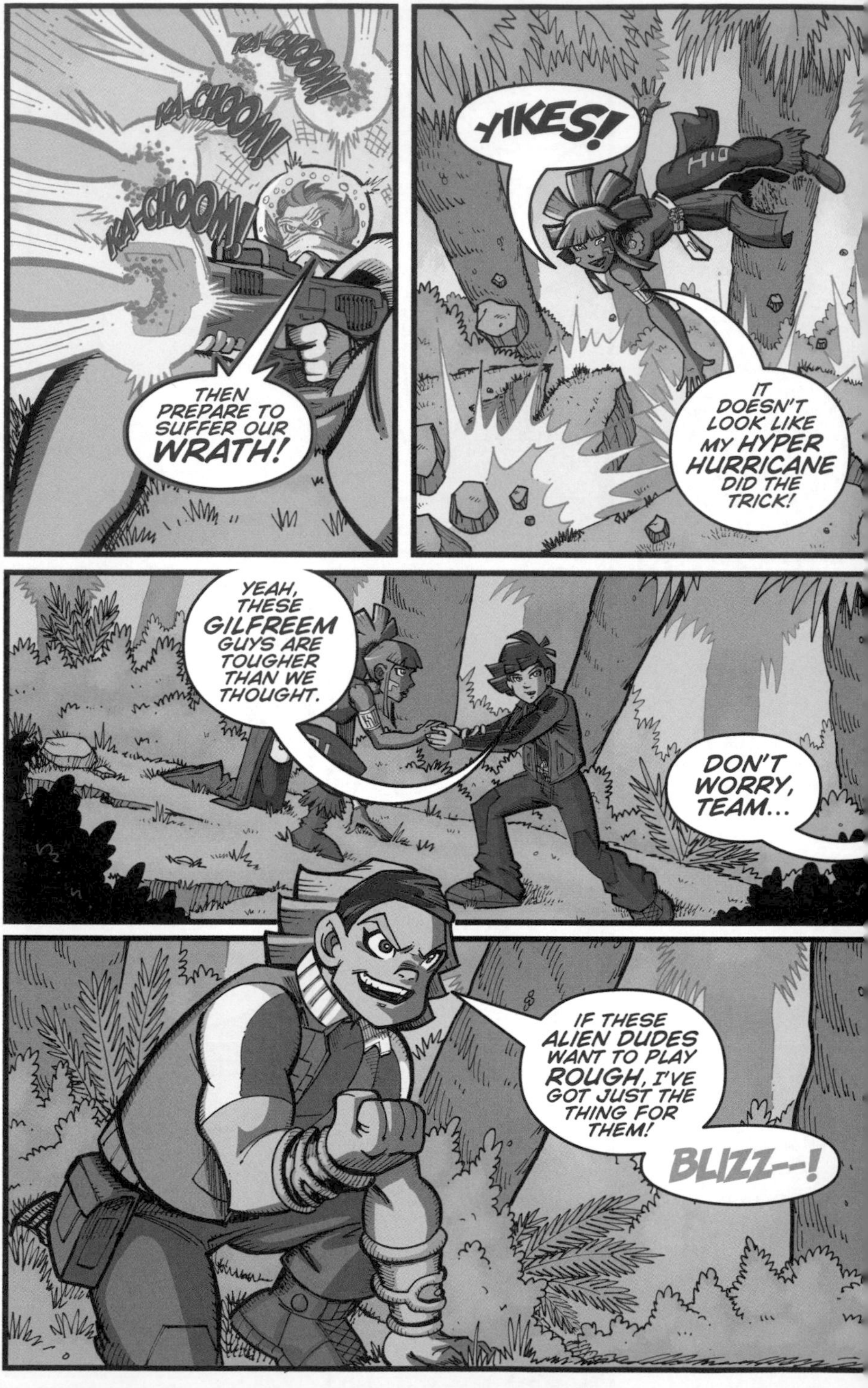
KA-CHOOM!
KA-CHOOM!
KA-CHOOM!
THEN PREPARE TO SUFFER OUR WRATH!
YIKES!
IT DOESN'T LOOK LIKE MY HYPER HURRICANE DID THE TRICK!
YEAH, THESE GILFREEM GUYS ARE TOUGHER THAN WE THOUGHT.
DON'T WORRY, TEAM...
IF THESE ALIEN DUDES WANT TO PLAY ROUGH, I'VE GOT JUST THE THING FOR THEM!
BLIZZ--!

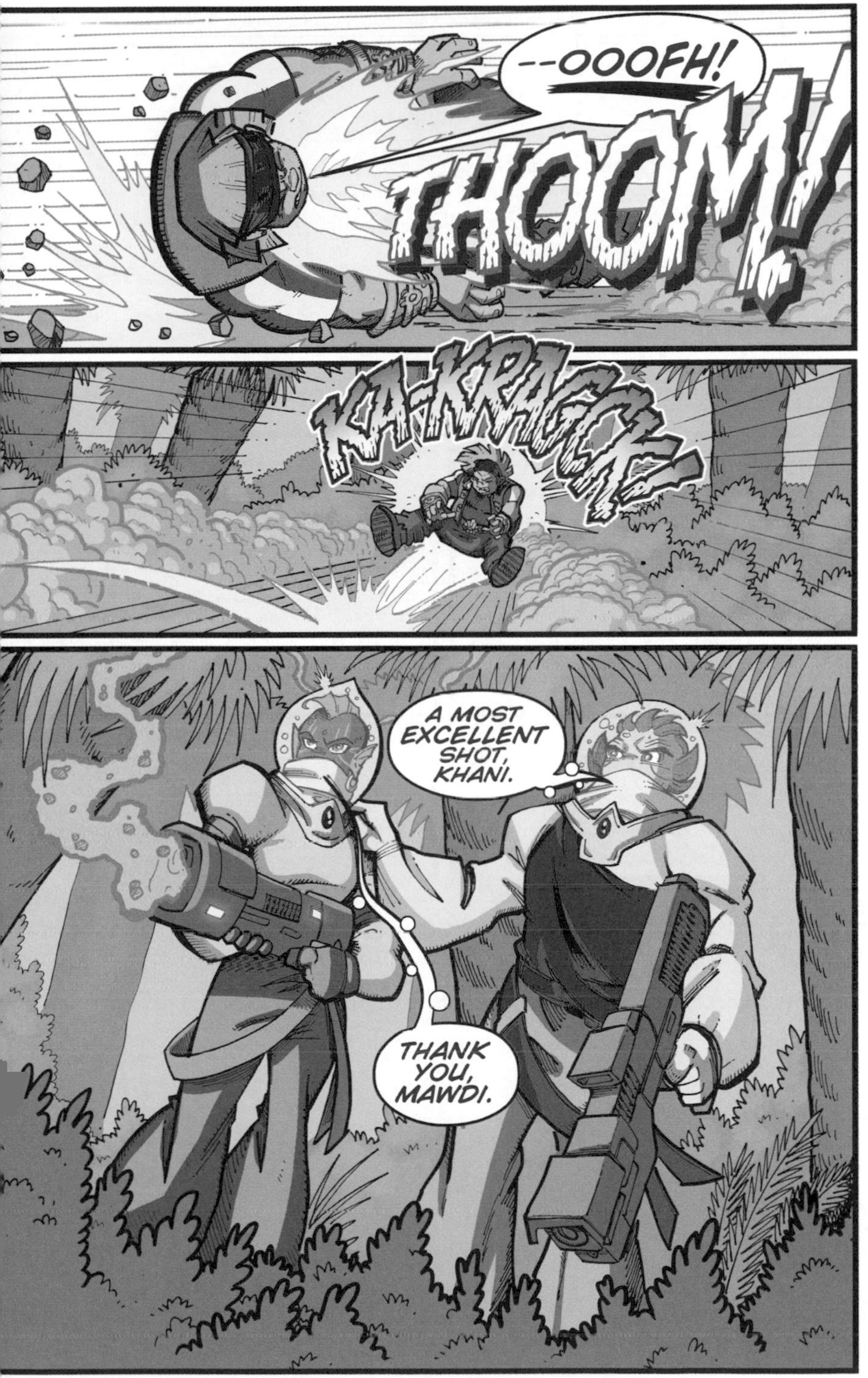
--OOOFH!
THOOM!
KA-KRACK!
A MOST EXCELLENT SHOT, KHANI.
THANK YOU, MAWDI.

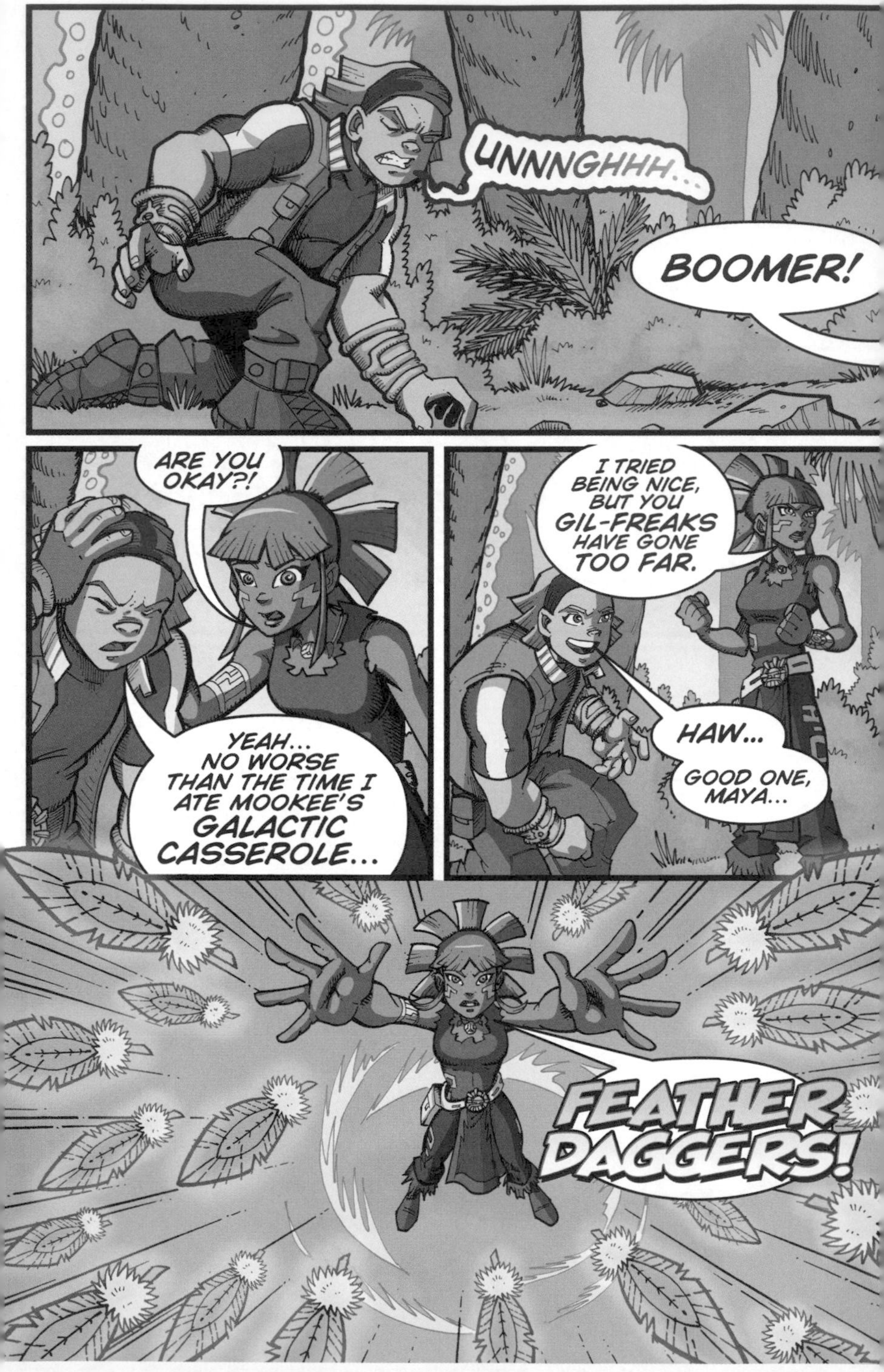
UNNNGHHH...
BOOMER!
ARE YOU OKAY?!
YEAH... NO WORSE THAN THE TIME I ATE MOOKEE'S GALACTIC CASSEROLE...
I TRIED BEING NICE, BUT YOU GIL-FREAKS HAVE GONE TOO FAR.
HAW...
GOOD ONE, MAYA...
FEATHER DAGGERS!

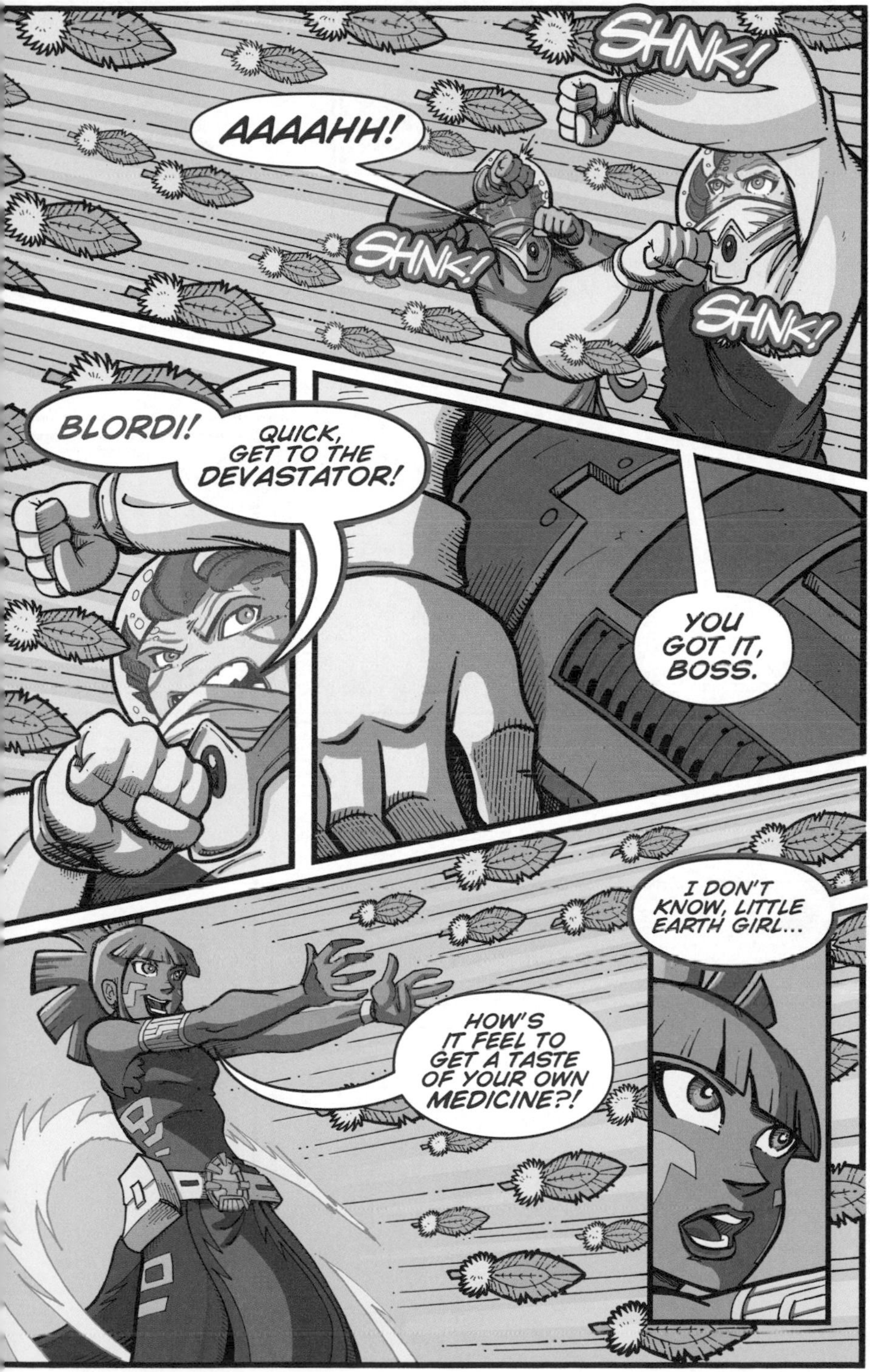
SHNK!
AAAAHH!
SHNK!
SHNK!
BLORDI!
QUICK, GET TO THE DEVASTATOR!
YOU GOT IT, BOSS.
HOW'S IT FEEL TO GET A TASTE OF YOUR OWN MEDICINE?!
I DON'T KNOW, LITTLE EARTH GIRL...

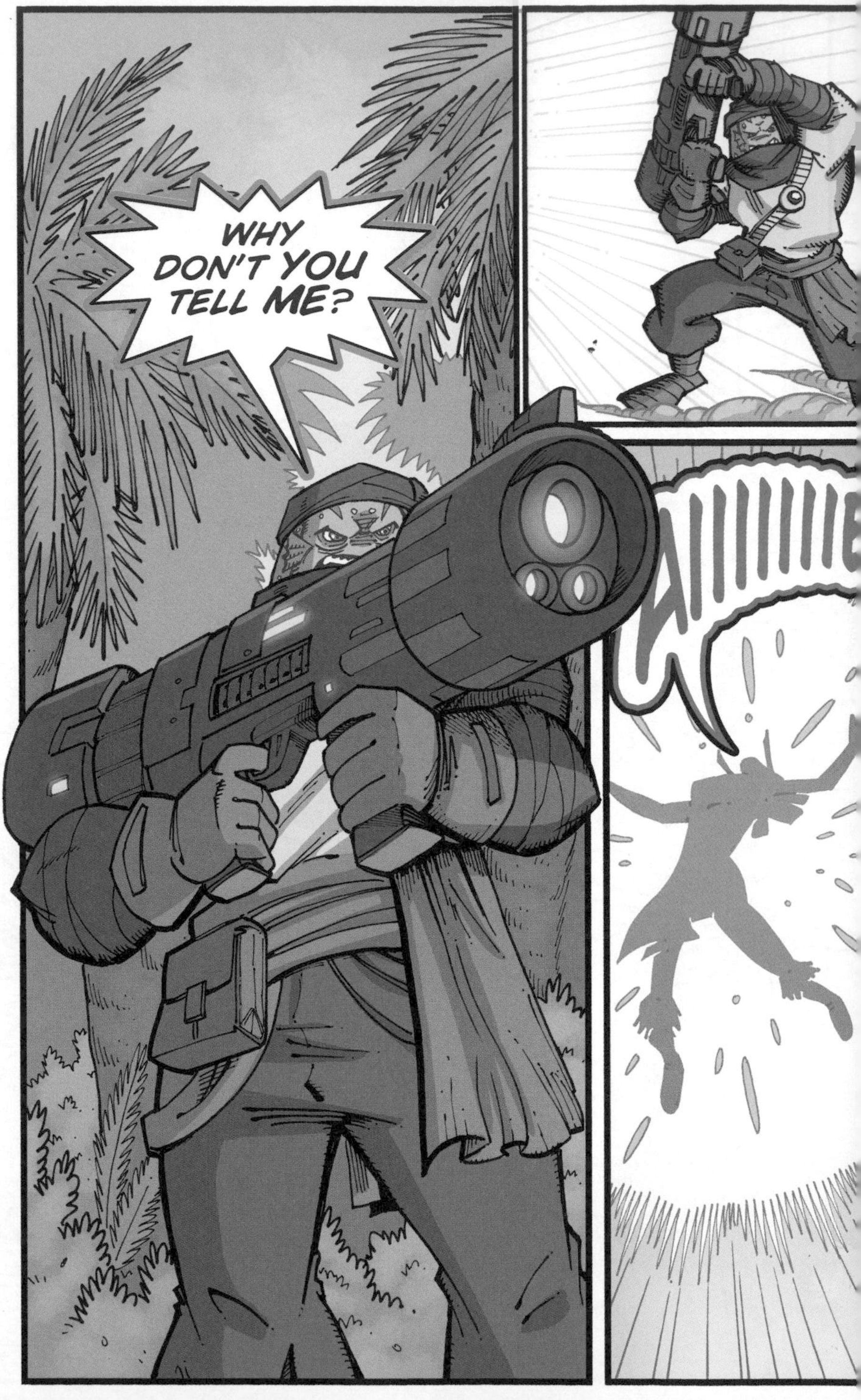
WHY DON'T YOU TELL ME?
AIIIIIIIE

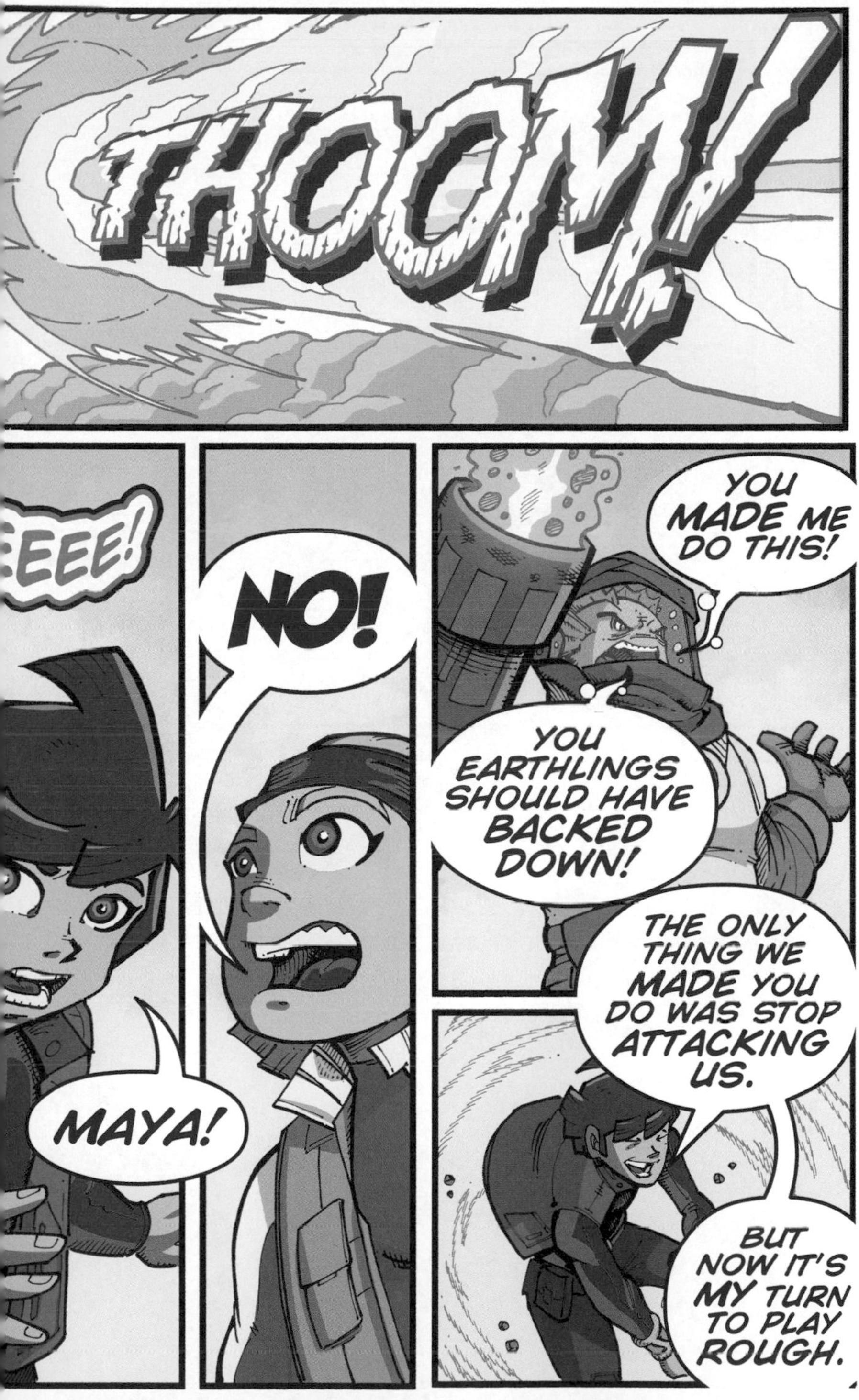
THOOM!
EEEE!
MAYA!
NO!
YOU MADE ME DO THIS!
YOU EARTHLINGS SHOULD HAVE BACKED DOWN!
THE ONLY THING WE MADE YOU DO WAS STOP ATTACKING US.
BUT NOW IT'S MY TURN TO PLAY ROUGH.

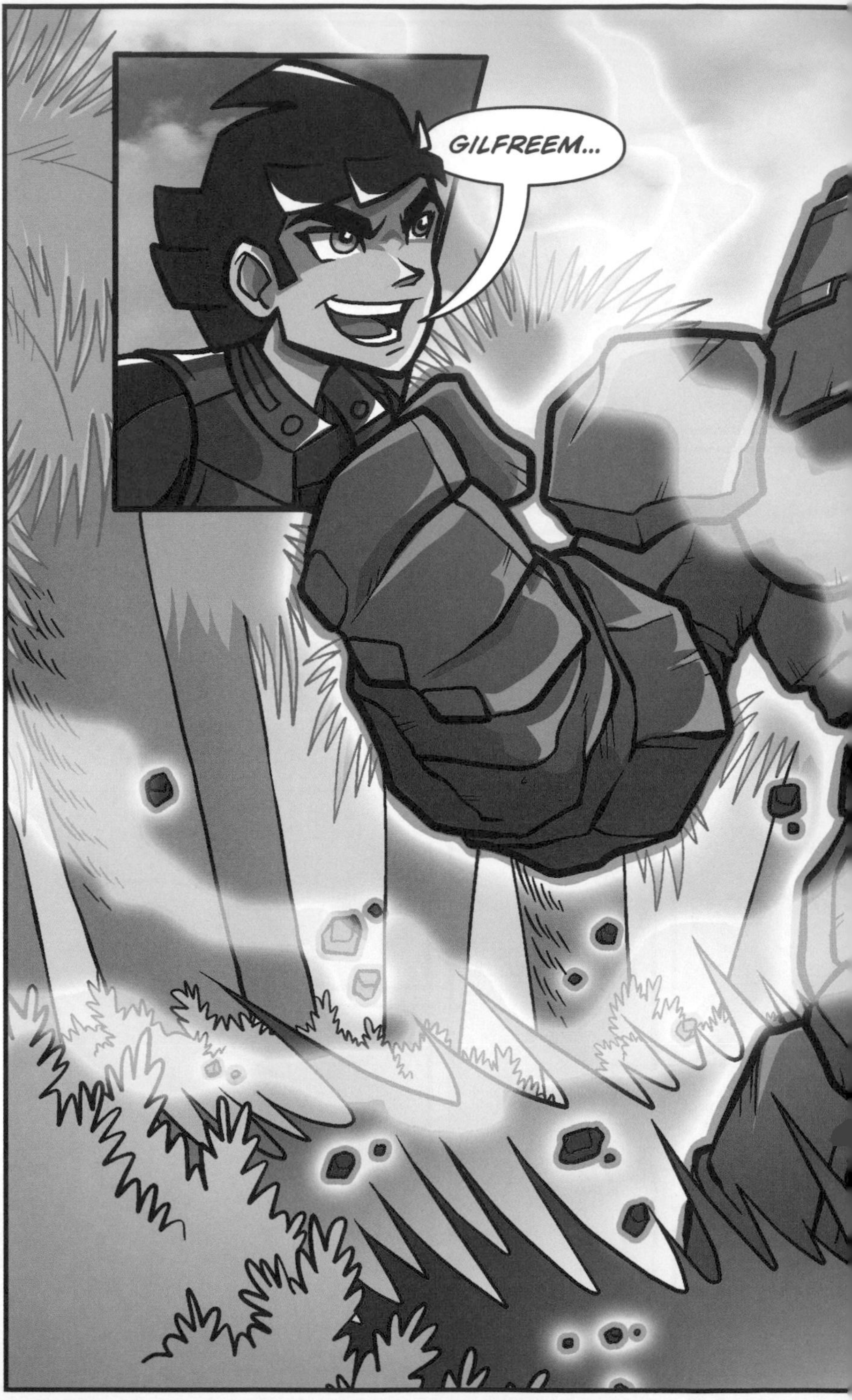
GILFREEM...

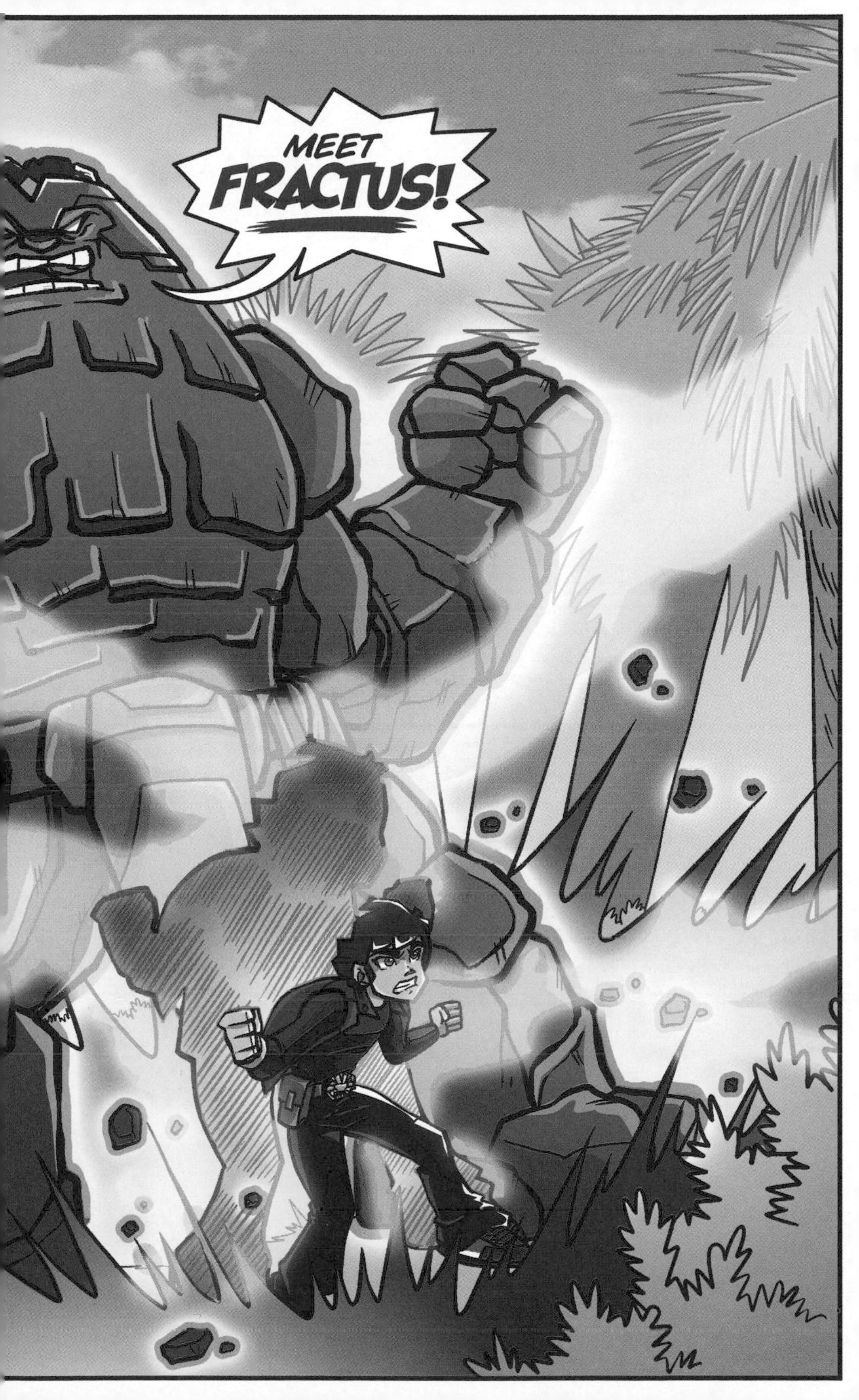
MEET
FRACTUS!

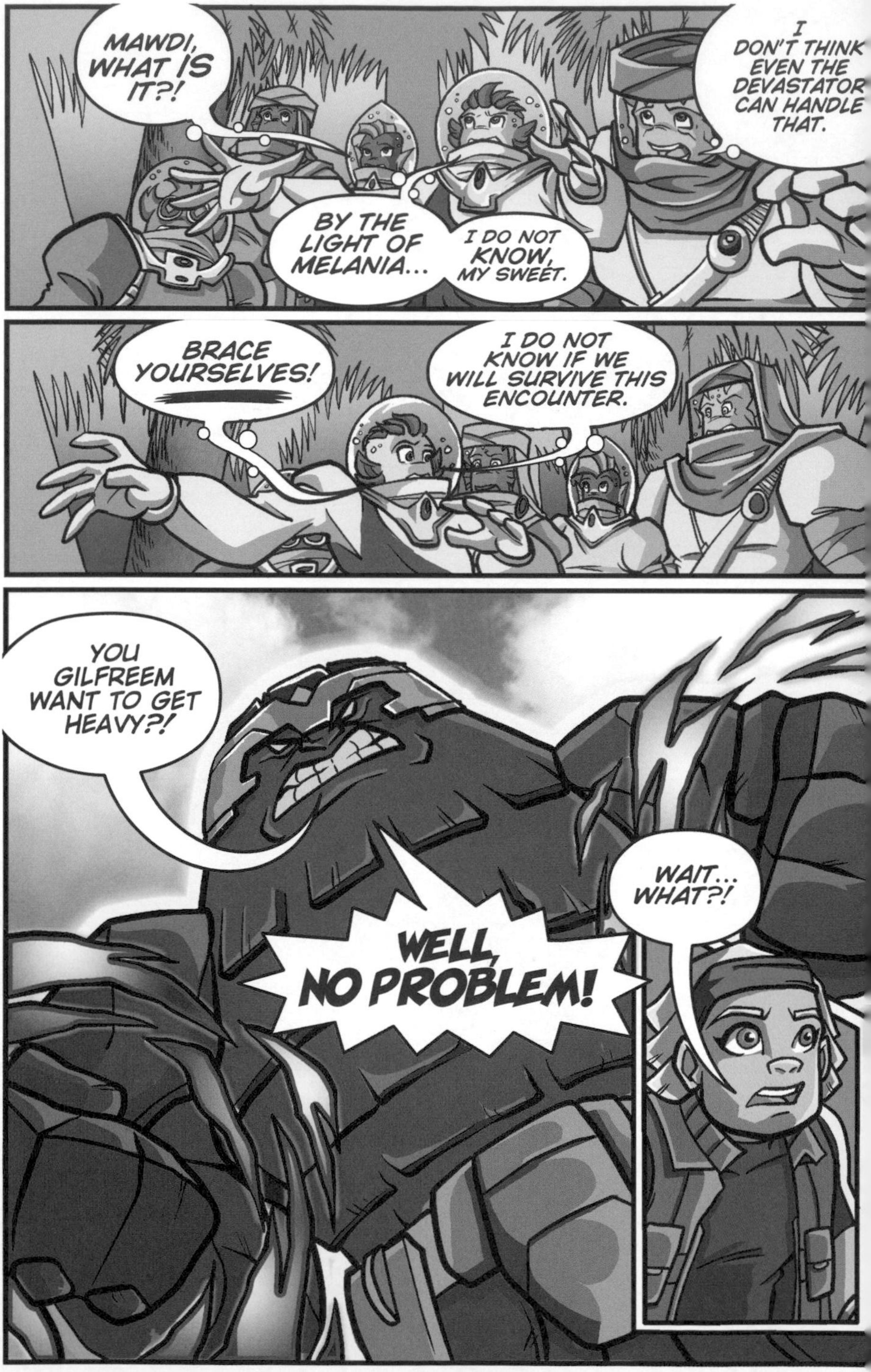
MAWDI, WHAT IS IT?!
I DON'T THINK EVEN THE DEVASTATOR CAN HANDLE THAT.
BY THE LIGHT OF MELANIA...
I DO NOT KNOW, MY SWEET.
BRACE YOURSELVES!
I DO NOT KNOW IF WE WILL SURVIVE THIS ENCOUNTER.
YOU GILFREEM WANT TO GET HEAVY?!
WELL, NO PROBLEM!
WAIT... WHAT?!

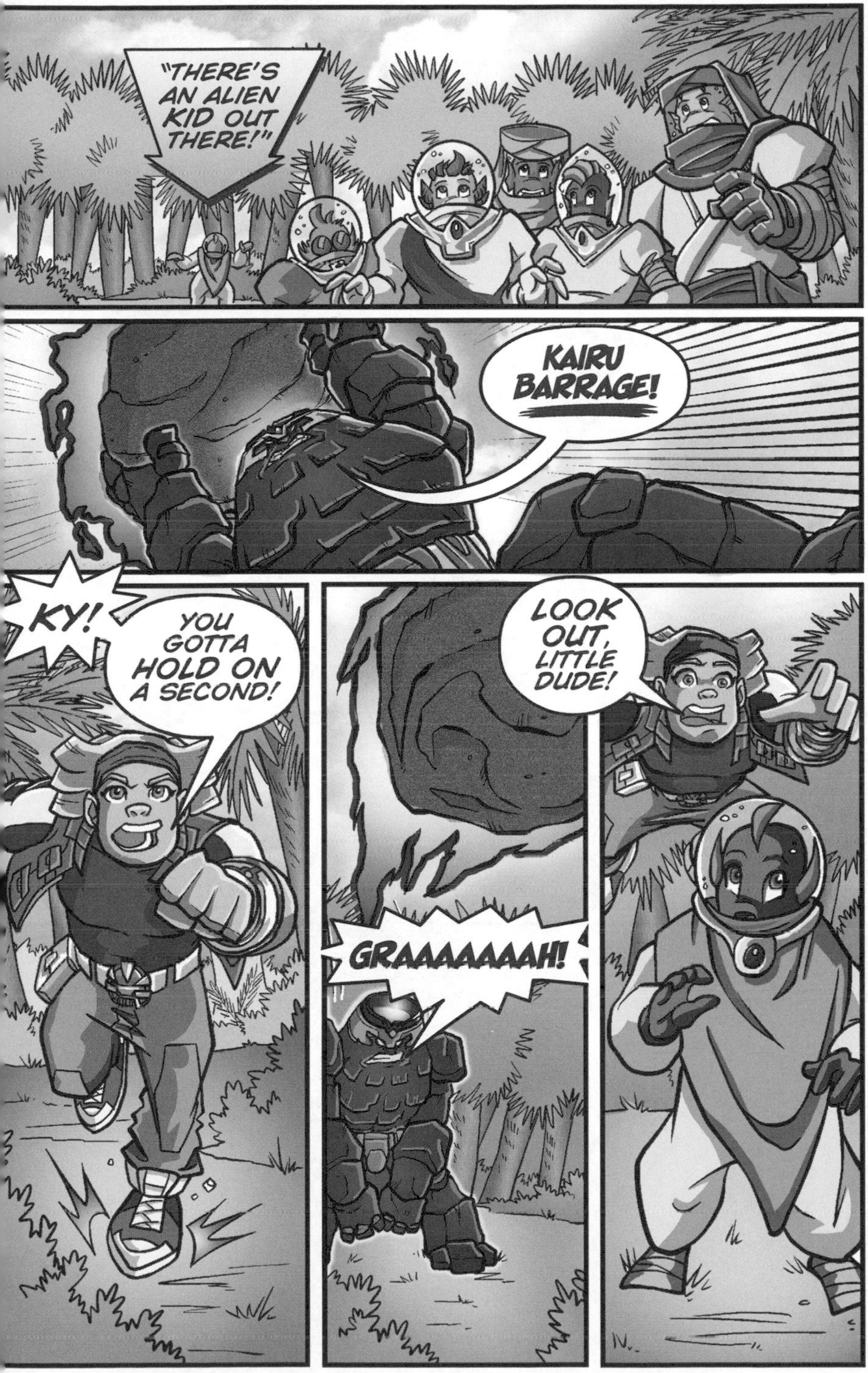
"THERE'S AN ALIEN KID OUT THERE!"
KAIRU BARRAGE!
KY!
YOU GOTTA HOLD ON A SECOND!
LOOK OUT, LITTLE DUDE!
GRAAAAAAAH!

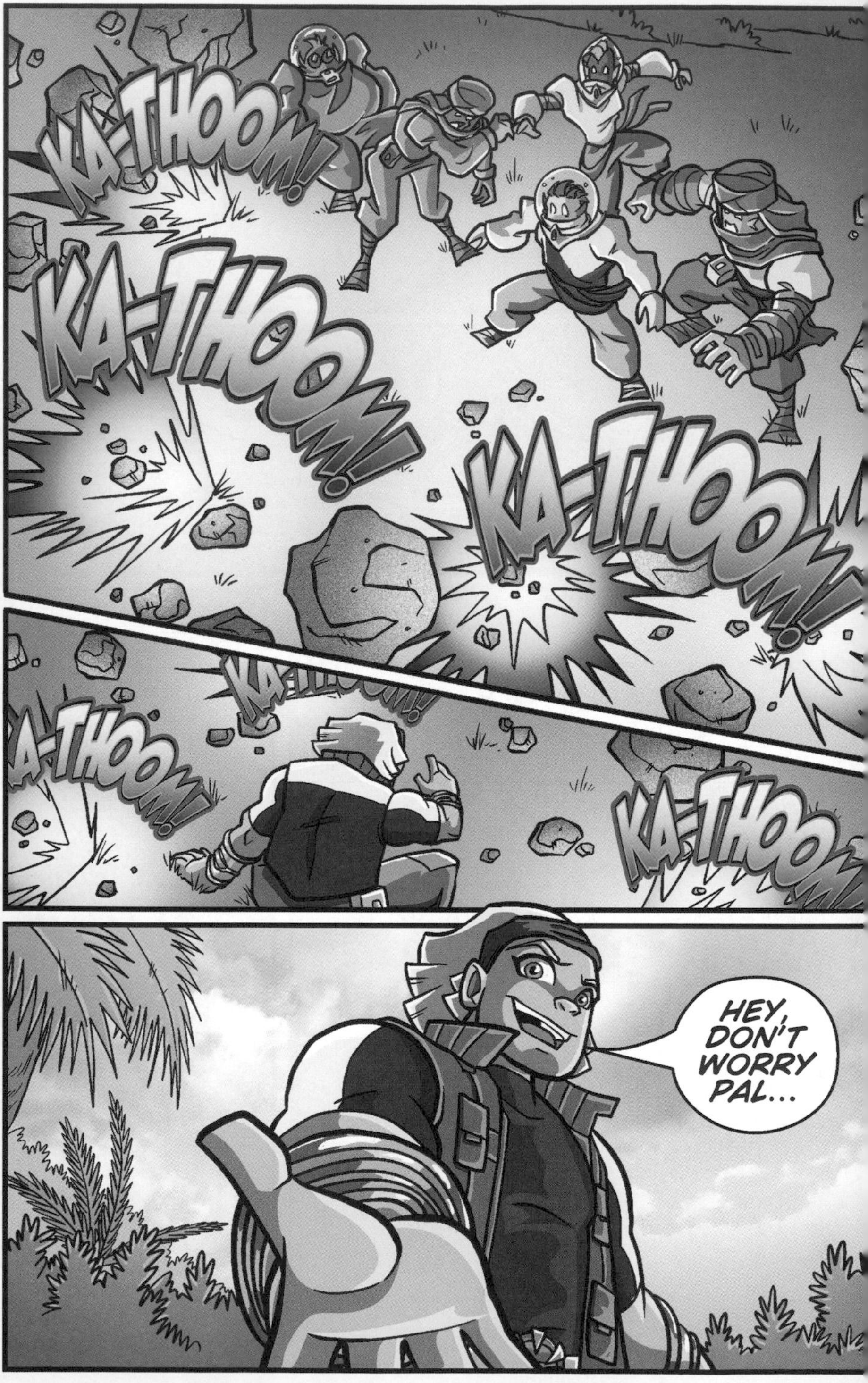
KA-THOOM!
KA-THOOM!
KA-THOOM!
KA-THOOM!
A-THOOM!
KA-THOOM
HEY, DON'T WORRY PAL...

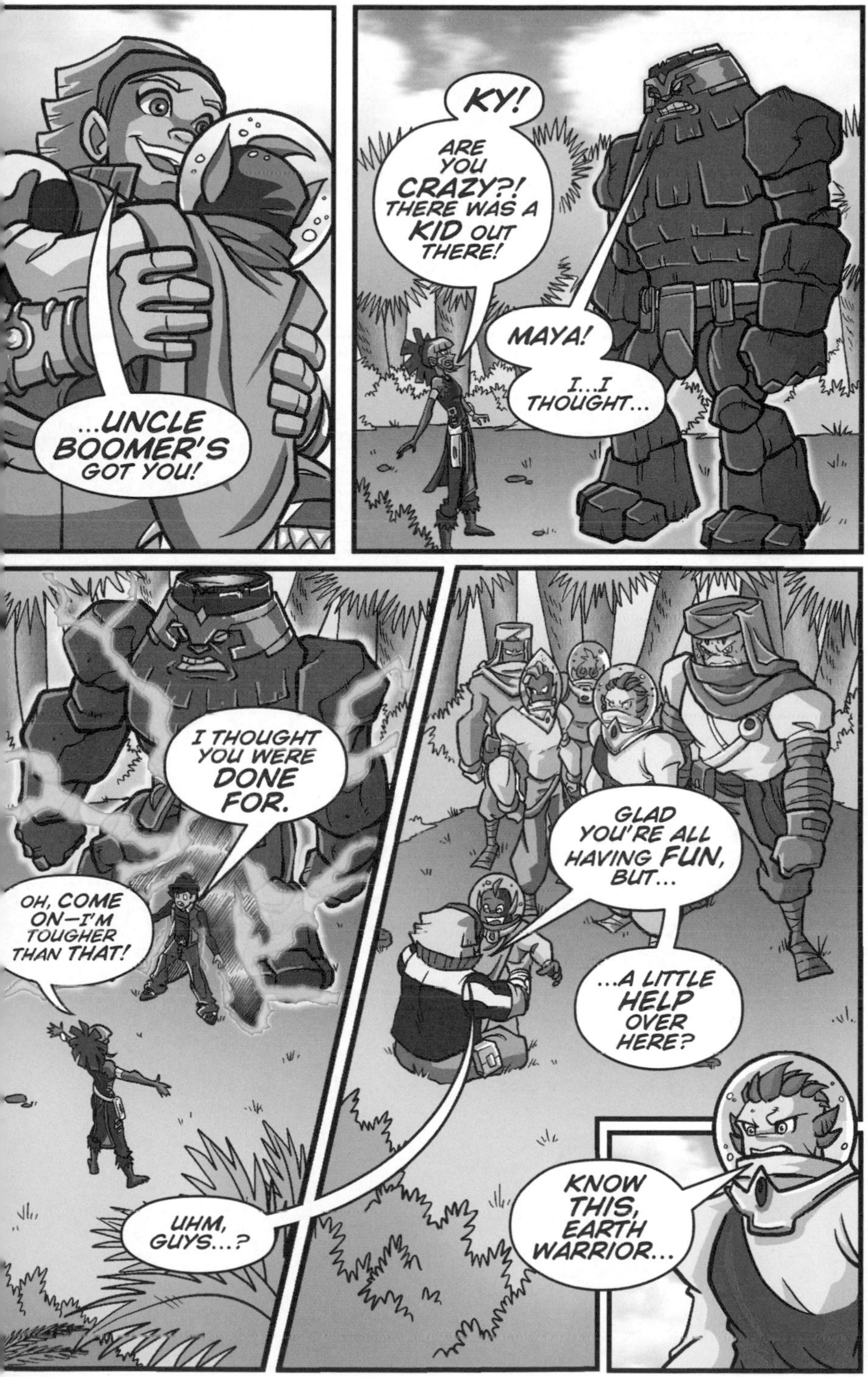
...UNCLE BOOMER'S GOT YOU!
KY!
ARE YOU CRAZY?! THERE WAS A KID OUT THERE!
MAYA!
I...I THOUGHT...
I THOUGHT YOU WERE DONE FOR.
OH, COME ON—I'M TOUGHER THAN THAT!
UHM, GUYS...?
GLAD YOU'RE ALL HAVING FUN, BUT...
...A LITTLE HELP OVER HERE?
KNOW THIS, EARTH WARRIOR...

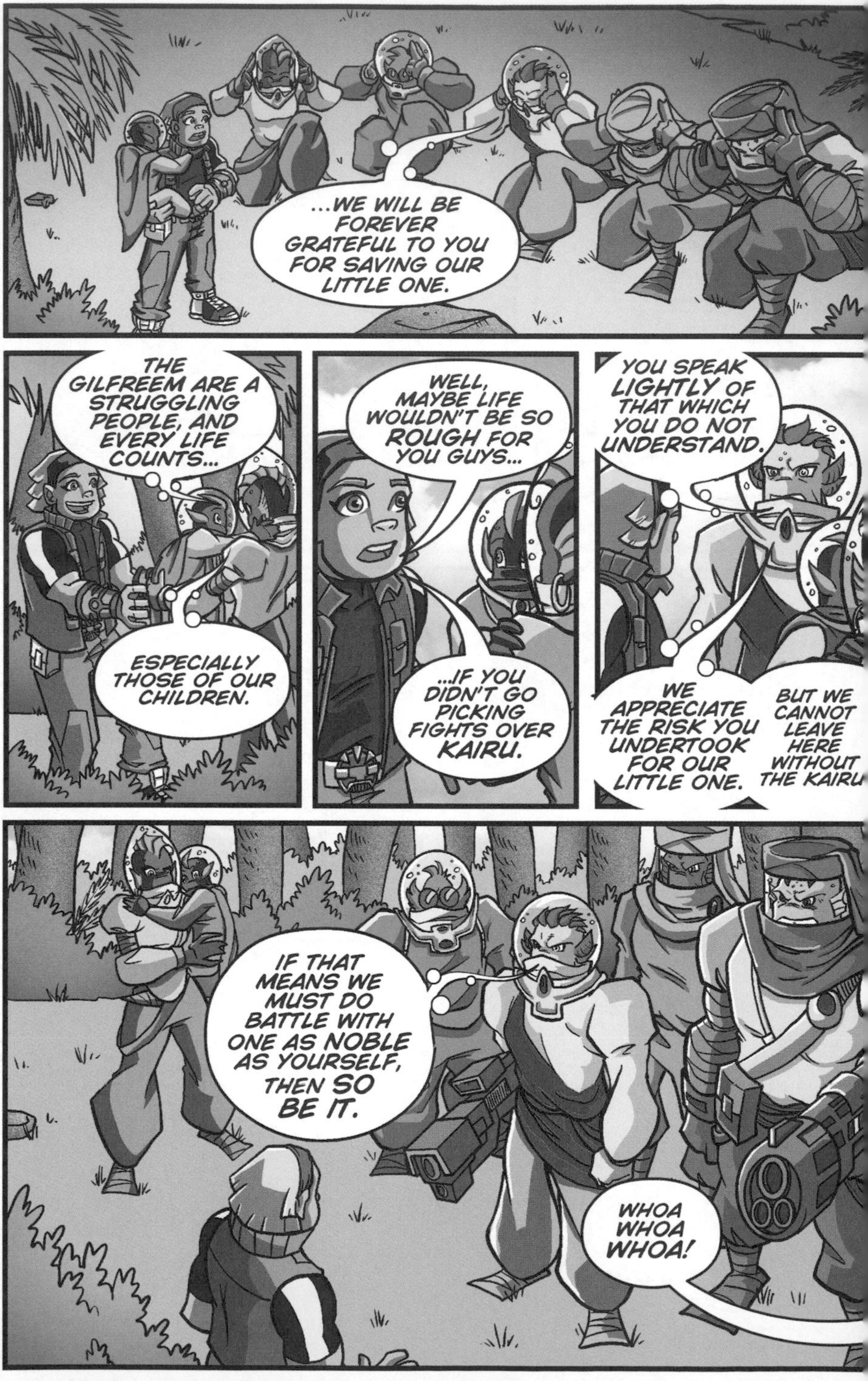
...WE WILL BE FOREVER GRATEFUL TO YOU FOR SAVING OUR LITTLE ONE.
THE GILFREEM ARE A STRUGGLING PEOPLE, AND EVERY LIFE COUNTS...
ESPECIALLY THOSE OF OUR CHILDREN.
WELL, MAYBE LIFE WOULDN'T BE SO ROUGH FOR YOU GUYS...
...IF YOU DIDN'T GO PICKING FIGHTS OVER KAIRU.
YOU SPEAK LIGHTLY OF THAT WHICH YOU DO NOT UNDERSTAND.
WE APPRECIATE THE RISK YOU UNDERTOOK FOR OUR LITTLE ONE.
BUT WE CANNOT LEAVE HERE WITHOUT THE KAIRU
IF THAT MEANS WE MUST DO BATTLE WITH ONE AS NOBLE AS YOURSELF, THEN SO BE IT.
WHOA WHOA WHOA!

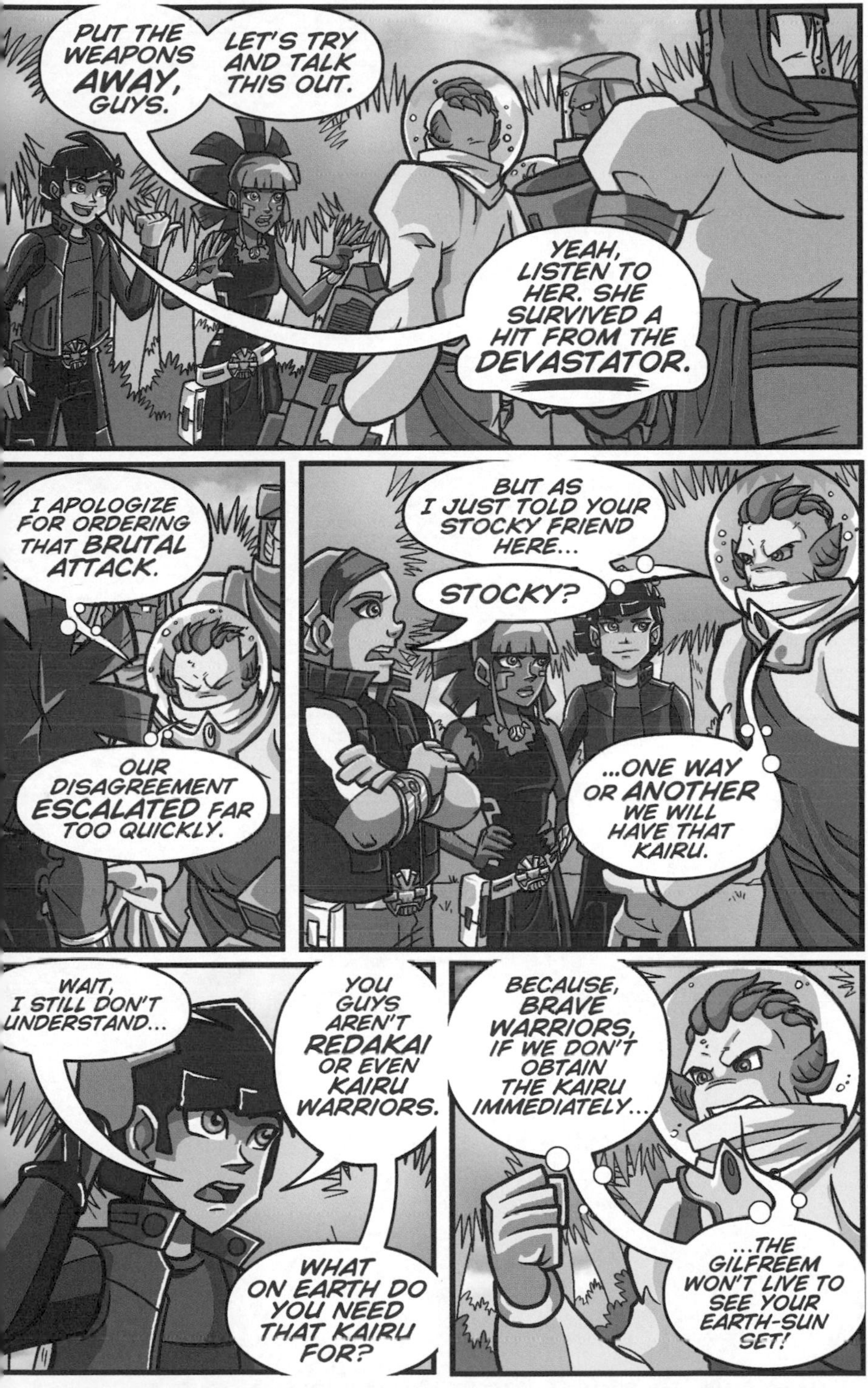
PUT THE WEAPONS AWAY, GUYS.
LET'S TRY AND TALK THIS OUT.
YEAH, LISTEN TO HER. SHE SURVIVED A HIT FROM THE DEVASTATOR.
I APOLOGIZE FOR ORDERING THAT BRUTAL ATTACK.
OUR DISAGREEMENT ESCALATED FAR TOO QUICKLY.
BUT AS I JUST TOLD YOUR STOCKY FRIEND HERE...
STOCKY?
...ONE WAY OR ANOTHER WE WILL HAVE THAT KAIRU.
WAIT, I STILL DON'T UNDERSTAND...
YOU GUYS AREN'T REDAKAI OR EVEN KAIRU WARRIORS.
WHAT ON EARTH DO YOU NEED THAT KAIRU FOR?
BECAUSE, BRAVE WARRIORS, IF WE DON'T OBTAIN THE KAIRU IMMEDIATELY...
...THE GILFREEM WON'T LIVE TO SEE YOUR EARTH-SUN SET!

INVASION OF THE GILFREEM
CHAPTER 3
Gilfrea Exodus

Story by **Aubrey Sitterson**
Art by **Zack Turner**

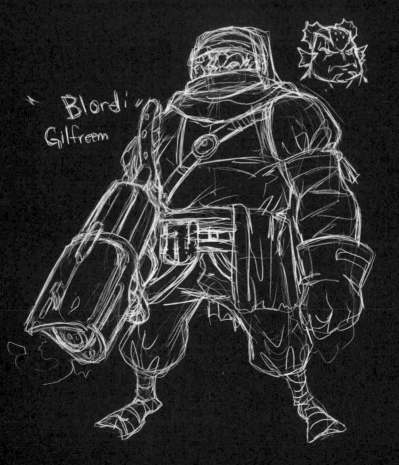

"Blordi"
Gilfreem

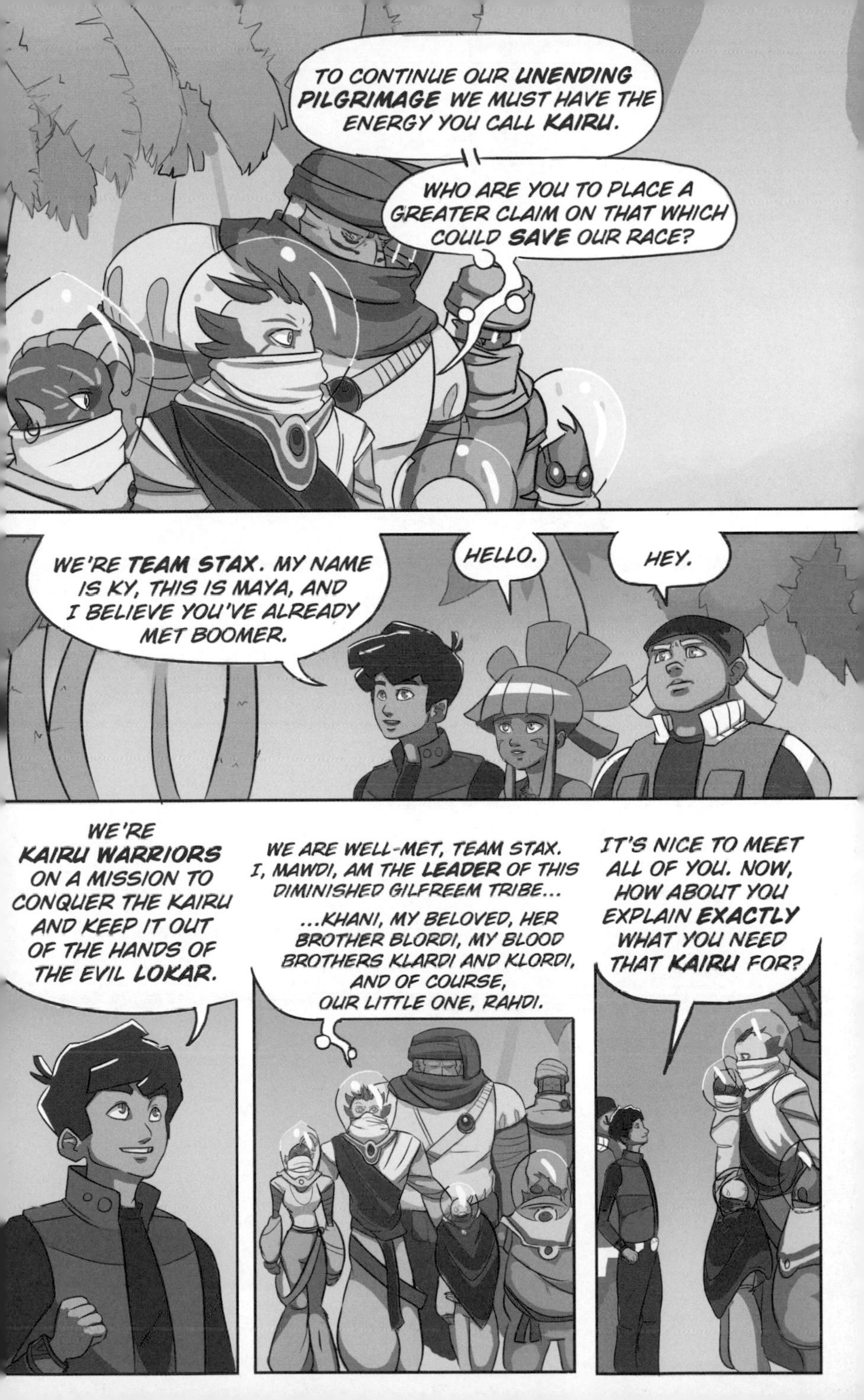
TO CONTINUE OUR UNENDING PILGRIMAGE WE MUST HAVE THE ENERGY YOU CALL KAIRU.
WHO ARE YOU TO PLACE A GREATER CLAIM ON THAT WHICH COULD SAVE OUR RACE?
WE'RE TEAM STAX. MY NAME IS KY, THIS IS MAYA, AND I BELIEVE YOU'VE ALREADY MET BOOMER.
HELLO.
HEY.
WE'RE KAIRU WARRIORS ON A MISSION TO CONQUER THE KAIRU AND KEEP IT OUT OF THE HANDS OF THE EVIL LOKAR.
WE ARE WELL-MET, TEAM STAX. I, MAWDI, AM THE LEADER OF THIS DIMINISHED GILFREEM TRIBE...
...KHANI, MY BELOVED, HER BROTHER BLORDI, MY BLOOD BROTHERS KLARDI AND KLORDI, AND OF COURSE, OUR LITTLE ONE, RAHDI.
IT'S NICE TO MEET ALL OF YOU. NOW, HOW ABOUT YOU EXPLAIN EXACTLY WHAT YOU NEED THAT KAIRU FOR?

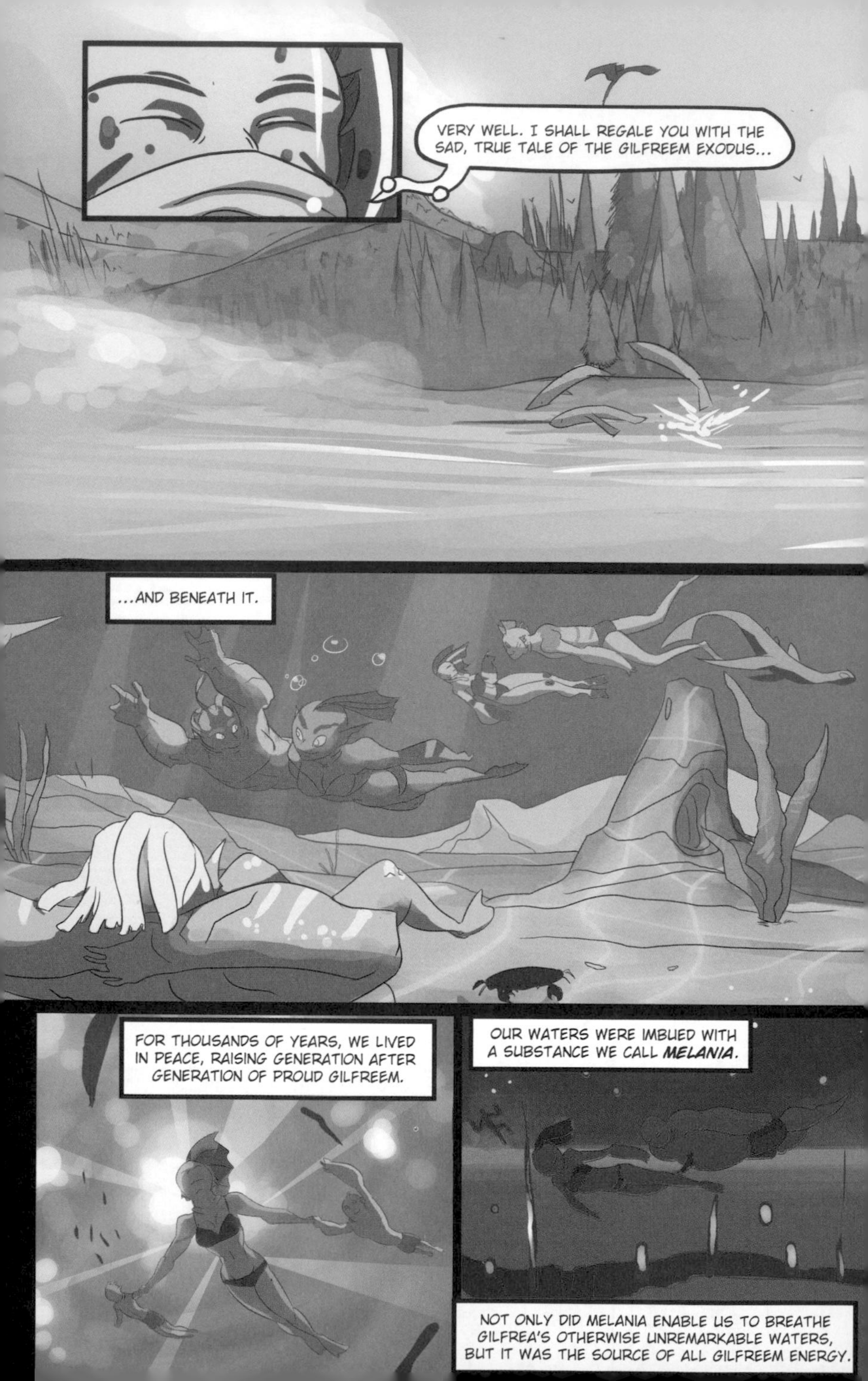

VERY WELL. I SHALL REGALE YOU WITH THE SAD, TRUE TALE OF THE GILFREEM EXODUS...
...AND BENEATH IT.
FOR THOUSANDS OF YEARS, WE LIVED IN PEACE, RAISING GENERATION AFTER GENERATION OF PROUD GILFREEM.
OUR WATERS WERE IMBUED WITH A SUBSTANCE WE CALL MELANIA.
NOT ONLY DID MELANIA ENABLE US TO BREATHE GILFREA'S OTHERWISE UNREMARKABLE WATERS, BUT IT WAS THE SOURCE OF ALL GILFREEM ENERGY.

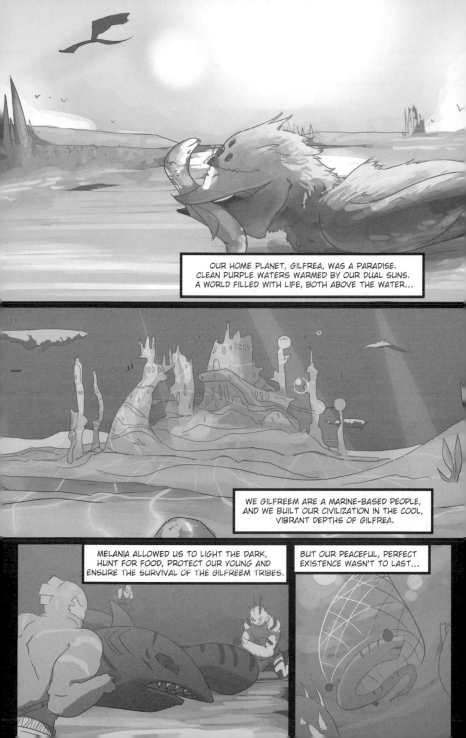

OUR HOME PLANET, GILFREA, WAS A PARADISE.
CLEAN PURPLE WATERS WARMED BY OUR DUAL SUNS.
A WORLD FILLED WITH LIFE, BOTH ABOVE THE WATER...

WE GILFREEM ARE A MARINE-BASED PEOPLE,
AND WE BUILT OUR CIVILIZATION IN THE COOL,
VIBRANT DEPTHS OF GILFREA.

MELANIA ALLOWED US TO LIGHT THE DARK,
HUNT FOR FOOD, PROTECT OUR YOUNG AND
ENSURE THE SURVIVAL OF THE GILFREEM TRIBES.

BUT OUR PEACEFUL, PERFECT
EXISTENCE WASN'T TO LAST...

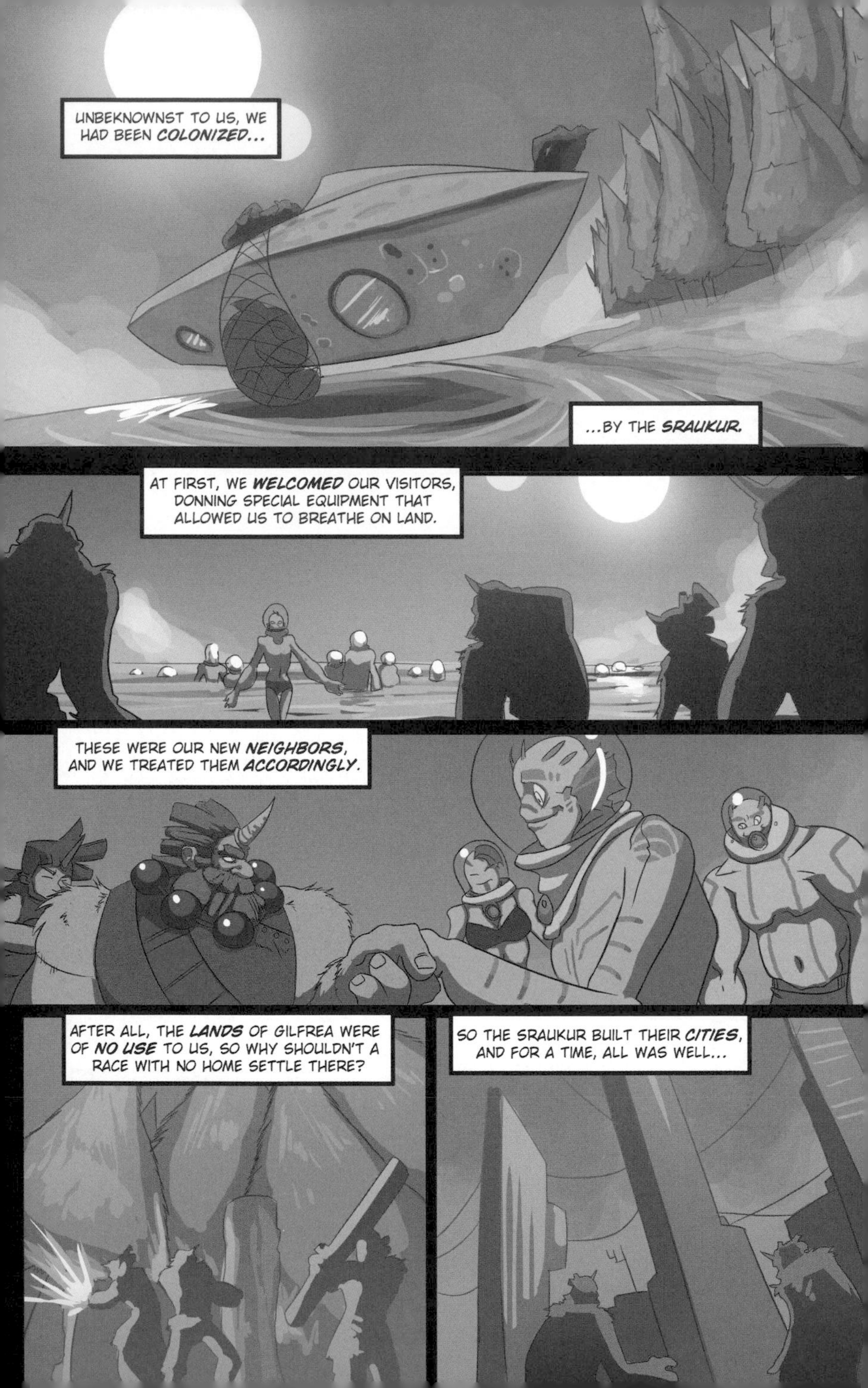
UNBEKNOWNST TO US, WE HAD BEEN COLONIZED...
...BY THE SRAUKUR.
AT FIRST, WE WELCOMED OUR VISITORS, DONNING SPECIAL EQUIPMENT THAT ALLOWED US TO BREATHE ON LAND.
THESE WERE OUR NEW NEIGHBORS, AND WE TREATED THEM ACCORDINGLY.
AFTER ALL, THE LANDS OF GILFREA WERE OF NO USE TO US, SO WHY SHOULDN'T A RACE WITH NO HOME SETTLE THERE?
SO THE SRAUKUR BUILT THEIR CITIES, AND FOR A TIME, ALL WAS WELL...

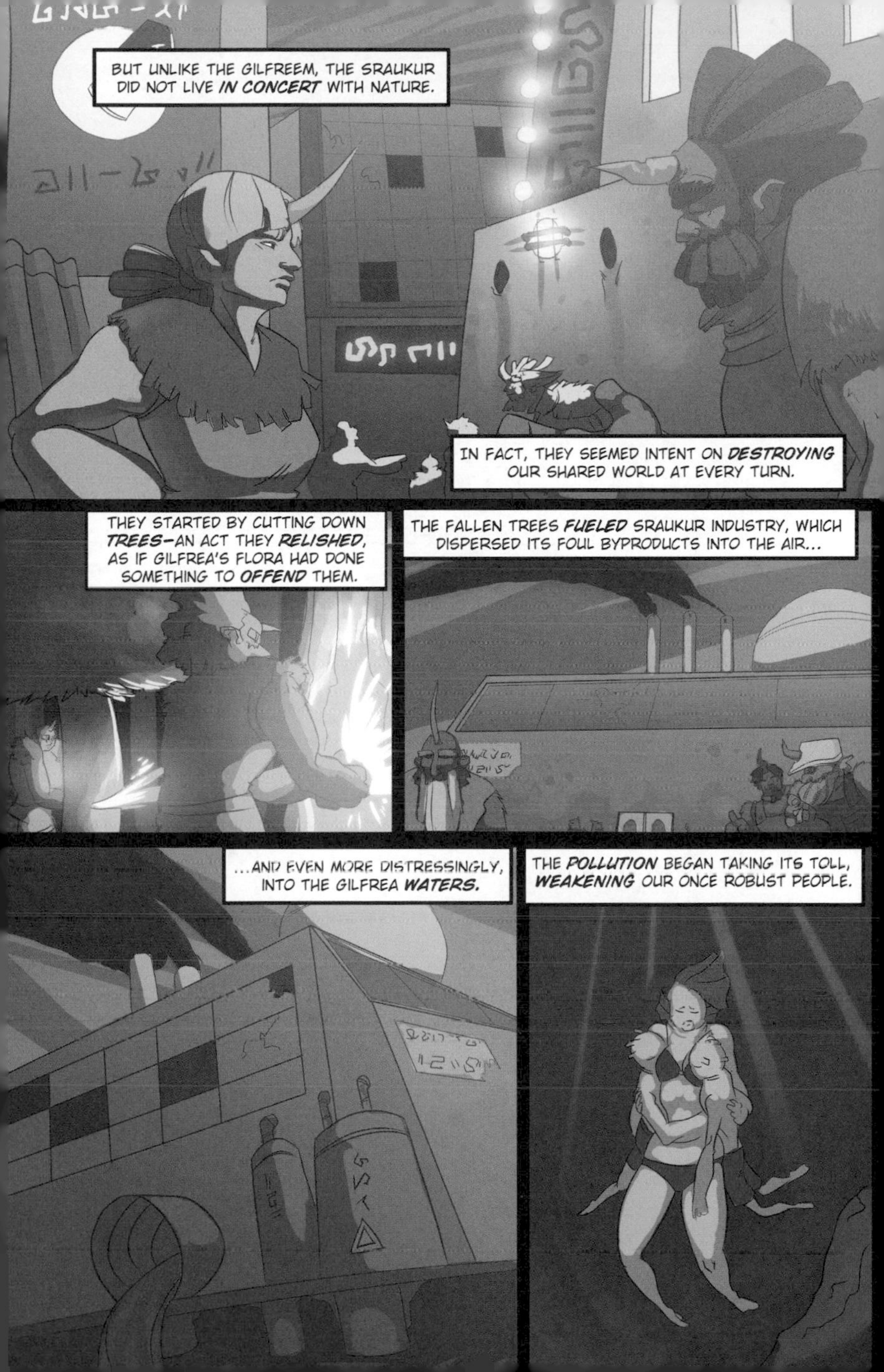
BUT UNLIKE THE GILFREEM, THE SRAUKUR DID NOT LIVE *IN CONCERT* WITH NATURE.
IN FACT, THEY SEEMED INTENT ON *DESTROYING* OUR SHARED WORLD AT EVERY TURN.
THEY STARTED BY CUTTING DOWN *TREES*—AN ACT THEY *RELISHED*, AS IF GILFREA'S FLORA HAD DONE SOMETHING TO *OFFEND* THEM.
THE FALLEN TREES *FUELED* SRAUKUR INDUSTRY, WHICH DISPERSED ITS FOUL BYPRODUCTS INTO THE AIR...
...AND EVEN MORE DISTRESSINGLY, INTO THE GILFREA *WATERS.*
THE *POLLUTION* BEGAN TAKING ITS TOLL, *WEAKENING* OUR ONCE ROBUST PEOPLE.

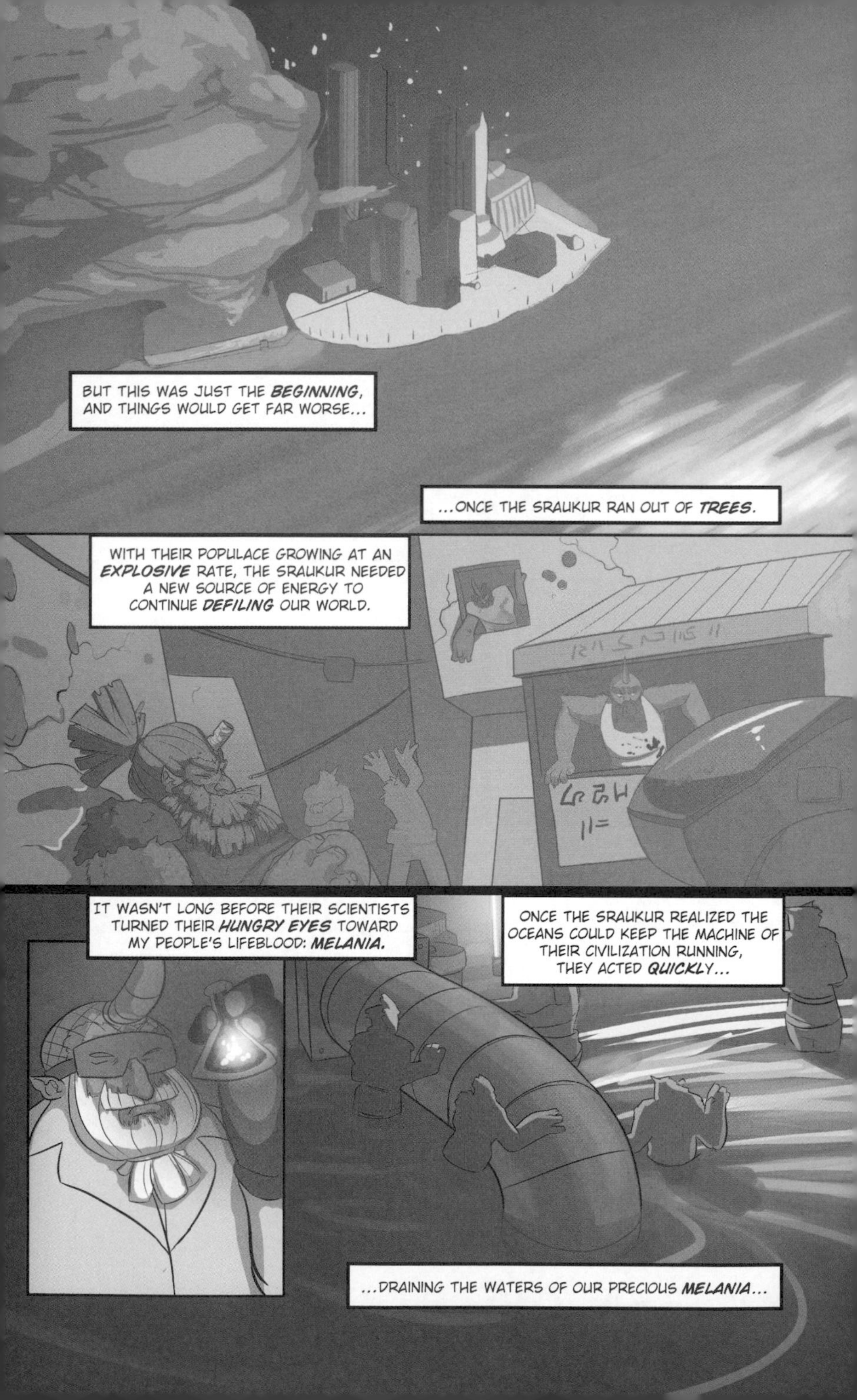
BUT THIS WAS JUST THE BEGINNING, AND THINGS WOULD GET FAR WORSE...
...ONCE THE SRAUKUR RAN OUT OF TREES.
WITH THEIR POPULACE GROWING AT AN EXPLOSIVE RATE, THE SRAUKUR NEEDED A NEW SOURCE OF ENERGY TO CONTINUE DEFILING OUR WORLD.
IT WASN'T LONG BEFORE THEIR SCIENTISTS TURNED THEIR HUNGRY EYES TOWARD MY PEOPLE'S LIFEBLOOD: MELANIA.
ONCE THE SRAUKUR REALIZED THE OCEANS COULD KEEP THE MACHINE OF THEIR CIVILIZATION RUNNING, THEY ACTED QUICKLY...
...DRAINING THE WATERS OF OUR PRECIOUS MELANIA...

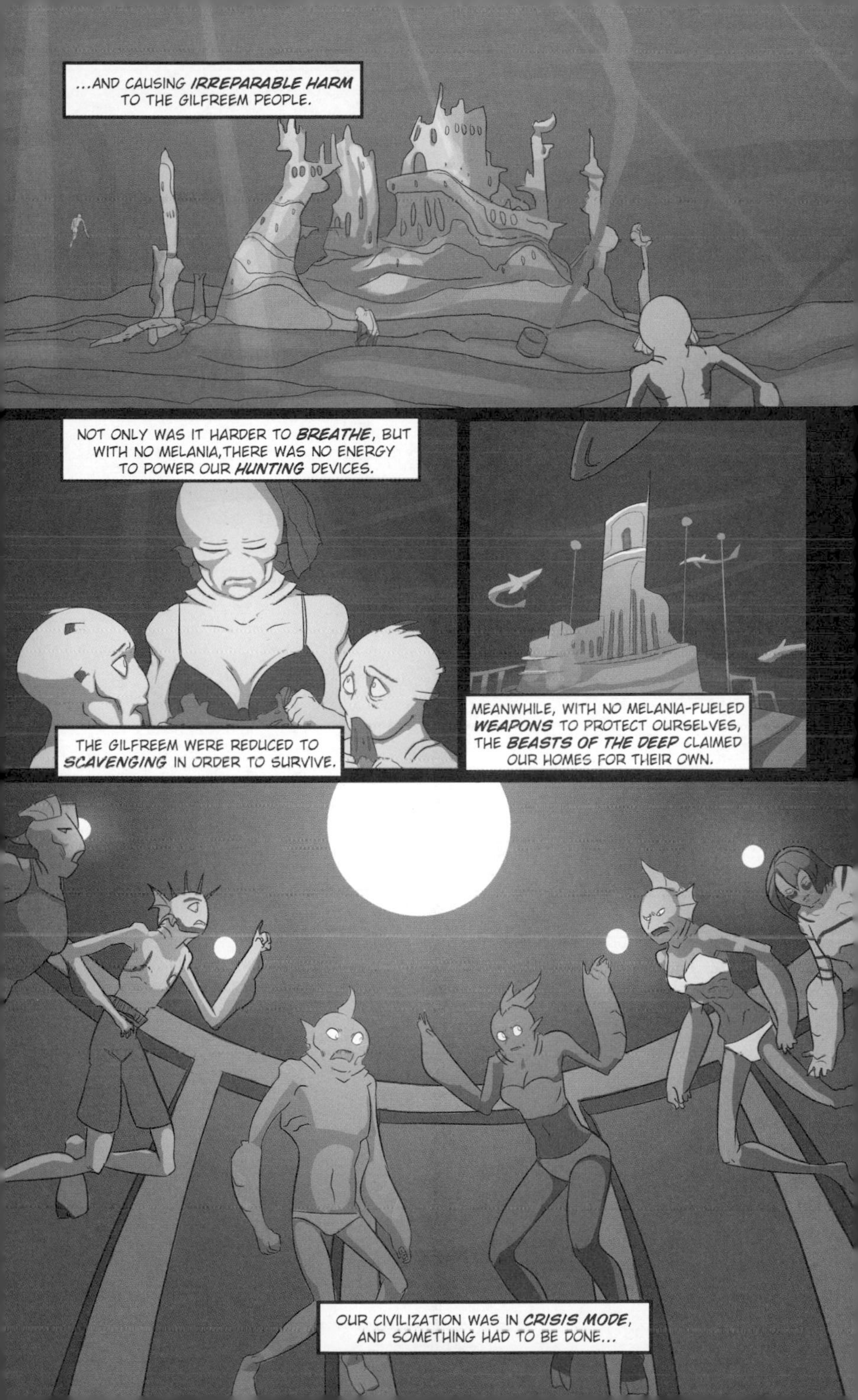
...AND CAUSING IRREPARABLE HARM TO THE GILFREEM PEOPLE.
NOT ONLY WAS IT HARDER TO BREATHE, BUT WITH NO MELANIA,THERE WAS NO ENERGY TO POWER OUR HUNTING DEVICES.
THE GILFREEM WERE REDUCED TO SCAVENGING IN ORDER TO SURVIVE.
MEANWHILE, WITH NO MELANIA-FUELED WEAPONS TO PROTECT OURSELVES, THE BEASTS OF THE DEEP CLAIMED OUR HOMES FOR THEIR OWN.
OUR CIVILIZATION WAS IN CRISIS MODE, AND SOMETHING HAD TO BE DONE...

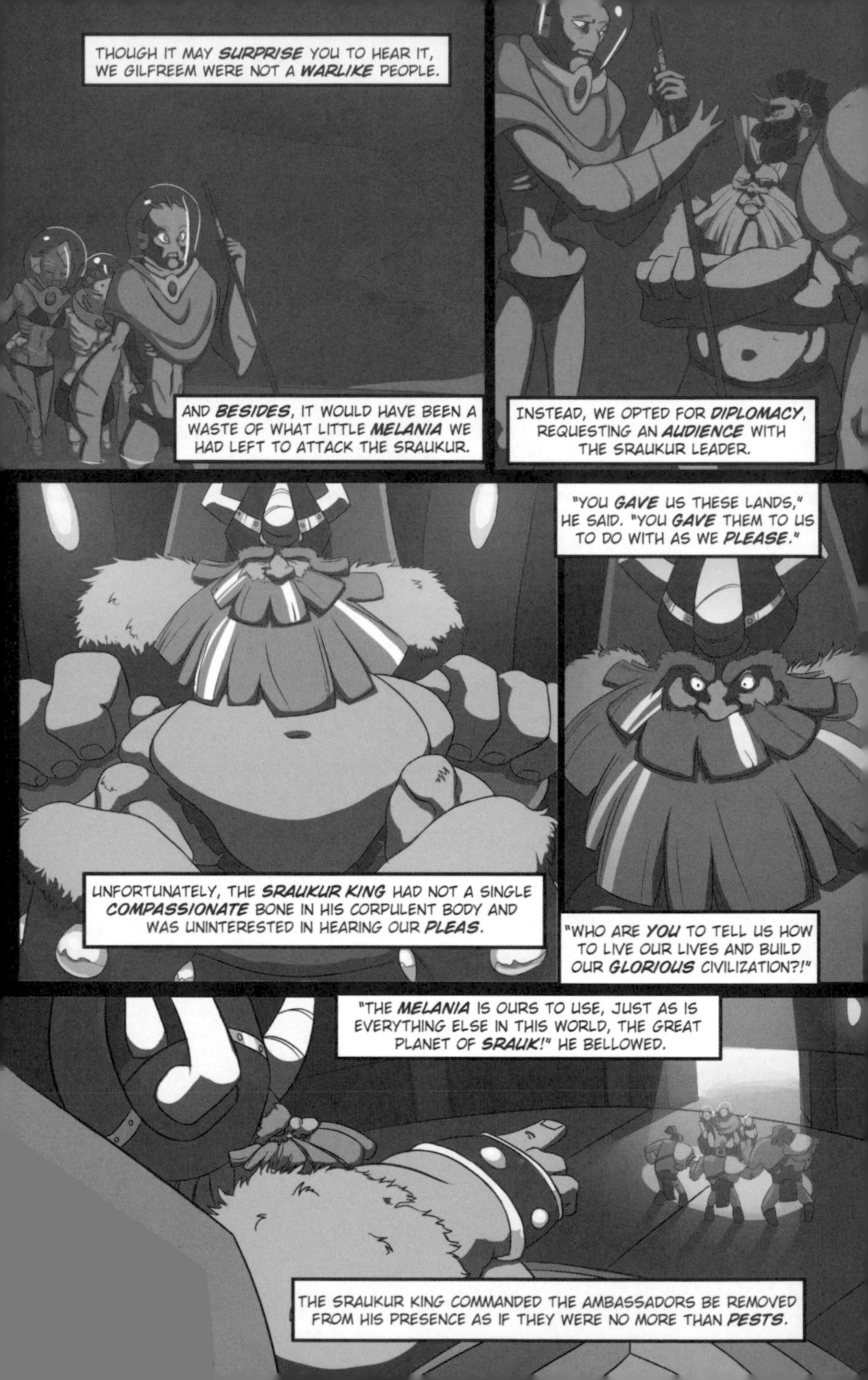
THOUGH IT MAY SURPRISE YOU TO HEAR IT, WE GILFREEM WERE NOT A WARLIKE PEOPLE.
AND BESIDES, IT WOULD HAVE BEEN A WASTE OF WHAT LITTLE MELANIA WE HAD LEFT TO ATTACK THE SRAUKUR.
INSTEAD, WE OPTED FOR DIPLOMACY, REQUESTING AN AUDIENCE WITH THE SRAUKUR LEADER.
UNFORTUNATELY, THE SRAUKUR KING HAD NOT A SINGLE COMPASSIONATE BONE IN HIS CORPULENT BODY AND WAS UNINTERESTED IN HEARING OUR PLEAS.
"YOU GAVE US THESE LANDS," HE SAID. "YOU GAVE THEM TO US TO DO WITH AS WE PLEASE."
"WHO ARE YOU TO TELL US HOW TO LIVE OUR LIVES AND BUILD OUR GLORIOUS CIVILIZATION?!"
"THE MELANIA IS OURS TO USE, JUST AS IS EVERYTHING ELSE IN THIS WORLD, THE GREAT PLANET OF SRAUK!" HE BELLOWED.
THE SRAUKUR KING COMMANDED THE AMBASSADORS BE REMOVED FROM HIS PRESENCE AS IF THEY WERE NO MORE THAN PESTS.

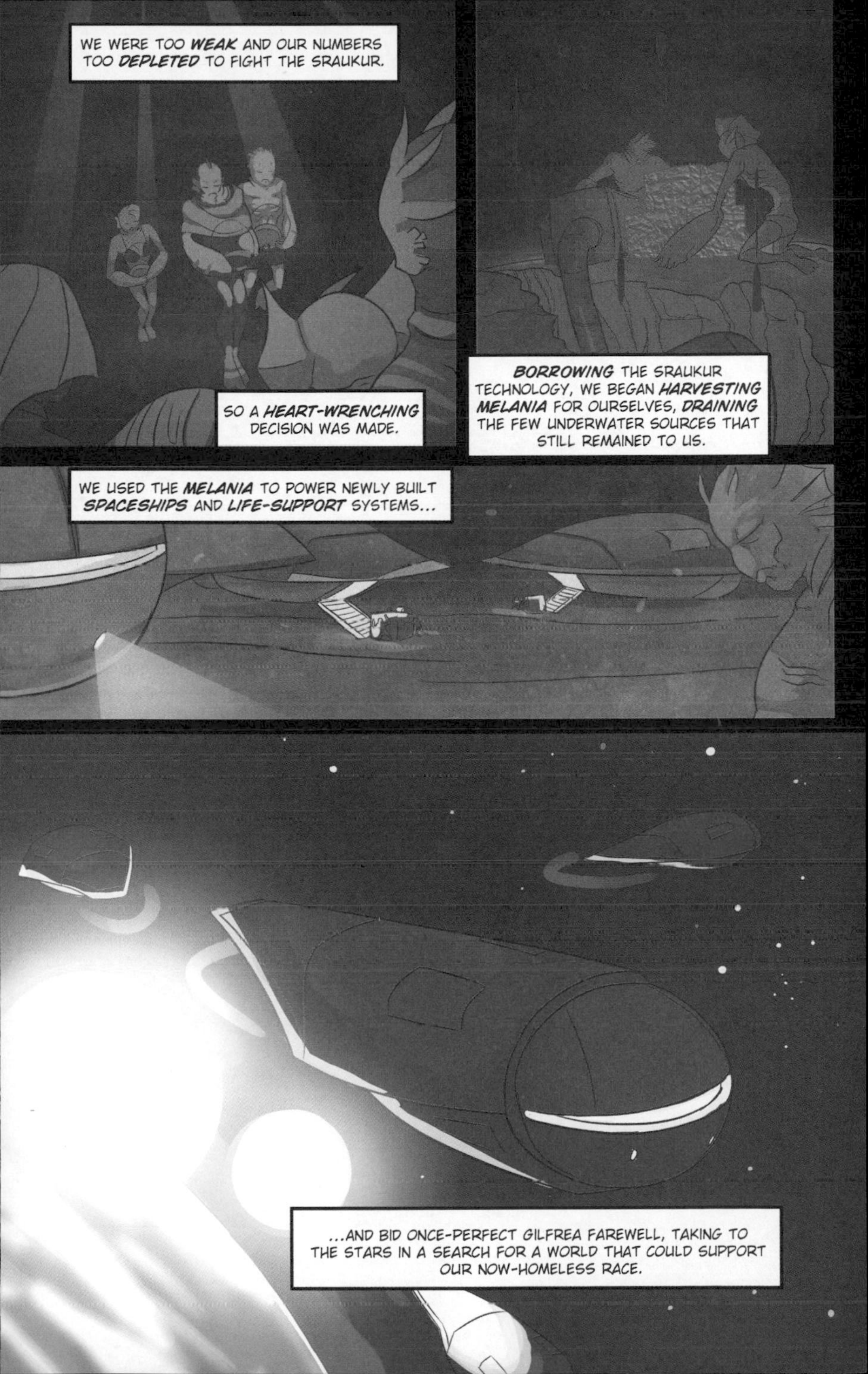
WE WERE TOO WEAK AND OUR NUMBERS TOO DEPLETED TO FIGHT THE SRAUKUR.
SO A HEART-WRENCHING DECISION WAS MADE.
BORROWING THE SRAUKUR TECHNOLOGY, WE BEGAN HARVESTING MELANIA FOR OURSELVES, DRAINING THE FEW UNDERWATER SOURCES THAT STILL REMAINED TO US.
WE USED THE MELANIA TO POWER NEWLY BUILT SPACESHIPS AND LIFE-SUPPORT SYSTEMS...
...AND BID ONCE-PERFECT GILFREA FAREWELL, TAKING TO THE STARS IN A SEARCH FOR A WORLD THAT COULD SUPPORT OUR NOW-HOMELESS RACE.

ONCE, WE WERE NOT A *VIOLENT* PEOPLE. THE IDEA OF FIGHTING DAILY FOR OUR SURVIVAL WAS COMPLETELY *FOREIGN* TO US.

BUT AS WE SPREAD OUT THROUGH THE *GALAXY*, WE FOUND *DANGERS* EVEN GREATER THAN THE SRAUKUR.

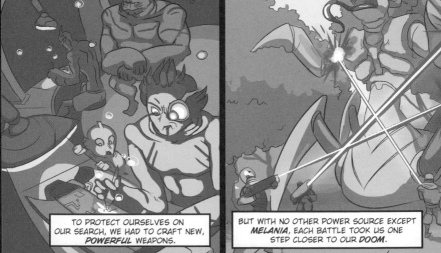

TO PROTECT OURSELVES ON OUR SEARCH, WE HAD TO CRAFT NEW, *POWERFUL* WEAPONS.

BUT WITH NO OTHER POWER SOURCE EXCEPT *MELANIA*, EACH BATTLE TOOK US ONE STEP CLOSER TO OUR *DOOM*.

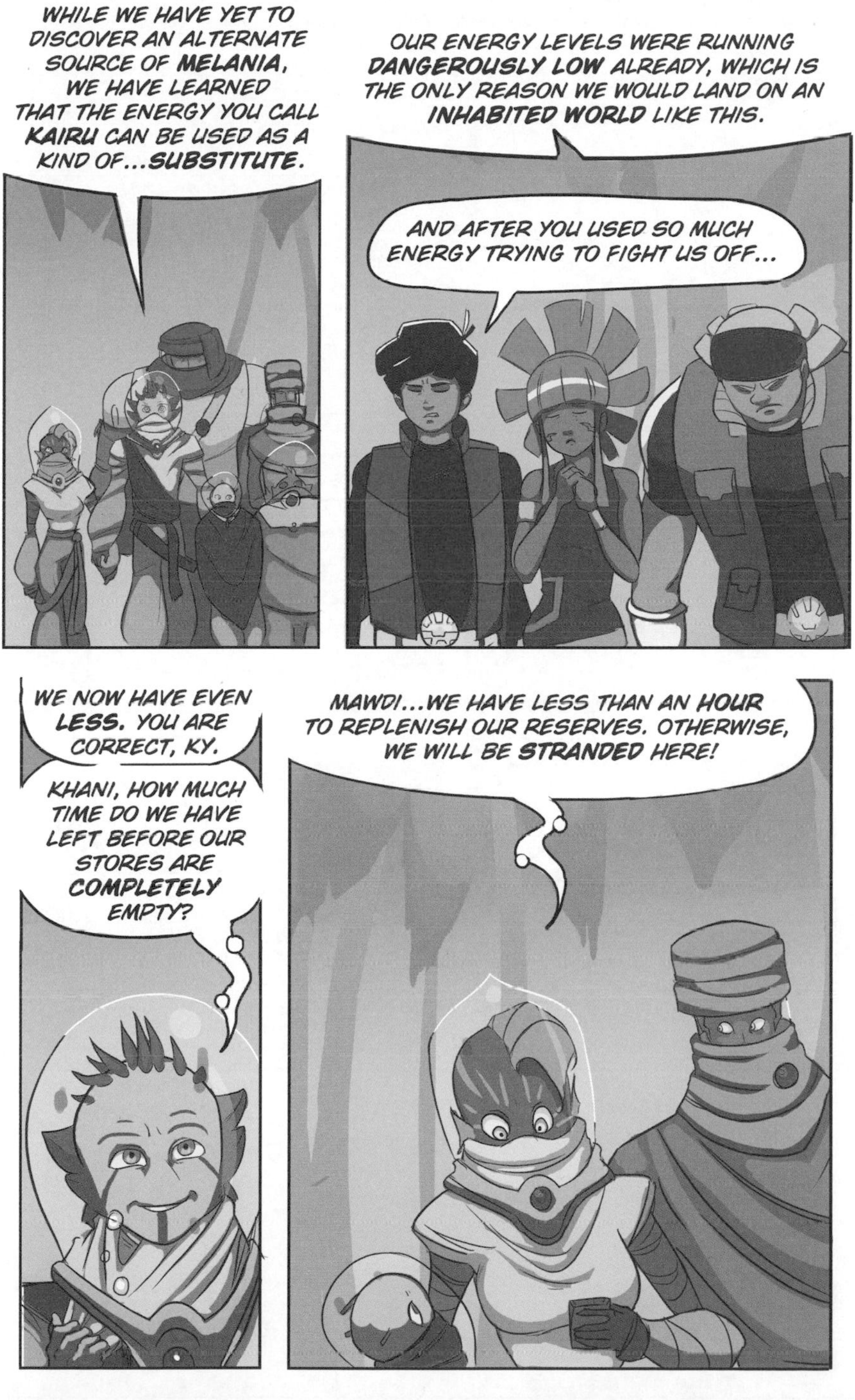
WHILE WE HAVE YET TO DISCOVER AN ALTERNATE SOURCE OF **MELANIA**, WE HAVE LEARNED THAT THE ENERGY YOU CALL **KAIRU** CAN BE USED AS A KIND OF... **SUBSTITUTE**.
OUR ENERGY LEVELS WERE RUNNING **DANGEROUSLY LOW** ALREADY, WHICH IS THE ONLY REASON WE WOULD LAND ON AN **INHABITED WORLD** LIKE THIS.
AND AFTER YOU USED SO MUCH ENERGY TRYING TO FIGHT US OFF...
WE NOW HAVE EVEN **LESS**. YOU ARE CORRECT, KY.
KHANI, HOW MUCH TIME DO WE HAVE LEFT BEFORE OUR STORES ARE **COMPLETELY** EMPTY?
MAWDI... WE HAVE LESS THAN AN **HOUR** TO REPLENISH OUR RESERVES. OTHERWISE, WE WILL BE **STRANDED** HERE!

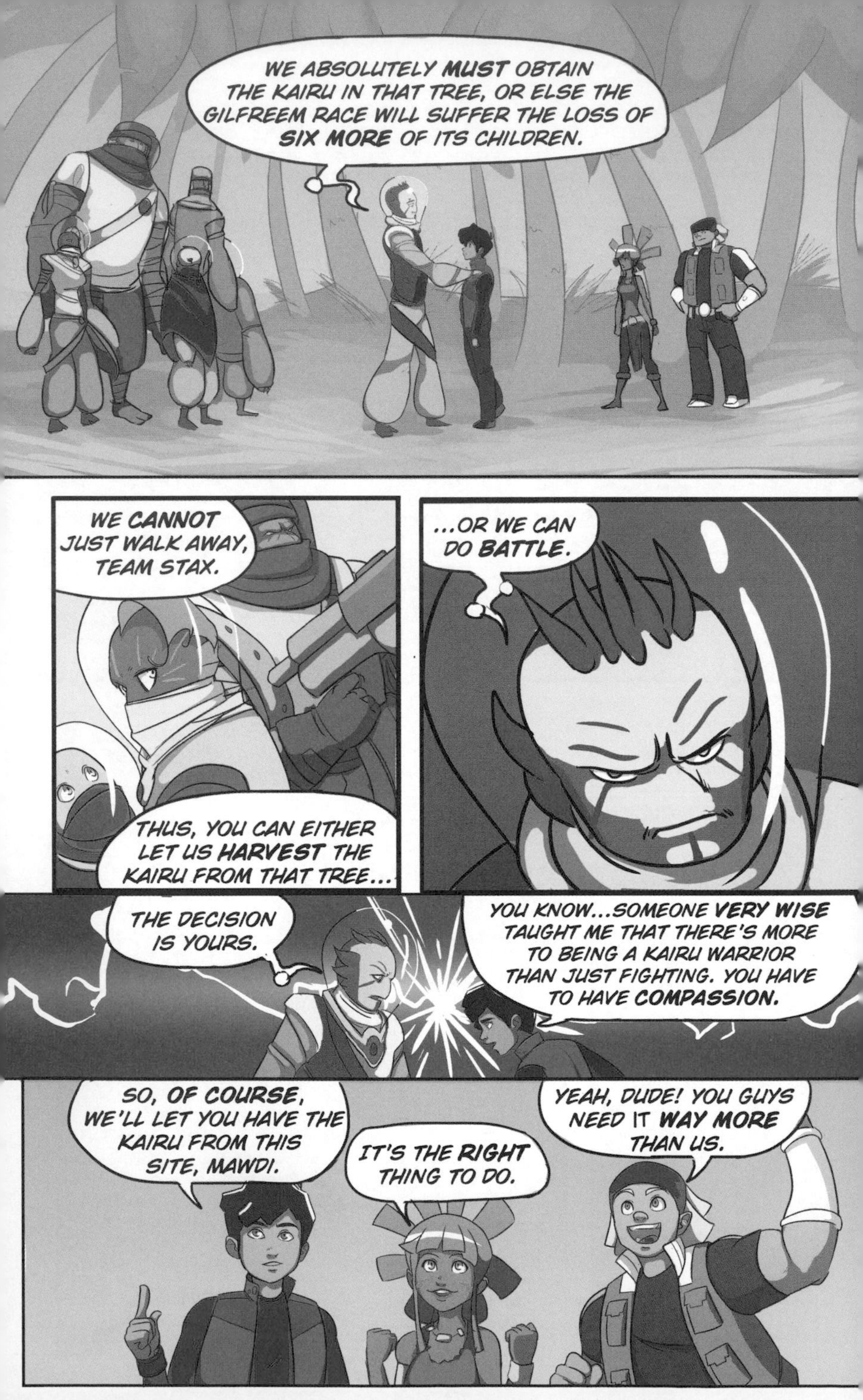
WE ABSOLUTELY MUST OBTAIN THE KAIRU IN THAT TREE, OR ELSE THE GILFREEM RACE WILL SUFFER THE LOSS OF SIX MORE OF ITS CHILDREN.
WE CANNOT JUST WALK AWAY, TEAM STAX.
THUS, YOU CAN EITHER LET US HARVEST THE KAIRU FROM THAT TREE...
...OR WE CAN DO BATTLE.
THE DECISION IS YOURS.
YOU KNOW...SOMEONE VERY WISE TAUGHT ME THAT THERE'S MORE TO BEING A KAIRU WARRIOR THAN JUST FIGHTING. YOU HAVE TO HAVE COMPASSION.
SO, OF COURSE, WE'LL LET YOU HAVE THE KAIRU FROM THIS SITE, MAWDI.
IT'S THE RIGHT THING TO DO.
YEAH, DUDE! YOU GUYS NEED IT WAY MORE THAN US.

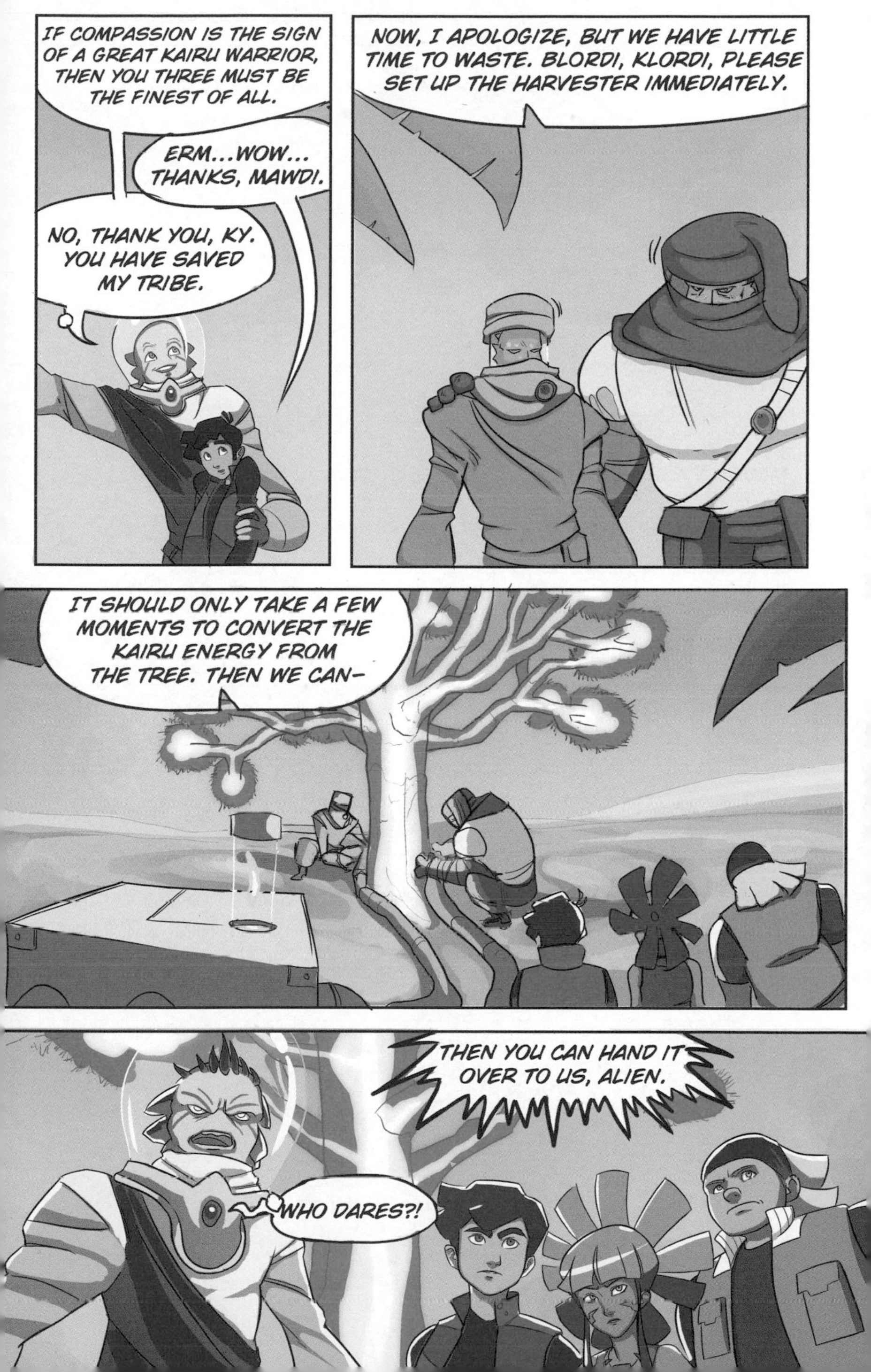
IF COMPASSION IS THE SIGN OF A GREAT KAIRU WARRIOR, THEN YOU THREE MUST BE THE FINEST OF ALL.
ERM...WOW... THANKS, MAWDI.
NO, THANK YOU, KY. YOU HAVE SAVED MY TRIBE.
NOW, I APOLOGIZE, BUT WE HAVE LITTLE TIME TO WASTE. BLORDI, KLORDI, PLEASE SET UP THE HARVESTER IMMEDIATELY.
IT SHOULD ONLY TAKE A FEW MOMENTS TO CONVERT THE KAIRU ENERGY FROM THE TREE. THEN WE CAN-
THEN YOU CAN HAND IT OVER TO US, ALIEN.
WHO DARES?!

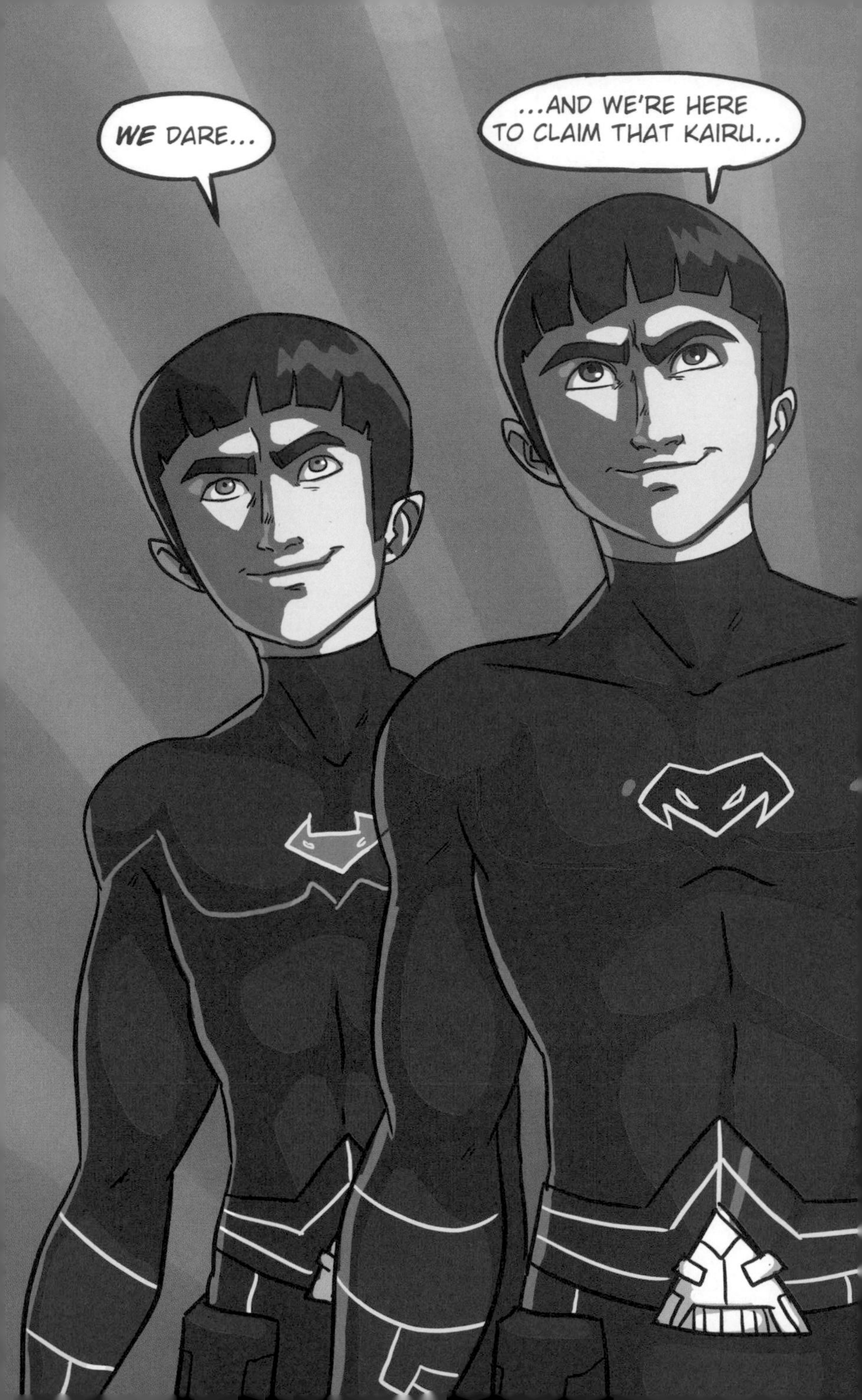
WE DARE...
...AND WE'RE HERE TO CLAIM THAT KAIRU...

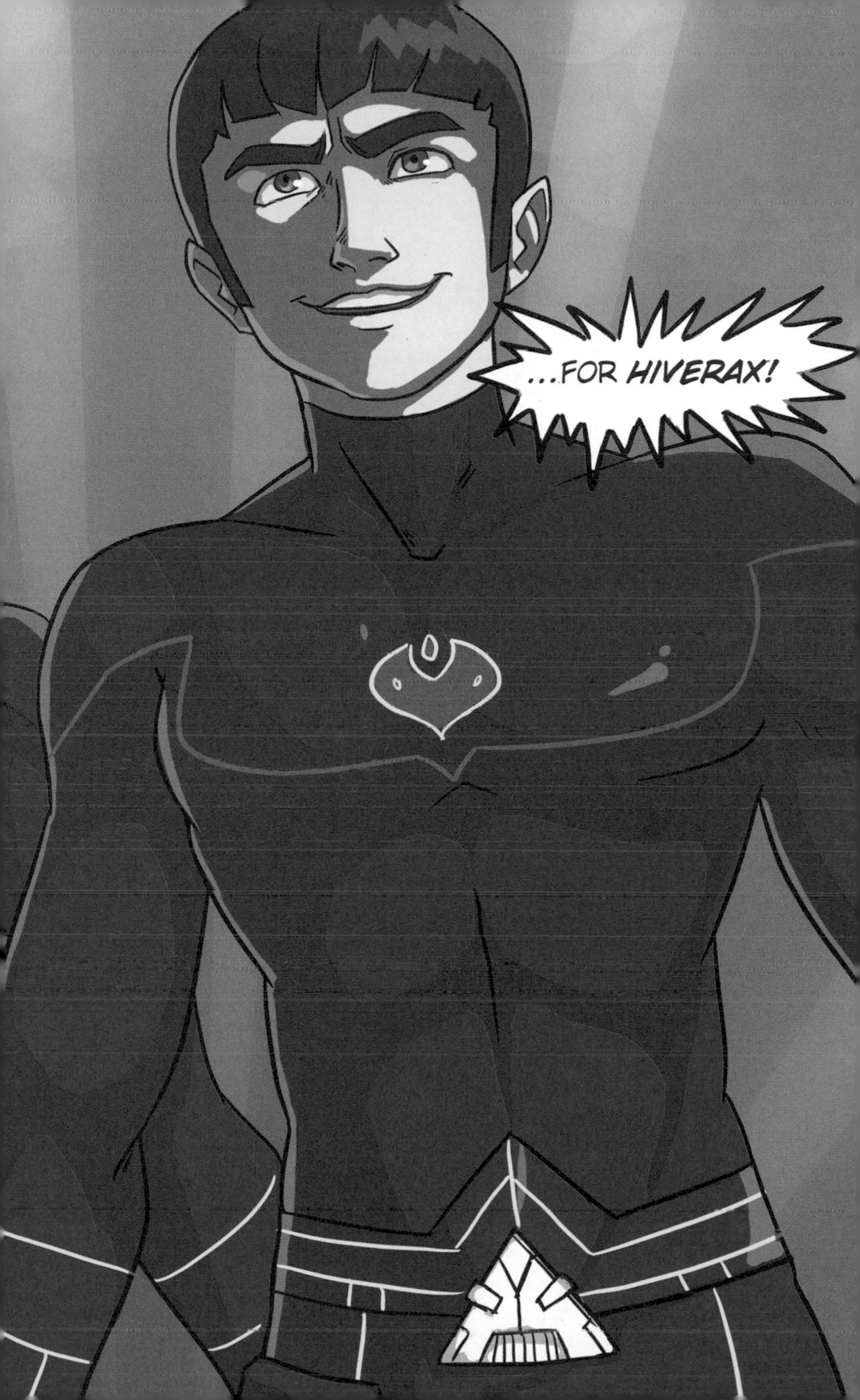
...FOR HIVERAX!

INVASION OF THE GILFREEM

CHAPTER 4
Hiverax Attack

Story by **Aubrey Sitterson**
Art by **Write Height Media**

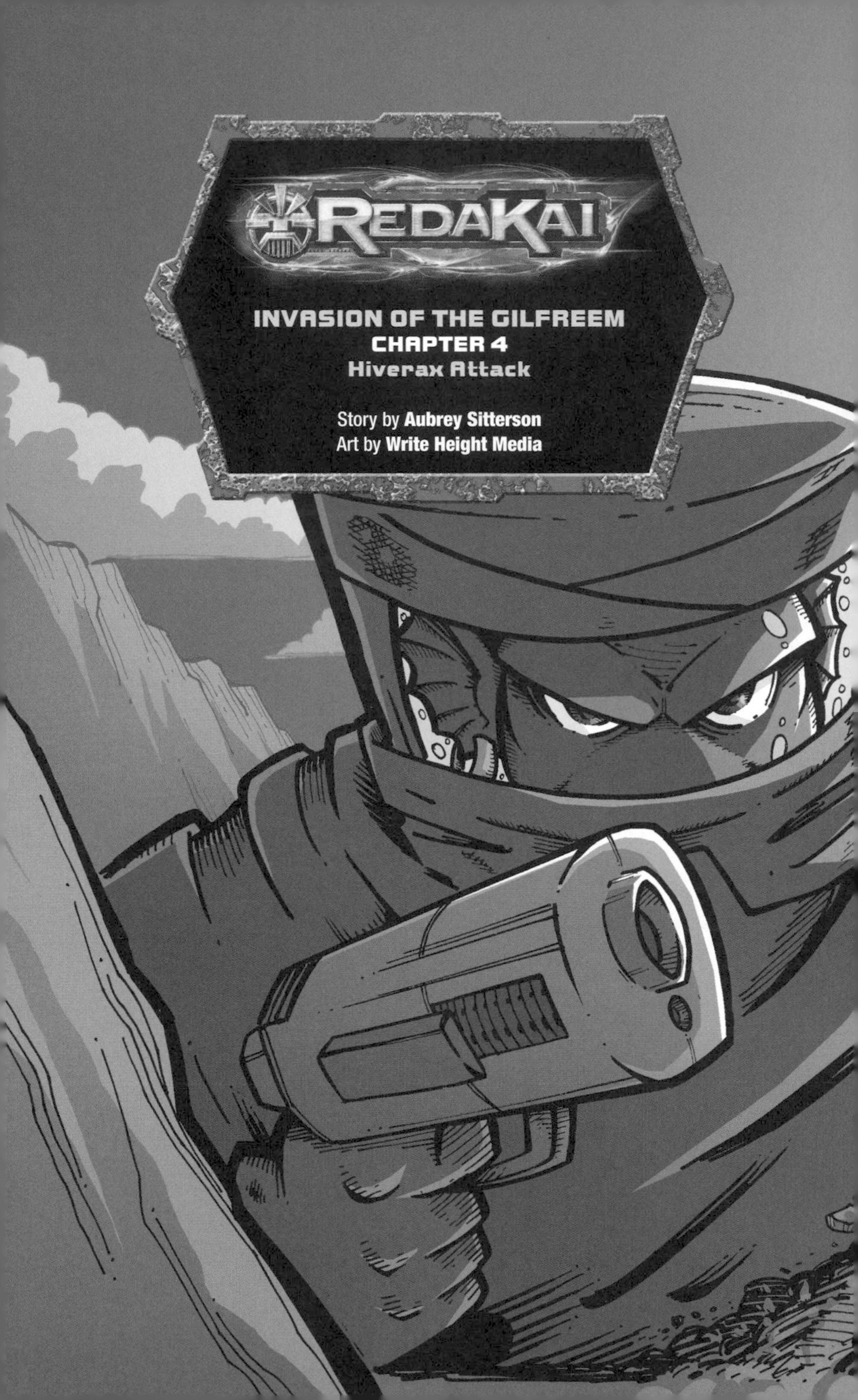
REDAKAI

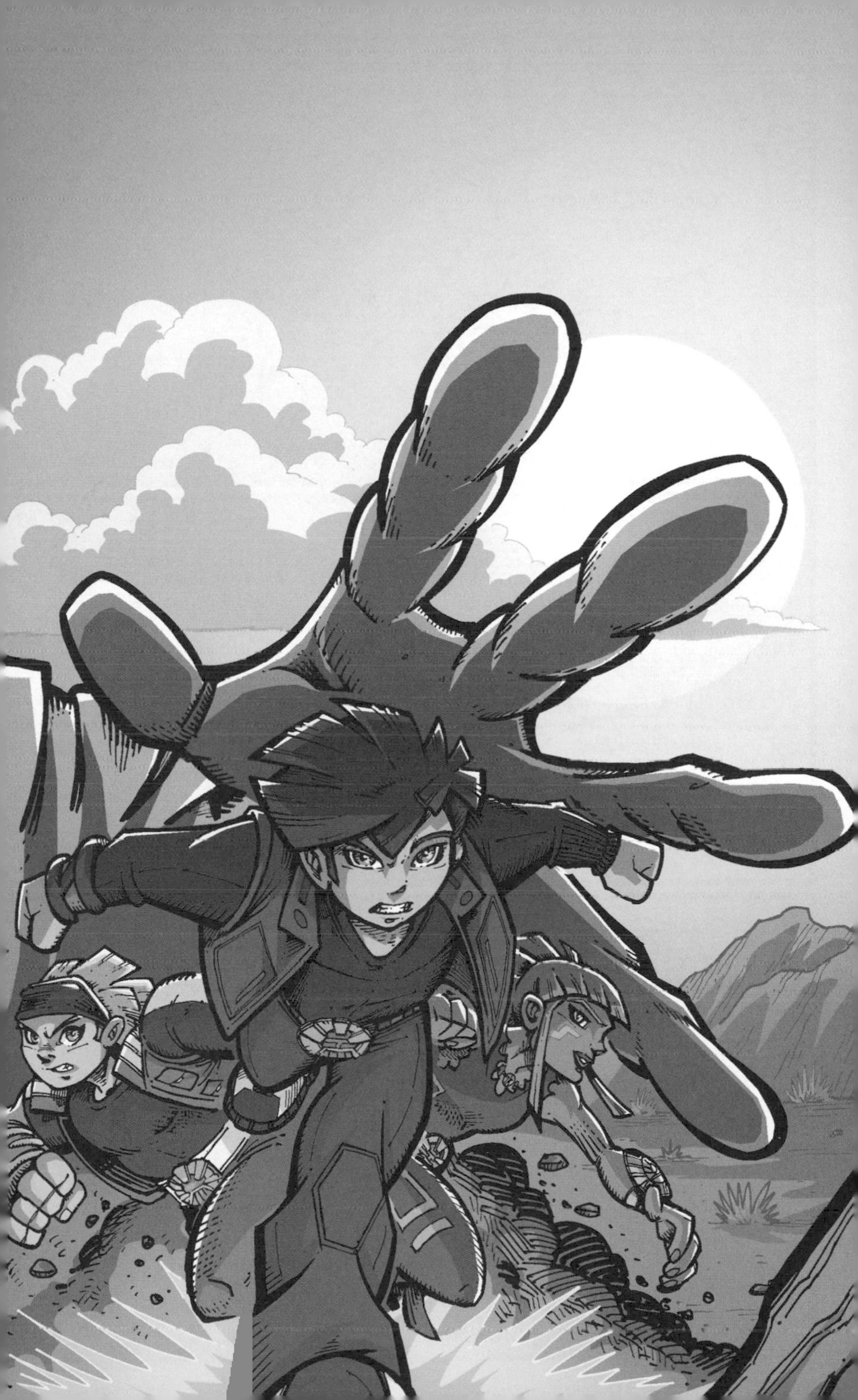

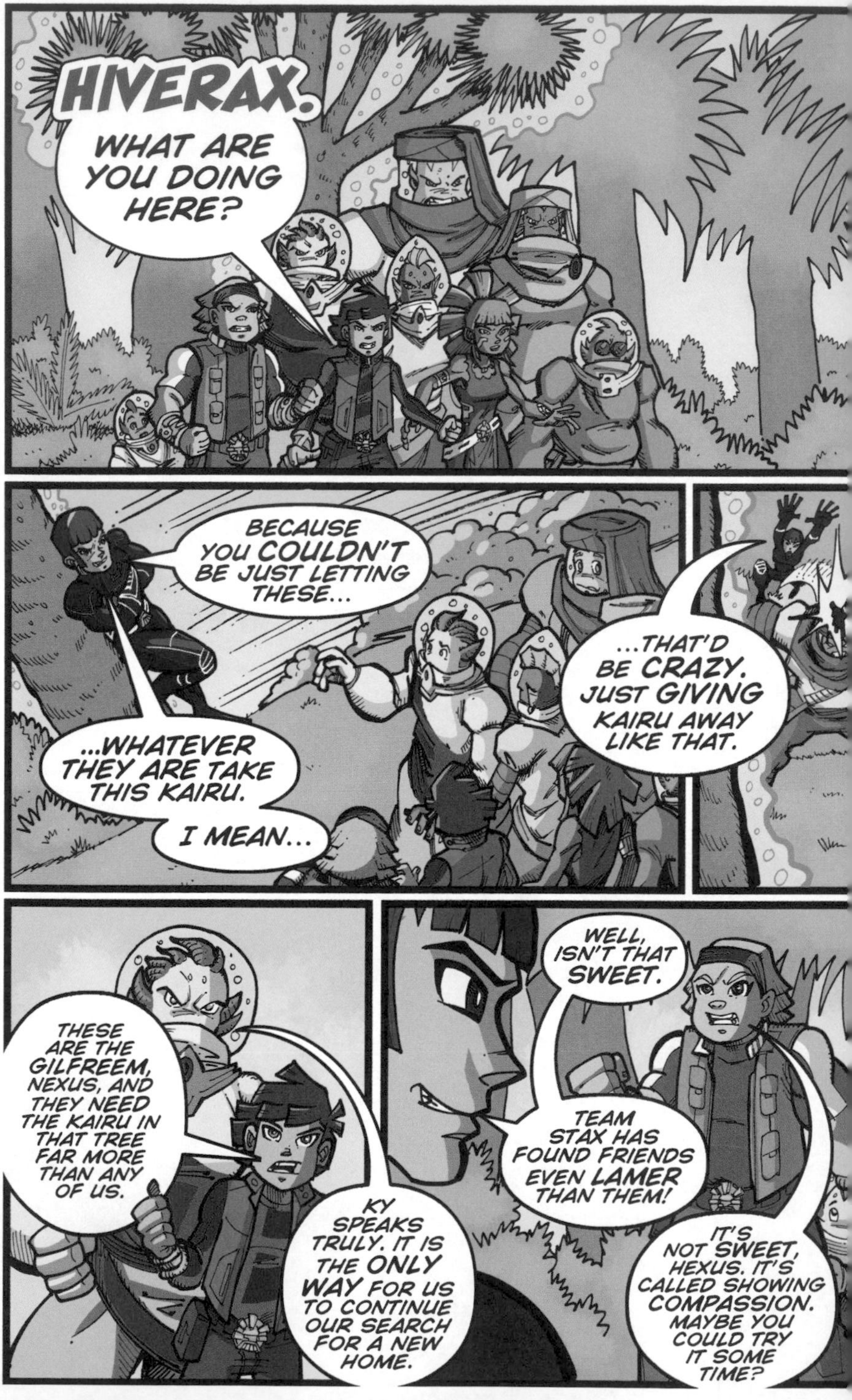
HIVERAX.
WHAT ARE YOU DOING HERE?
BECAUSE YOU COULDN'T BE JUST LETTING THESE...
...WHATEVER THEY ARE TAKE THIS KAIRU.
I MEAN...
...THAT'D BE CRAZY. JUST GIVING KAIRU AWAY LIKE THAT.
THESE ARE THE GILFREEM, NEXUS, AND THEY NEED THE KAIRU IN THAT TREE FAR MORE THAN ANY OF US.
KY SPEAKS TRULY. IT IS THE ONLY WAY FOR US TO CONTINUE OUR SEARCH FOR A NEW HOME.
WELL, ISN'T THAT SWEET.
TEAM STAX HAS FOUND FRIENDS EVEN LAMER THAN THEM!
IT'S NOT SWEET, HEXUS. IT'S CALLED SHOWING COMPASSION. MAYBE YOU COULD TRY IT SOME TIME?

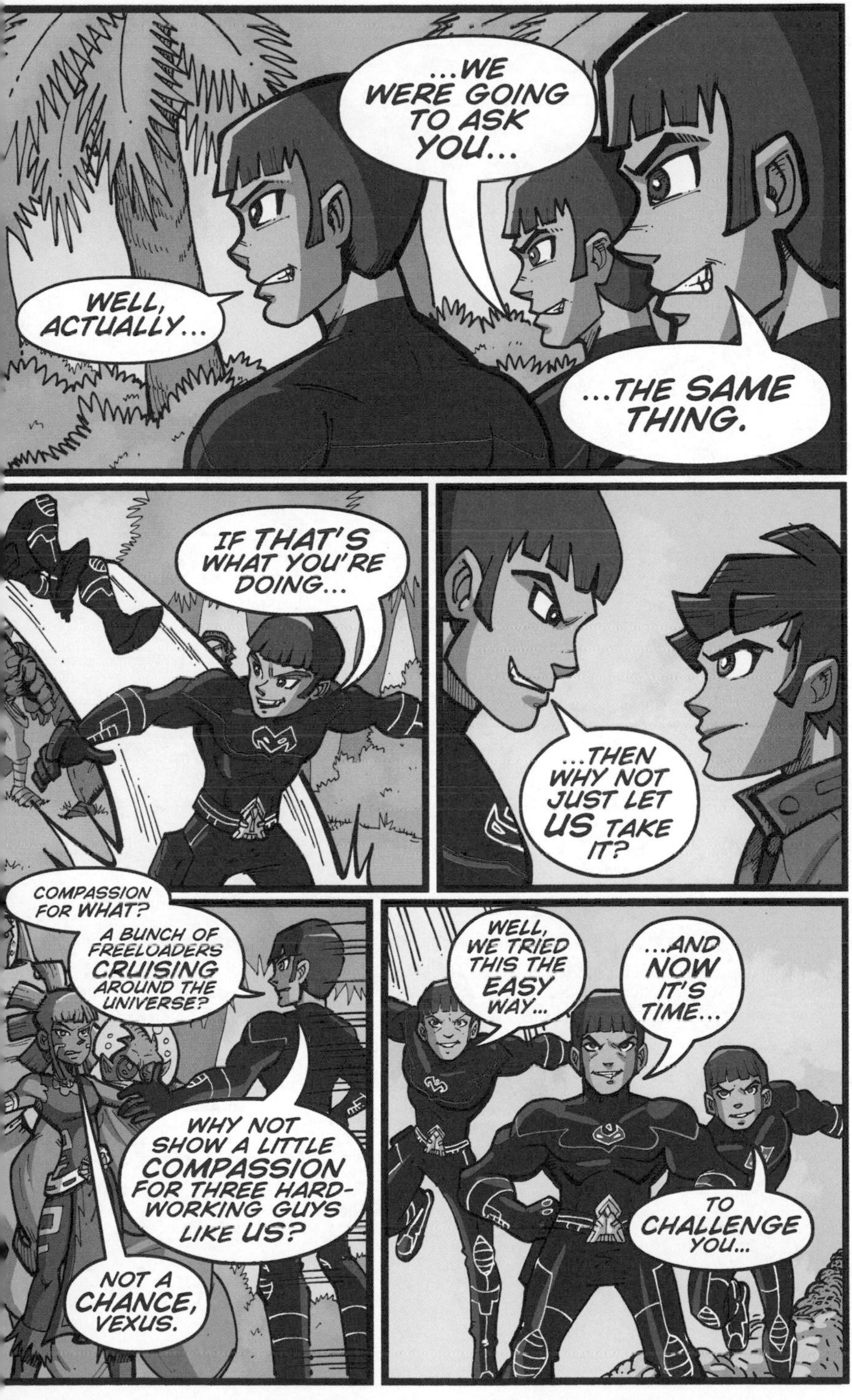
WELL, ACTUALLY...
...WE WERE GOING TO ASK YOU...
...THE SAME THING.
IF THAT'S WHAT YOU'RE DOING...
...THEN WHY NOT JUST LET US TAKE IT?
WHY NOT SHOW A LITTLE COMPASSION FOR THREE HARD-WORKING GUYS LIKE US?
COMPASSION FOR WHAT? A BUNCH OF FREELOADERS CRUISING AROUND THE UNIVERSE?
NOT A CHANCE, VEXUS.
WELL, WE TRIED THIS THE EASY WAY...
...AND NOW IT'S TIME...
TO CHALLENGE YOU...

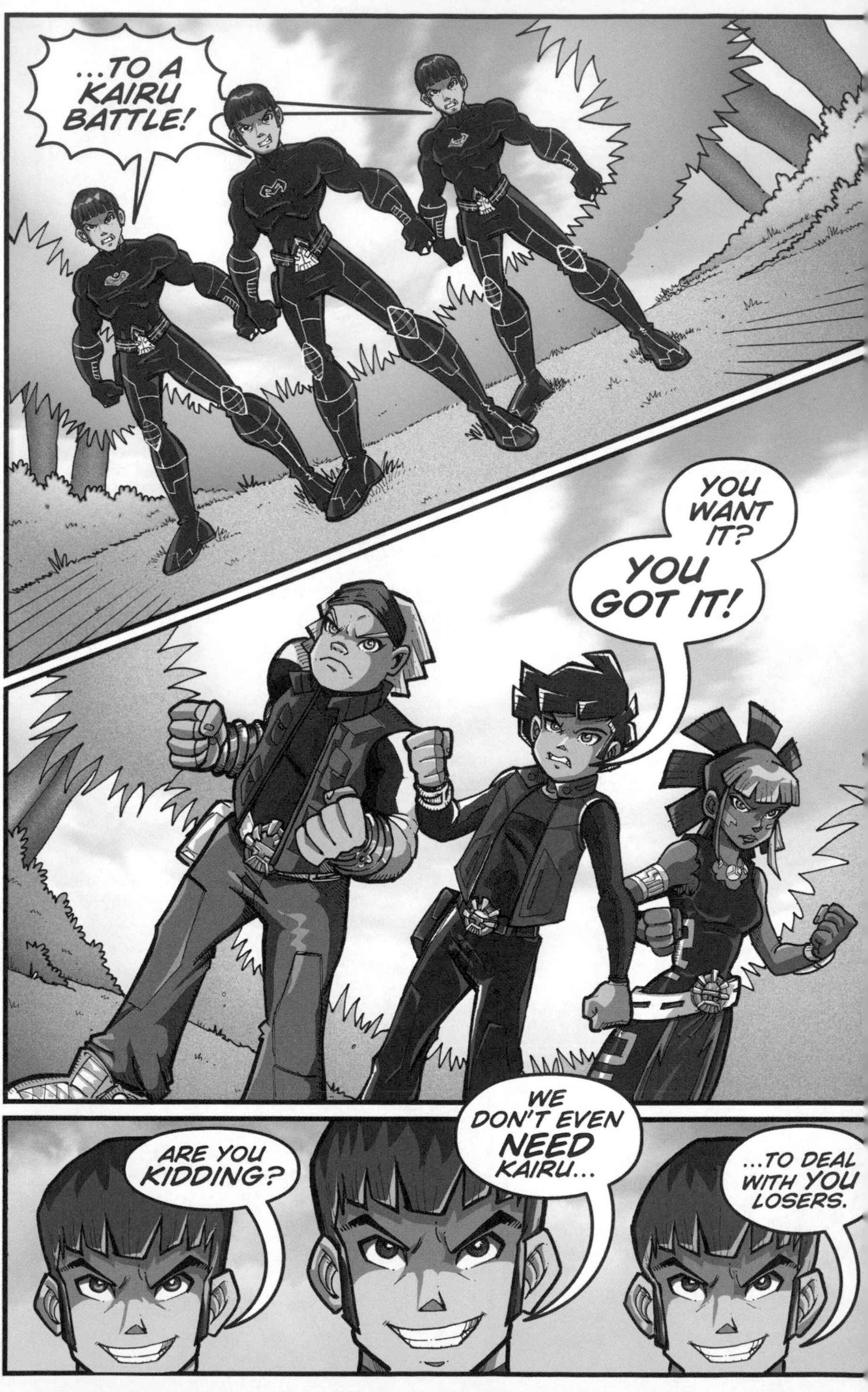
...TO A KAIRU BATTLE!
YOU WANT IT? YOU GOT IT!
ARE YOU KIDDING?
WE DON'T EVEN NEED KAIRU...
...TO DEAL WITH YOU LOSERS.

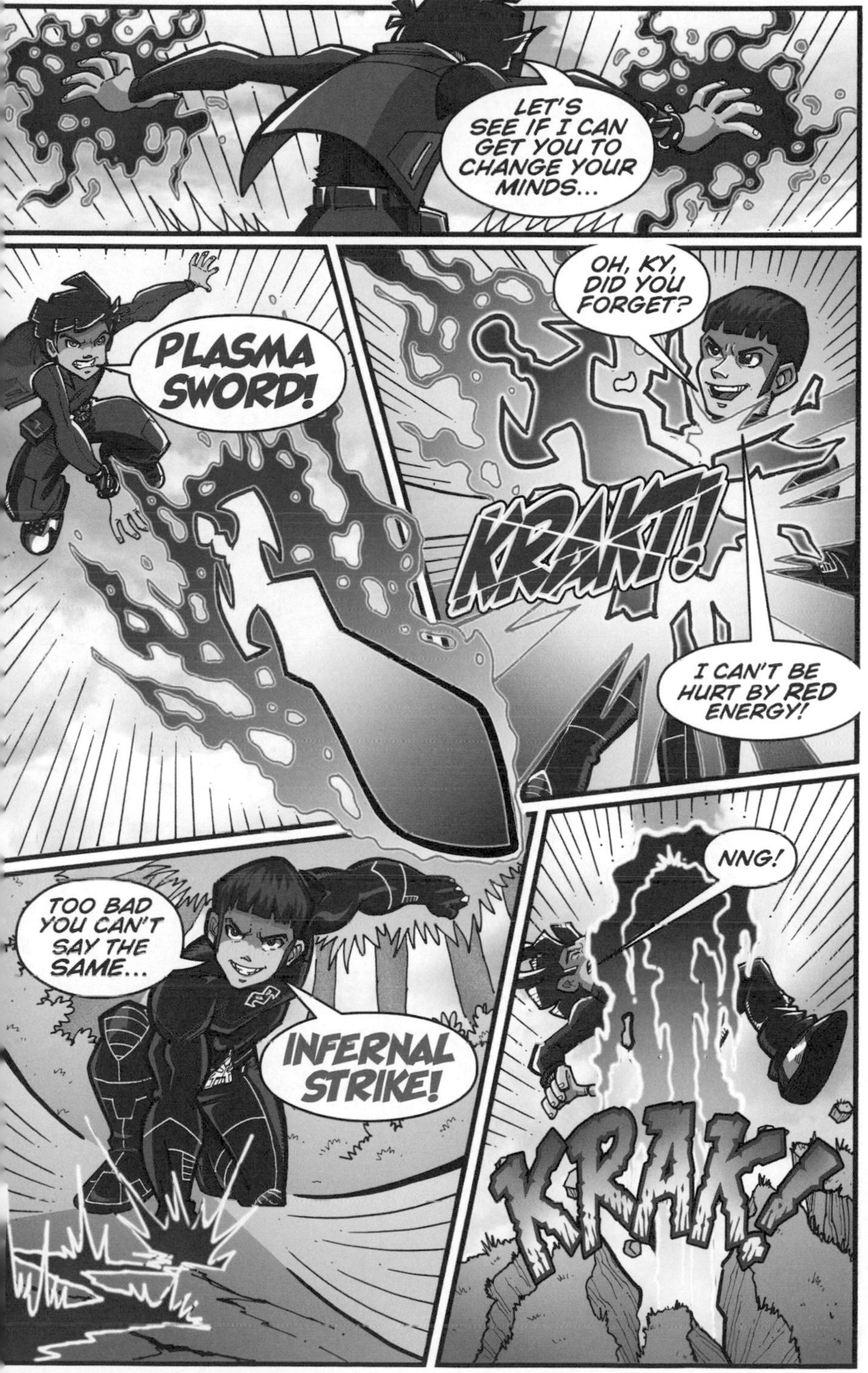
LET'S SEE IF I CAN GET YOU TO CHANGE YOUR MINDS...
PLASMA SWORD!
OH, KY, DID YOU FORGET?
KRAKT!
I CAN'T BE HURT BY RED ENERGY!
TOO BAD YOU CAN'T SAY THE SAME...
INFERNAL STRIKE!
NNG!
KRAK!

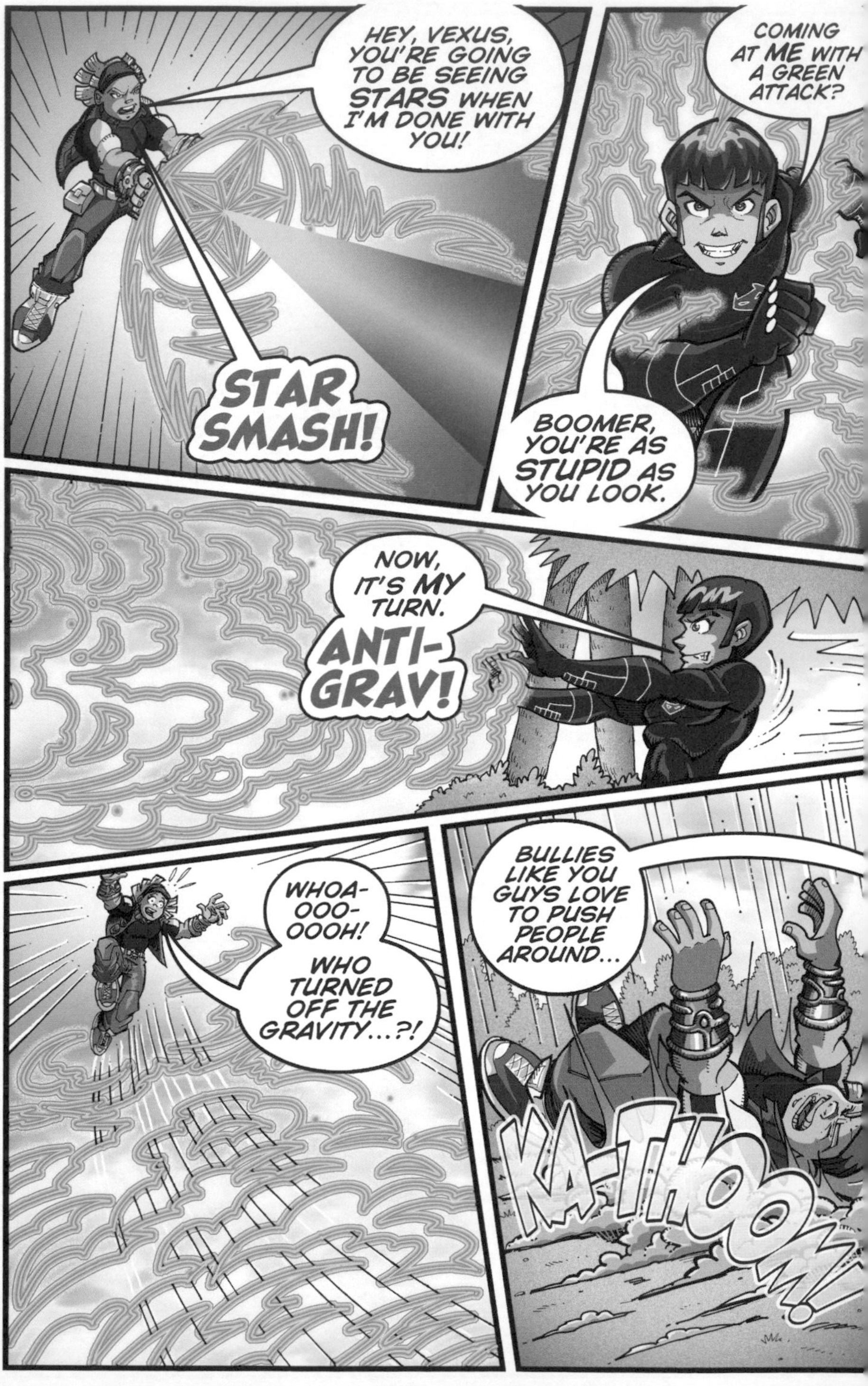
HEY, VEXUS, YOU'RE GOING TO BE SEEING STARS WHEN I'M DONE WITH YOU!
STAR SMASH!
COMING AT ME WITH A GREEN ATTACK?
BOOMER, YOU'RE AS STUPID AS YOU LOOK.
NOW, IT'S MY TURN.
ANTI-GRAV!
WHOA-OOO-OOOH!
WHO TURNED OFF THE GRAVITY...?!
BULLIES LIKE YOU GUYS LOVE TO PUSH PEOPLE AROUND...
KA-THOOM!

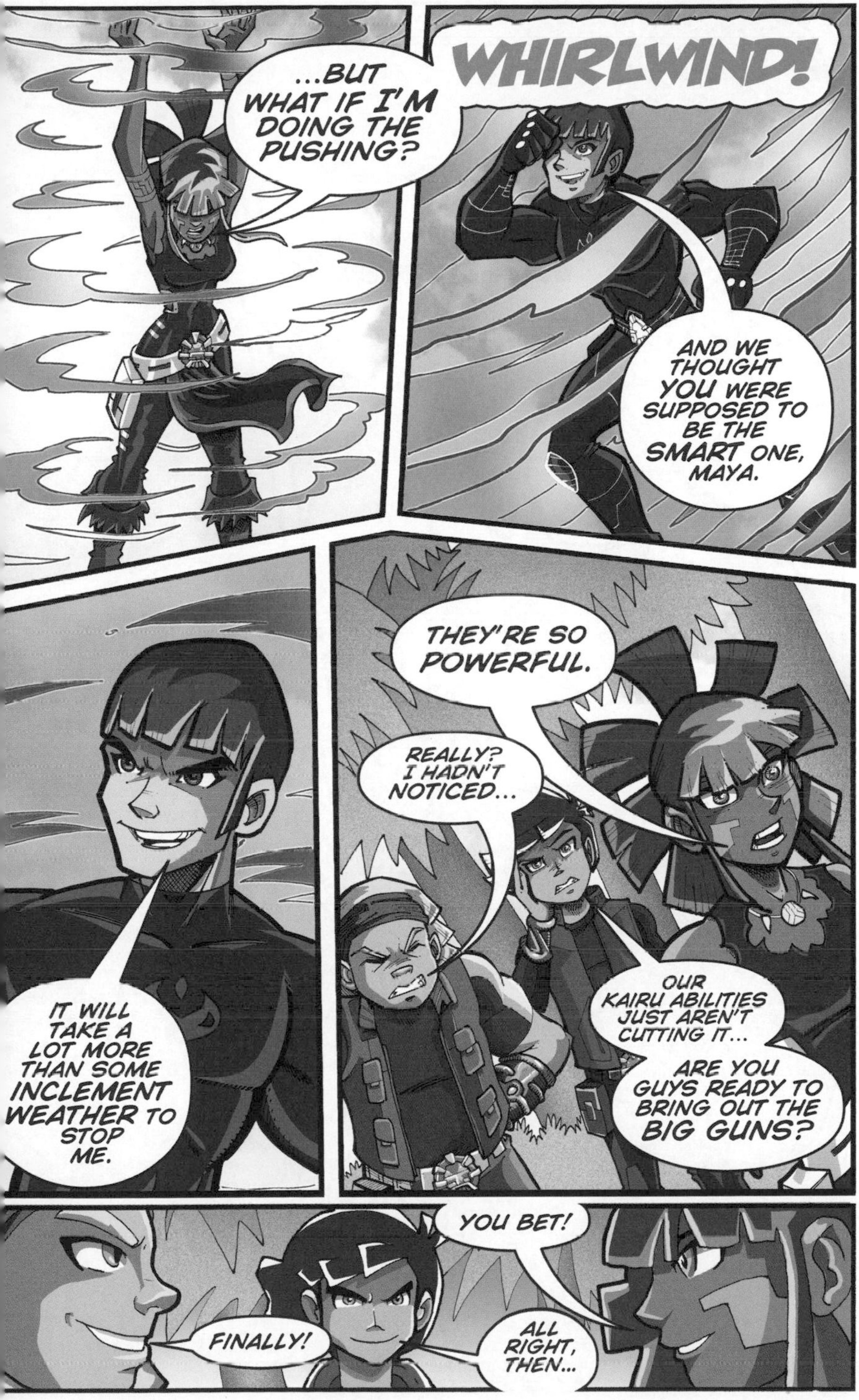
...BUT WHAT IF I'M DOING THE PUSHING?
WHIRLWIND!
AND WE THOUGHT YOU WERE SUPPOSED TO BE THE SMART ONE, MAYA.
IT WILL TAKE A LOT MORE THAN SOME INCLEMENT WEATHER TO STOP ME.
THEY'RE SO POWERFUL.
REALLY? I HADN'T NOTICED...
OUR KAIRU ABILITIES JUST AREN'T CUTTING IT...
ARE YOU GUYS READY TO BRING OUT THE BIG GUNS?
YOU BET!
FINALLY!
ALL RIGHT, THEN...

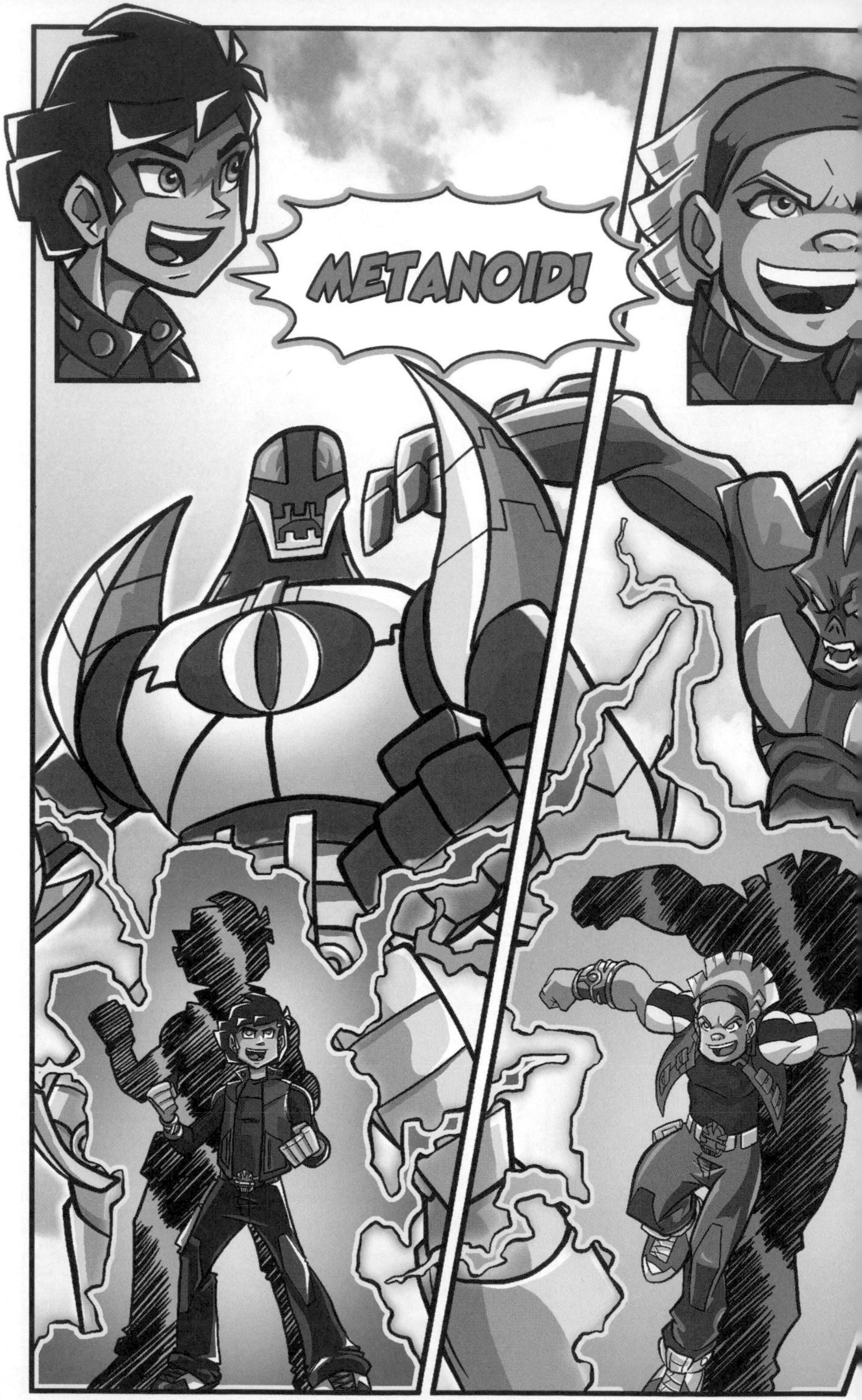
METANOID!

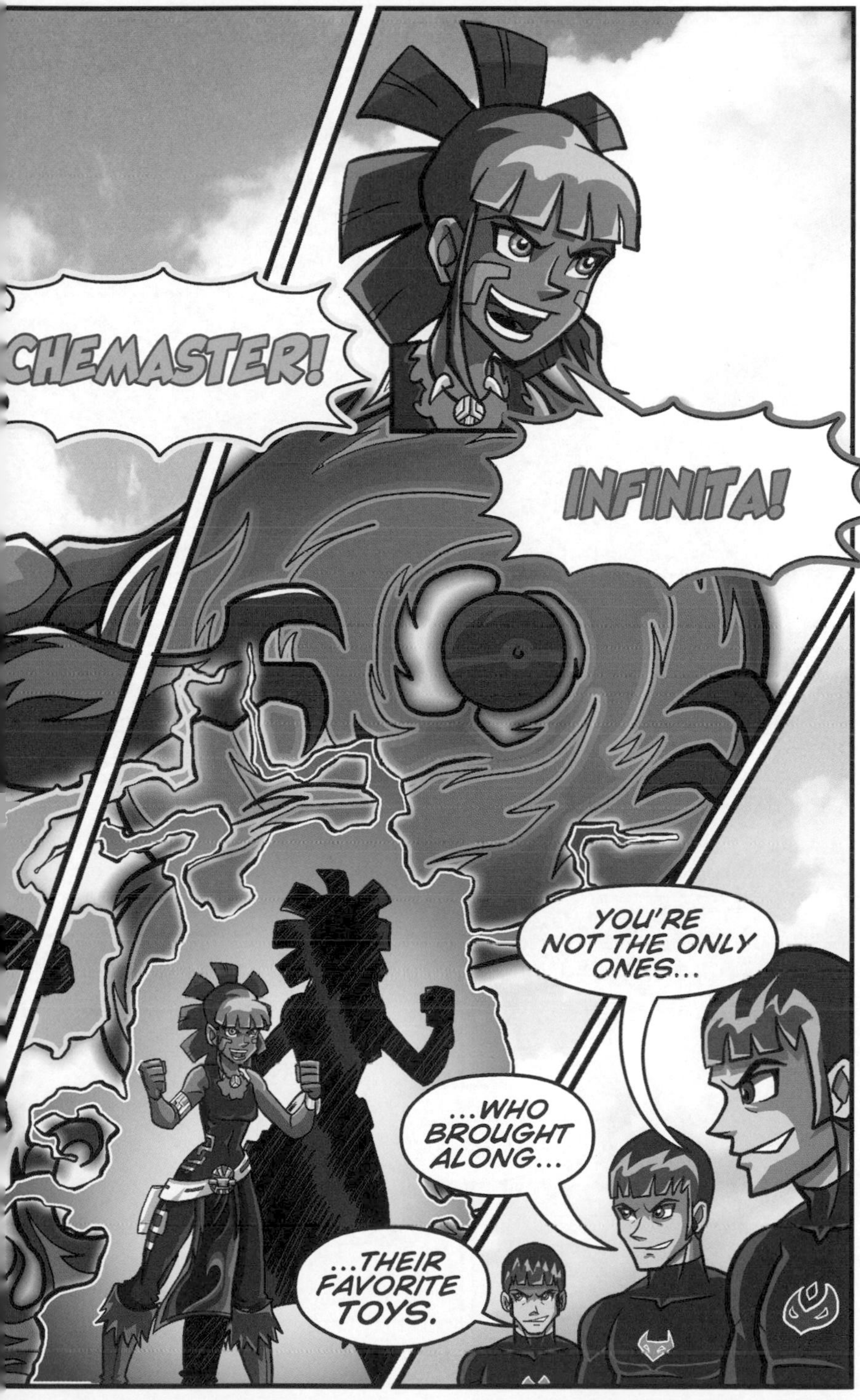
CHEMASTER!
INFINITA!
YOU'RE NOT THE ONLY ONES...
...WHO BROUGHT ALONG...
...THEIR FAVORITE TOYS.

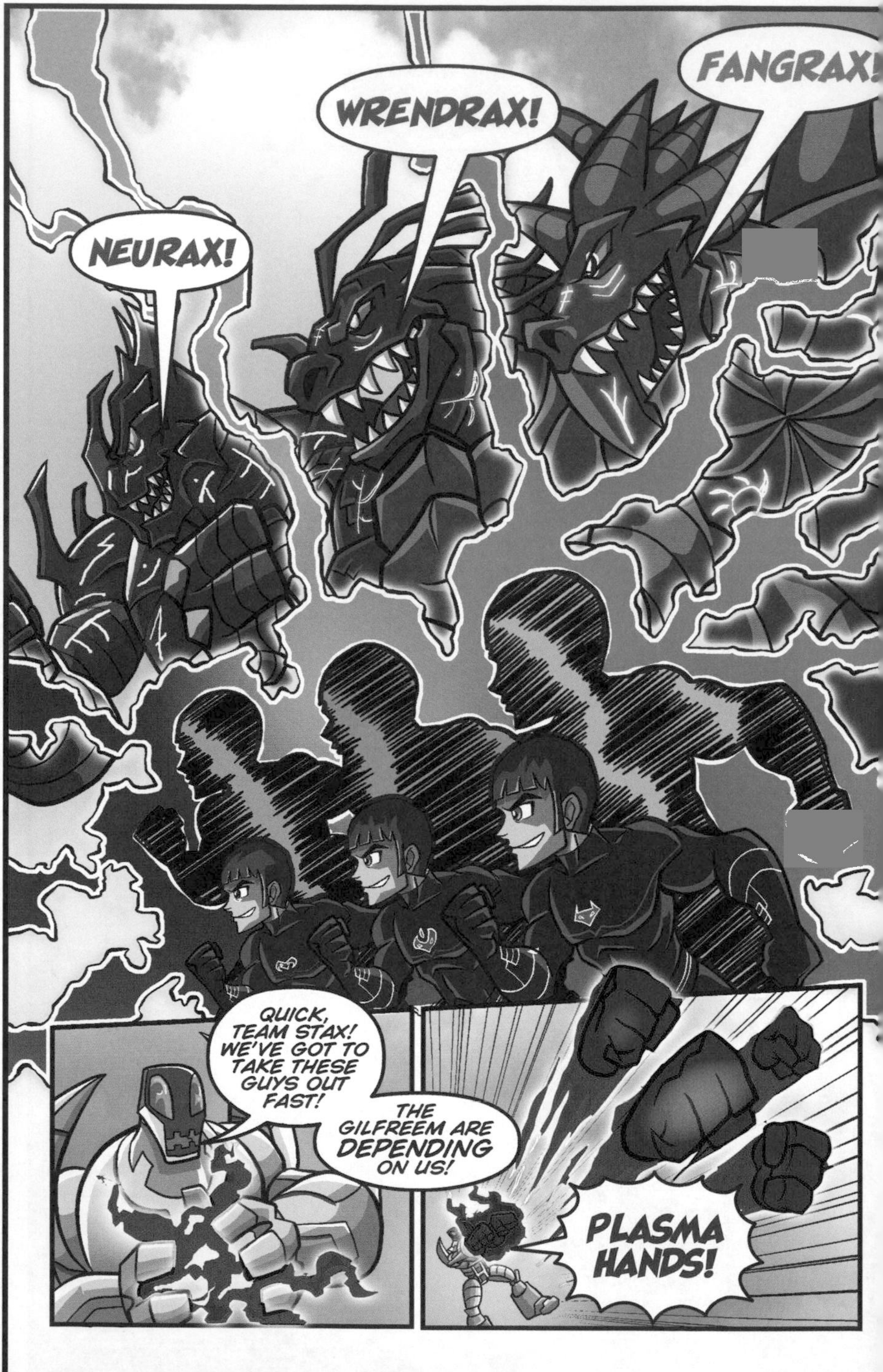
NEURAX!
WRENDRAX!
FANGRAX!
QUICK, TEAM STAX! WE'VE GOT TO TAKE THESE GUYS OUT FAST!
THE GILFREEM ARE DEPENDING ON US!
PLASMA HANDS!

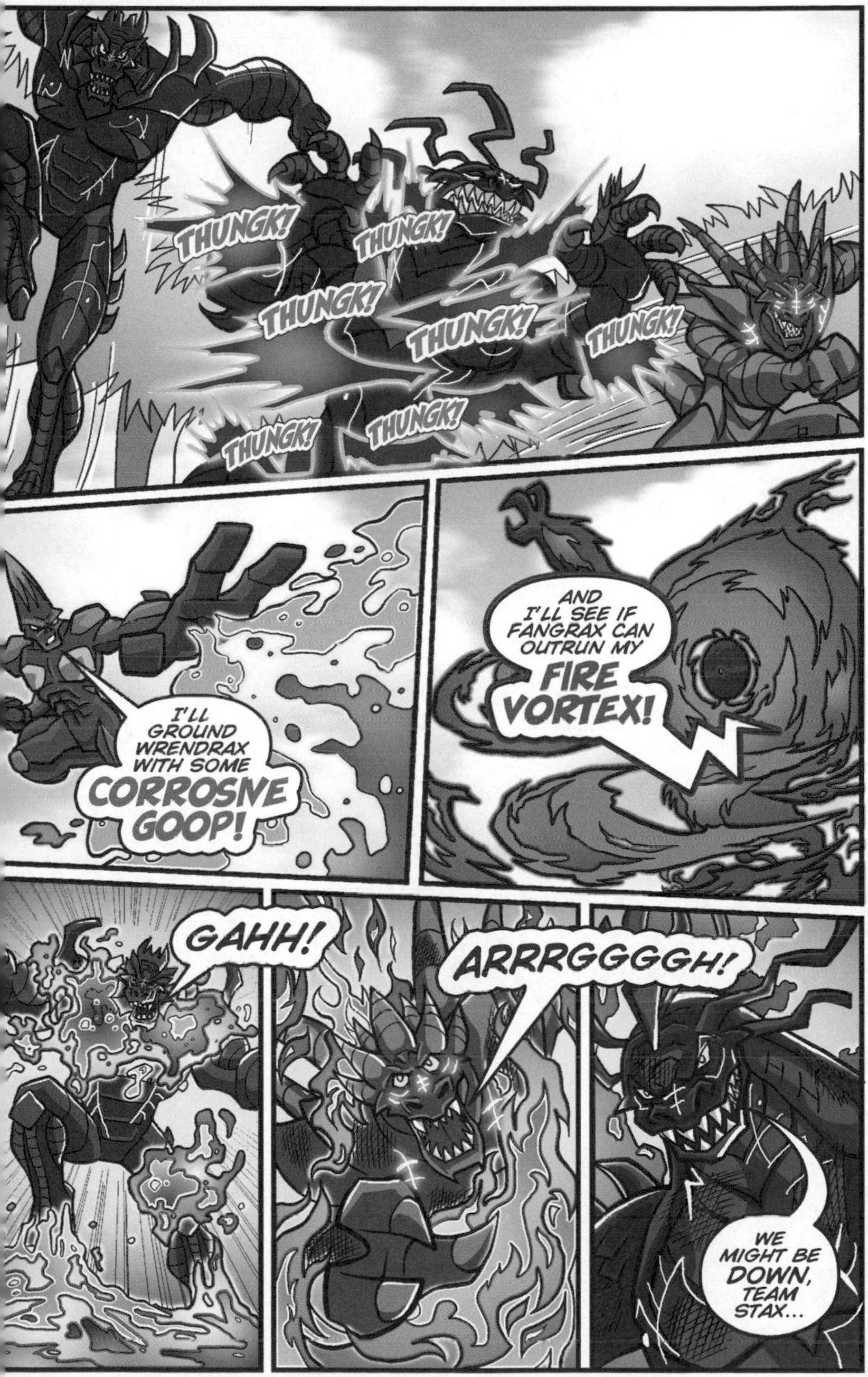
THUNGK!
THUNGK!
THUNGK!
THUNGK!
THUNGK!
THUNGK!
THUNGK!
I'LL GROUND WRENDRAX WITH SOME CORROSIVE GOOP!
AND I'LL SEE IF FANGRAX CAN OUTRUN MY FIRE VORTEX!
GAHH!
ARRRGGGGH!
WE MIGHT BE DOWN, TEAM STAX...

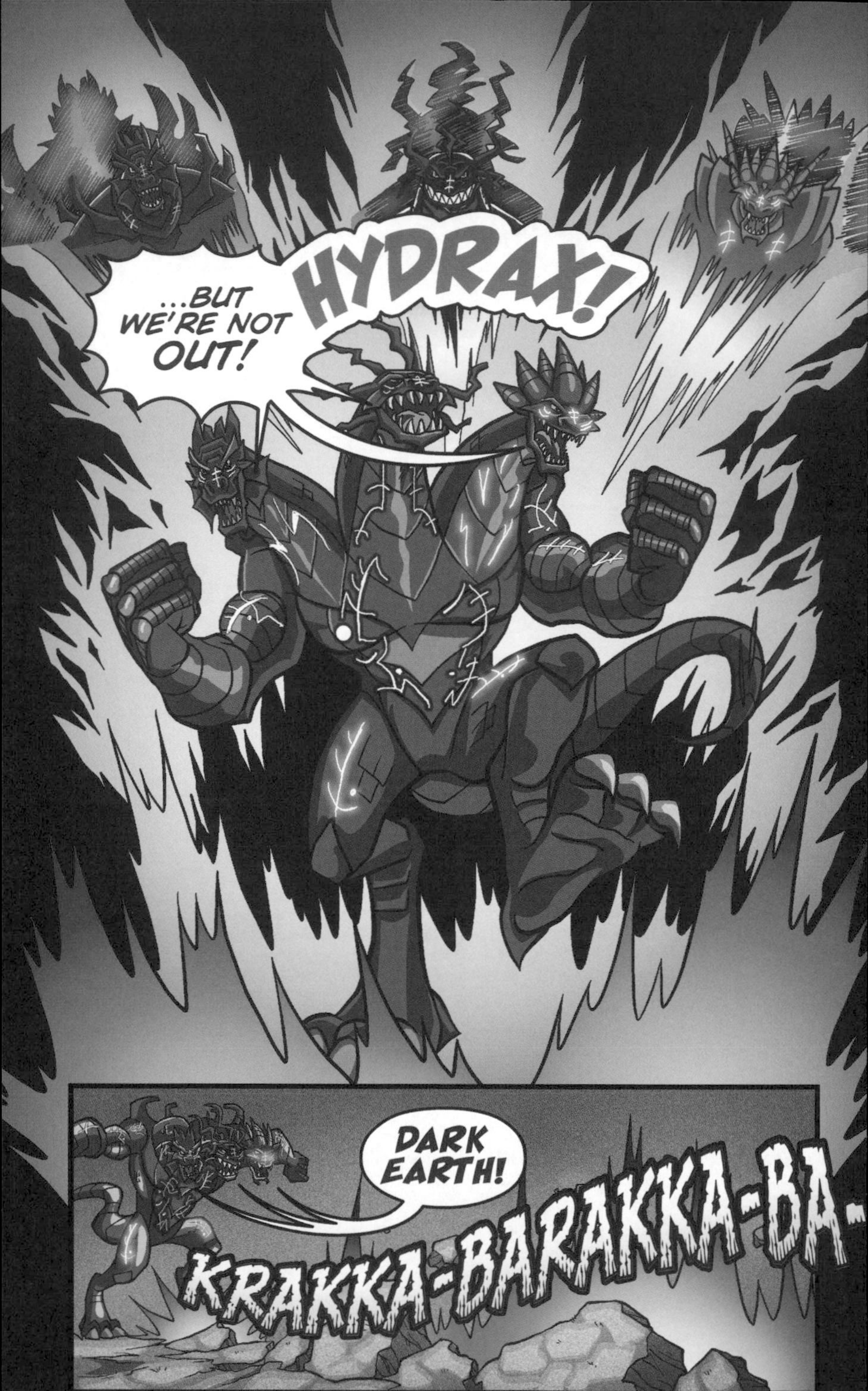
...BUT WE'RE NOT OUT!
HYDRAX!
DARK EARTH!
KRAKKA-BARAKKA-BA-

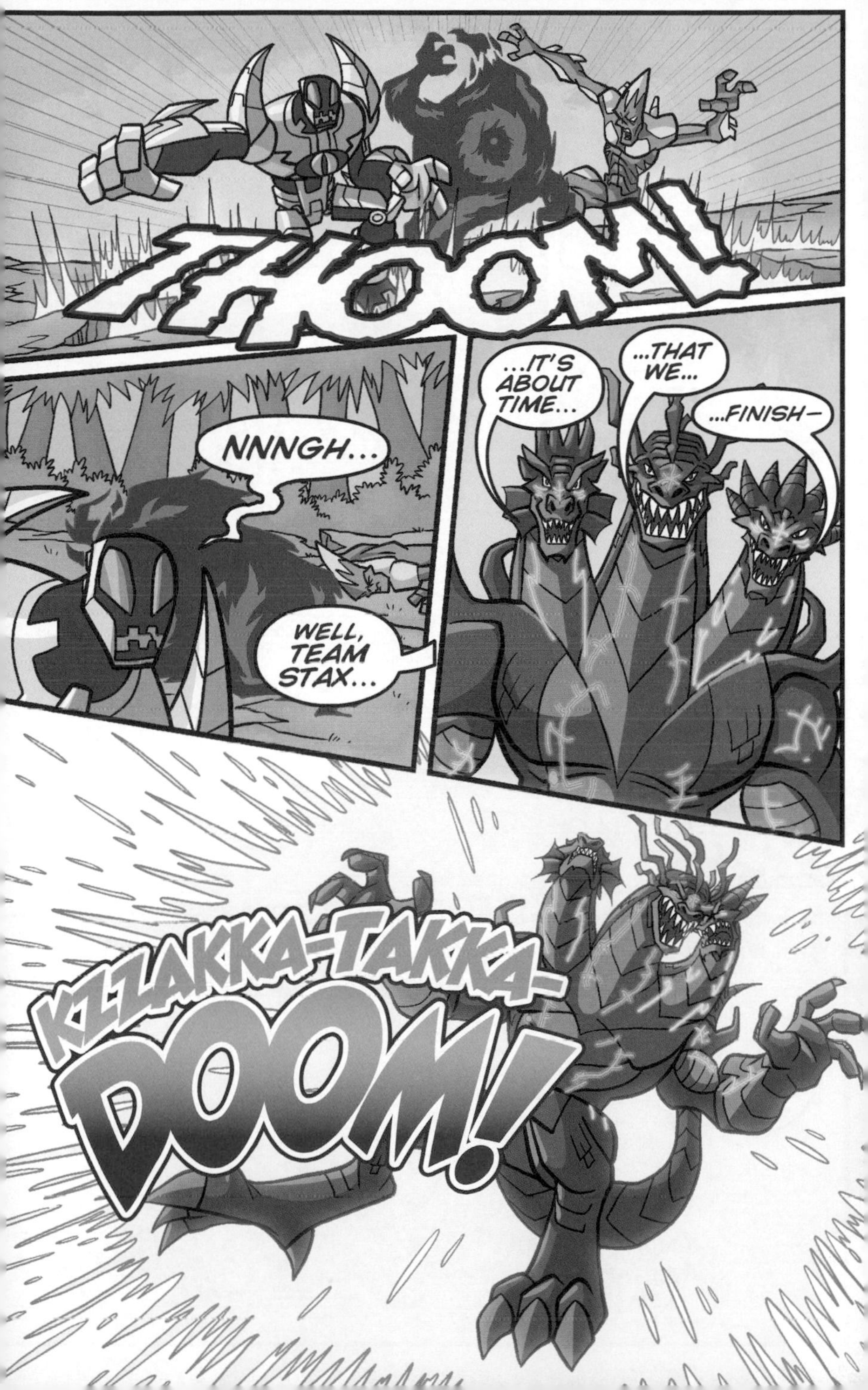
THOOM!
NNNGH...
WELL, TEAM STAX...
...IT'S ABOUT TIME...
...THAT WE...
...FINISH–
KZZAKKA-TAKKA-DOOM!

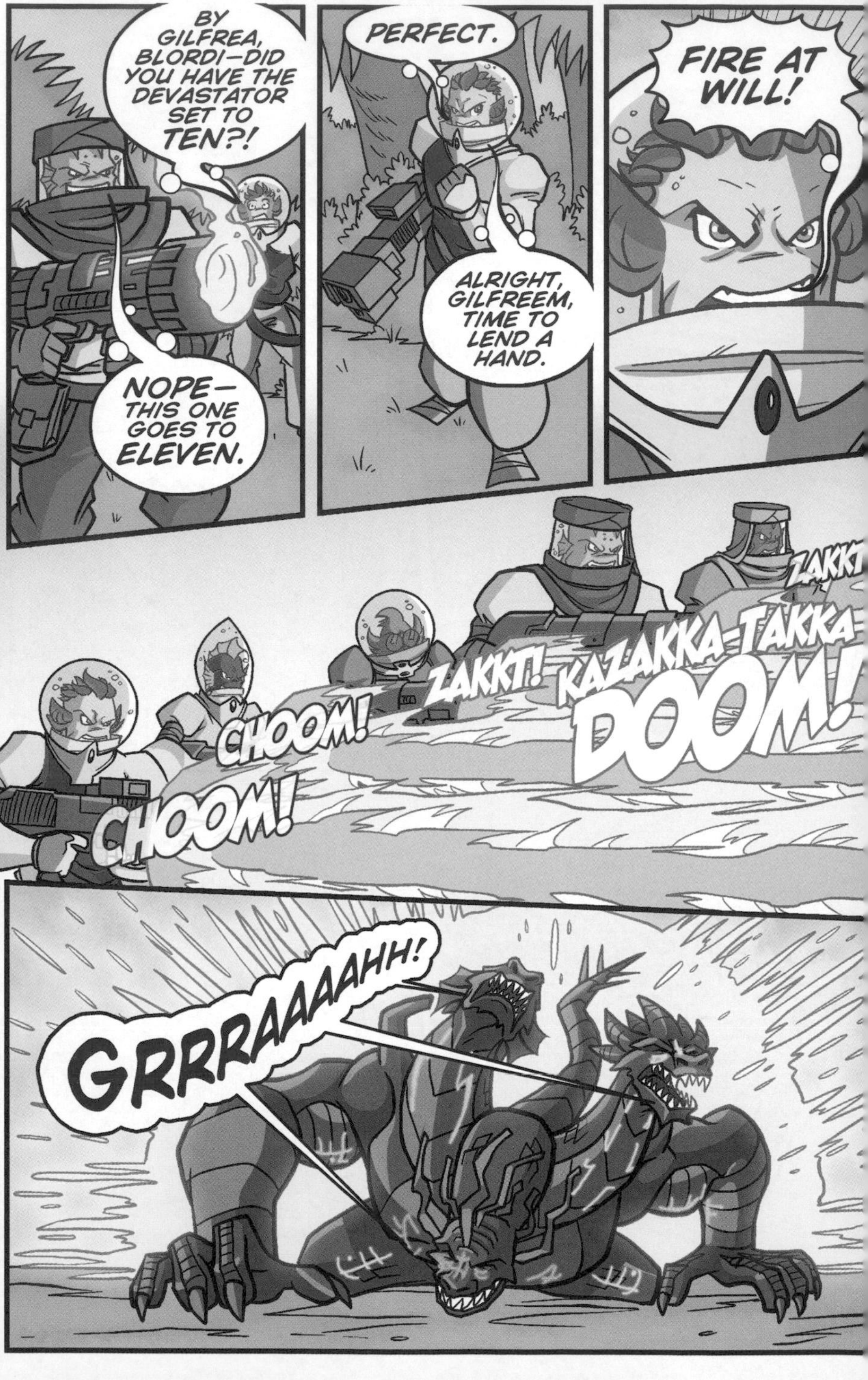
BY GILFREA, BLORDI—DID YOU HAVE THE DEVASTATOR SET TO TEN?!
NOPE— THIS ONE GOES TO ELEVEN.
PERFECT.
ALRIGHT, GILFREEM, TIME TO LEND A HAND.
FIRE AT WILL!
ZAKKT
KAZAKKA-TAKKA
ZAKKT!
DOOM!
CHOOM!
CHOOM!
GRRRAAAAHH!

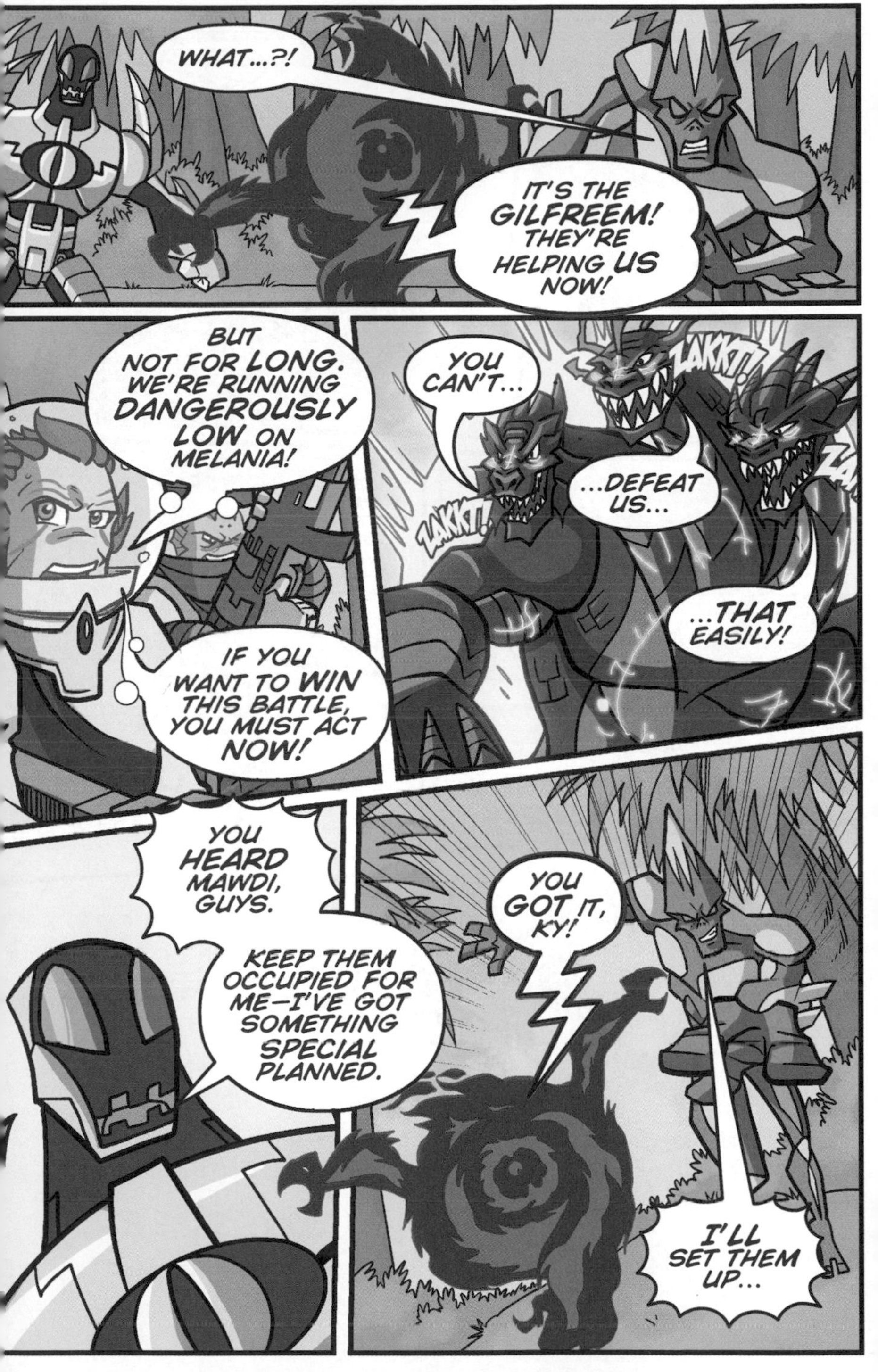
WHAT...?!
IT'S THE GILFREEM! THEY'RE HELPING US NOW!
BUT NOT FOR LONG. WE'RE RUNNING DANGEROUSLY LOW ON MELANIA!
IF YOU WANT TO WIN THIS BATTLE, YOU MUST ACT NOW!
ZAKKT!
YOU CAN'T...
...DEFEAT US...
...THAT EASILY!
ZAKKT!
YOU HEARD MAWDI, GUYS.
KEEP THEM OCCUPIED FOR ME—I'VE GOT SOMETHING SPECIAL PLANNED.
YOU GOT IT, KY!
I'LL SET THEM UP...

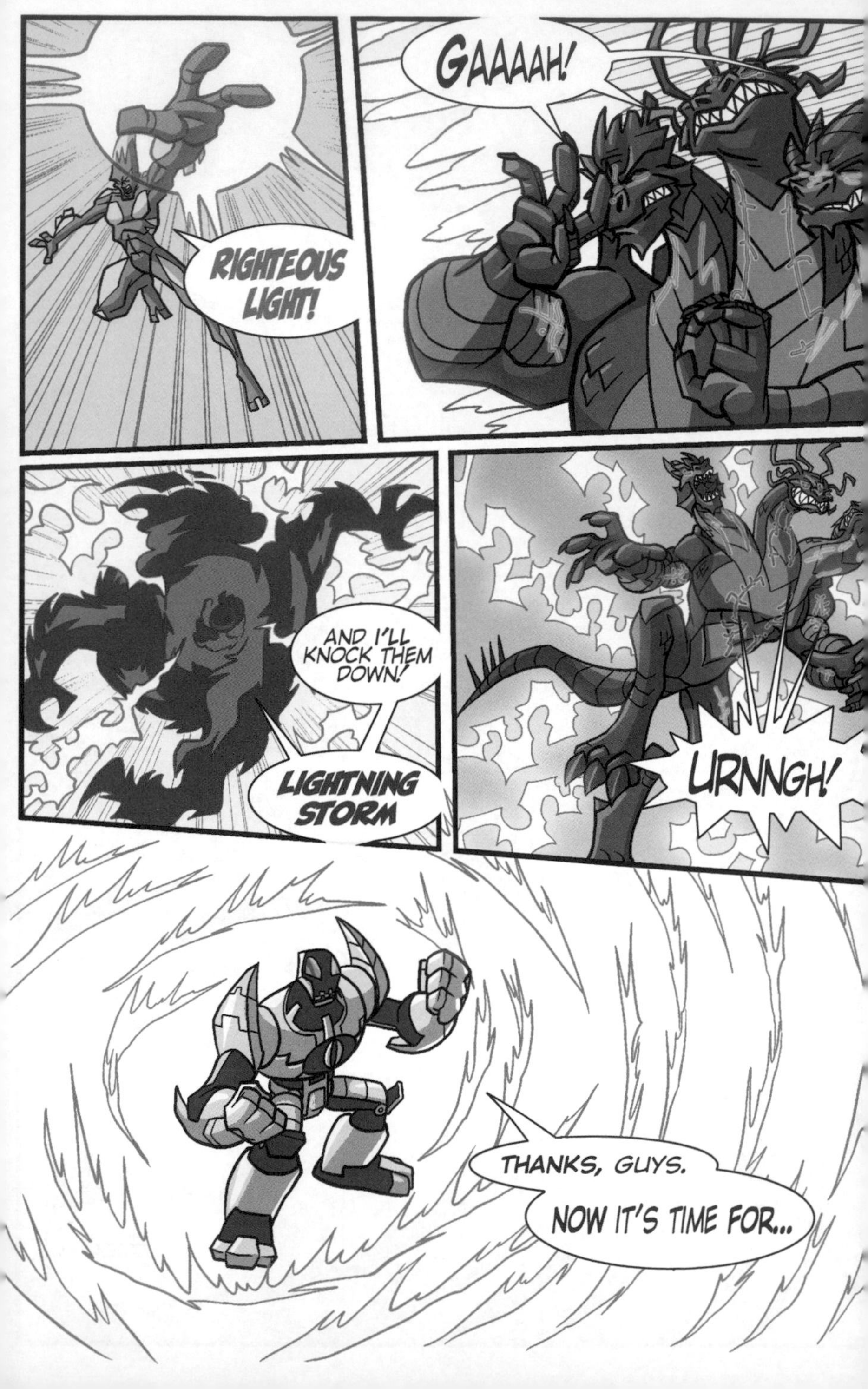
RIGHTEOUS LIGHT!
GAAAAH!
AND I'LL KNOCK THEM DOWN!
LIGHTNING STORM
URNNGH!
THANKS, GUYS.
NOW IT'S TIME FOR...

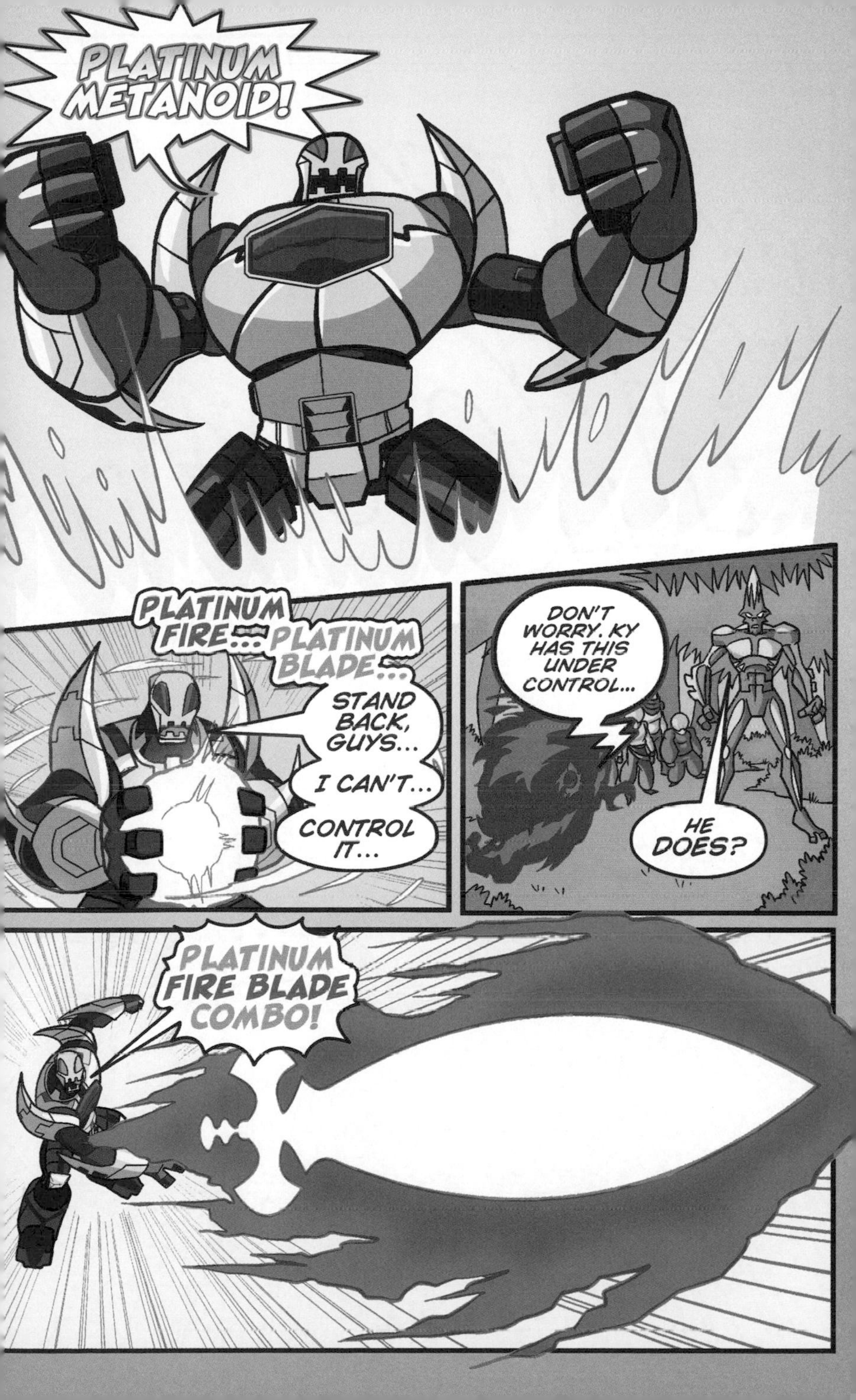
PLATINUM METANOID!
PLATINUM FIRE...
PLATINUM BLADE...
STAND BACK, GUYS...
I CAN'T...
CONTROL IT...
DON'T WORRY. KY HAS THIS UNDER CONTROL...
HE DOES?
PLATINUM FIRE BLADE COMBO!

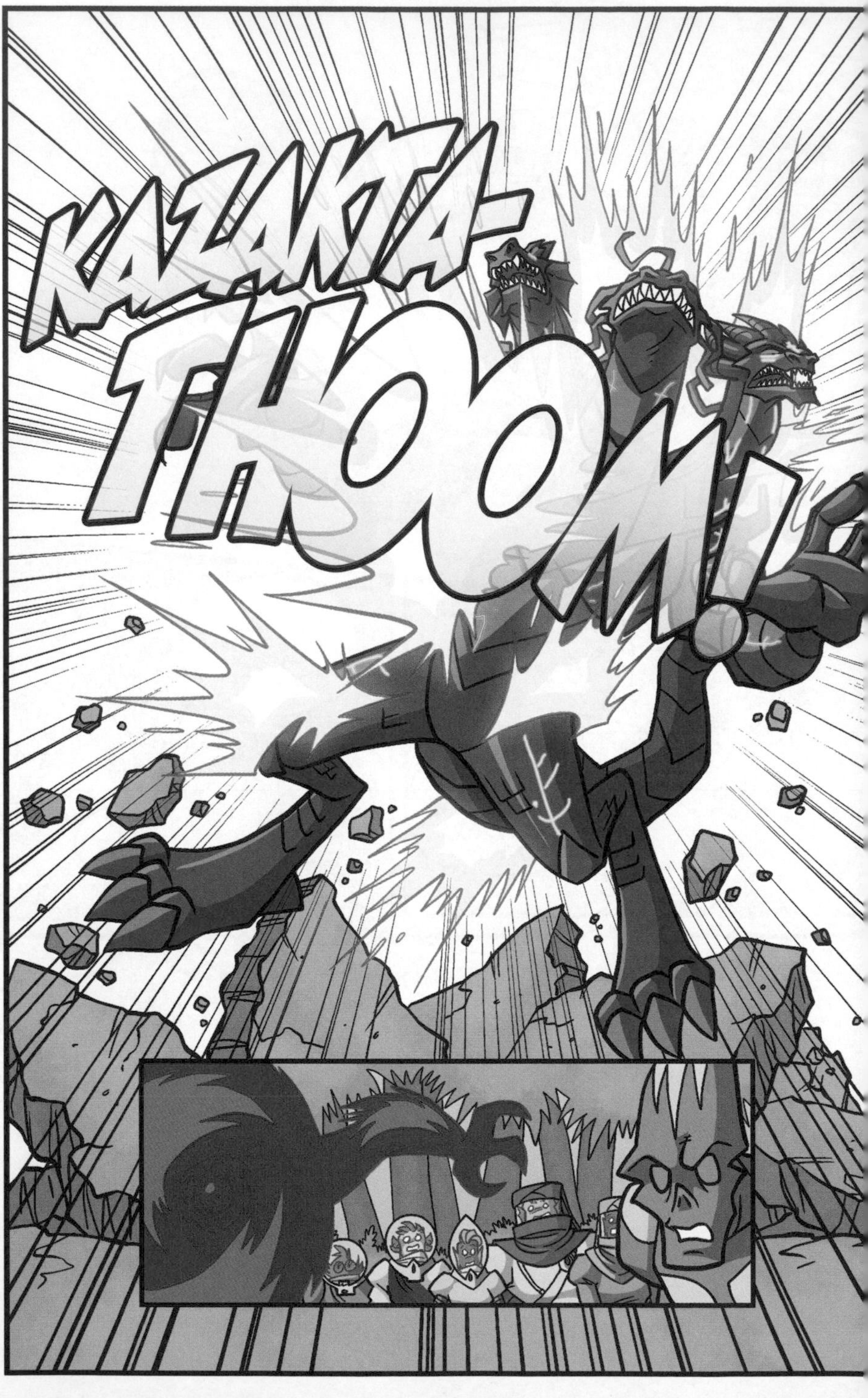
KAZAKTA-
THOOM!

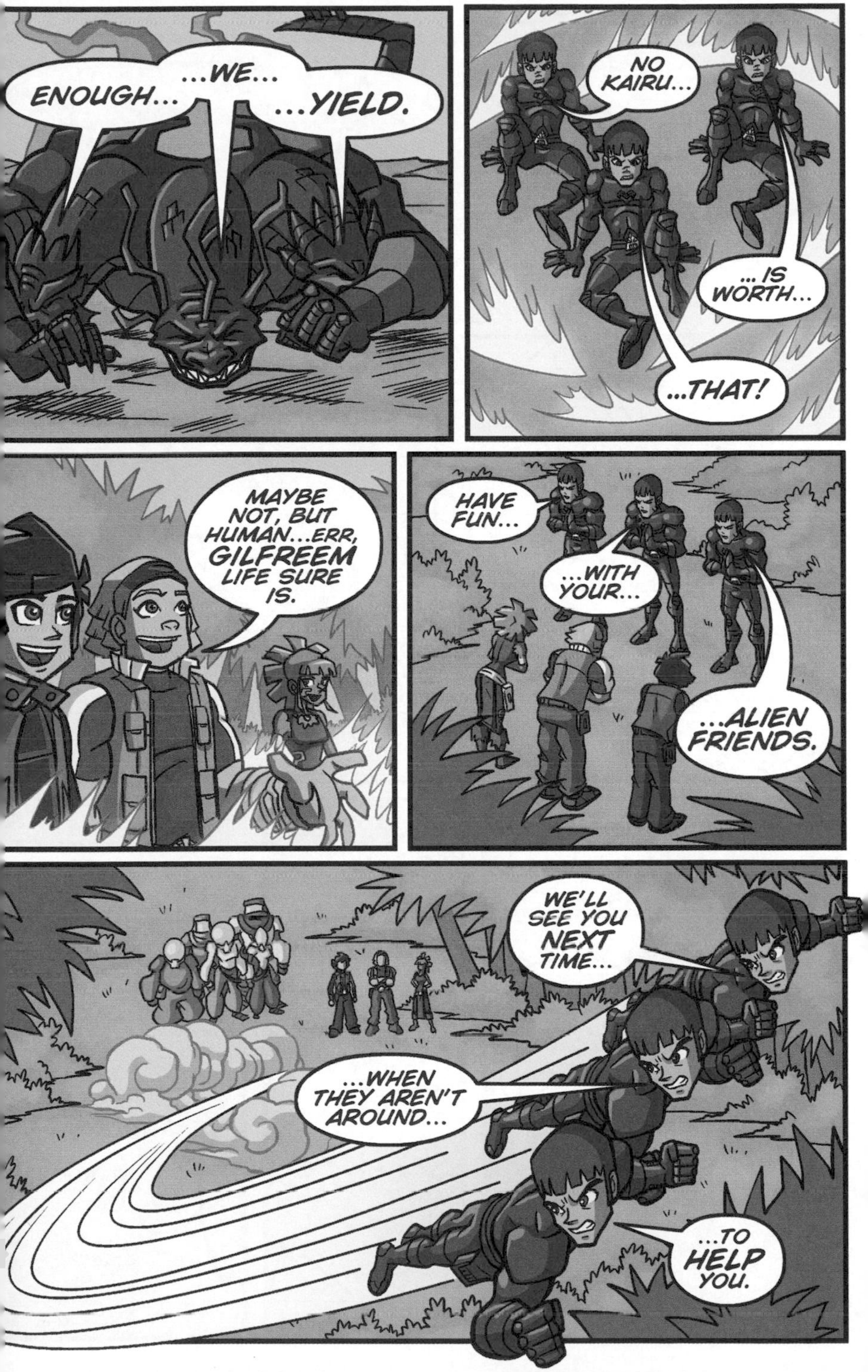
ENOUGH...
...WE...
...YIELD.
NO KAIRU...
...IS WORTH...
...THAT!
MAYBE NOT, BUT HUMAN...ERR, GILFREEM LIFE SURE IS.
HAVE FUN...
...WITH YOUR...
...ALIEN FRIENDS.
WE'LL SEE YOU NEXT TIME...
...WHEN THEY AREN'T AROUND...
...TO HELP YOU.

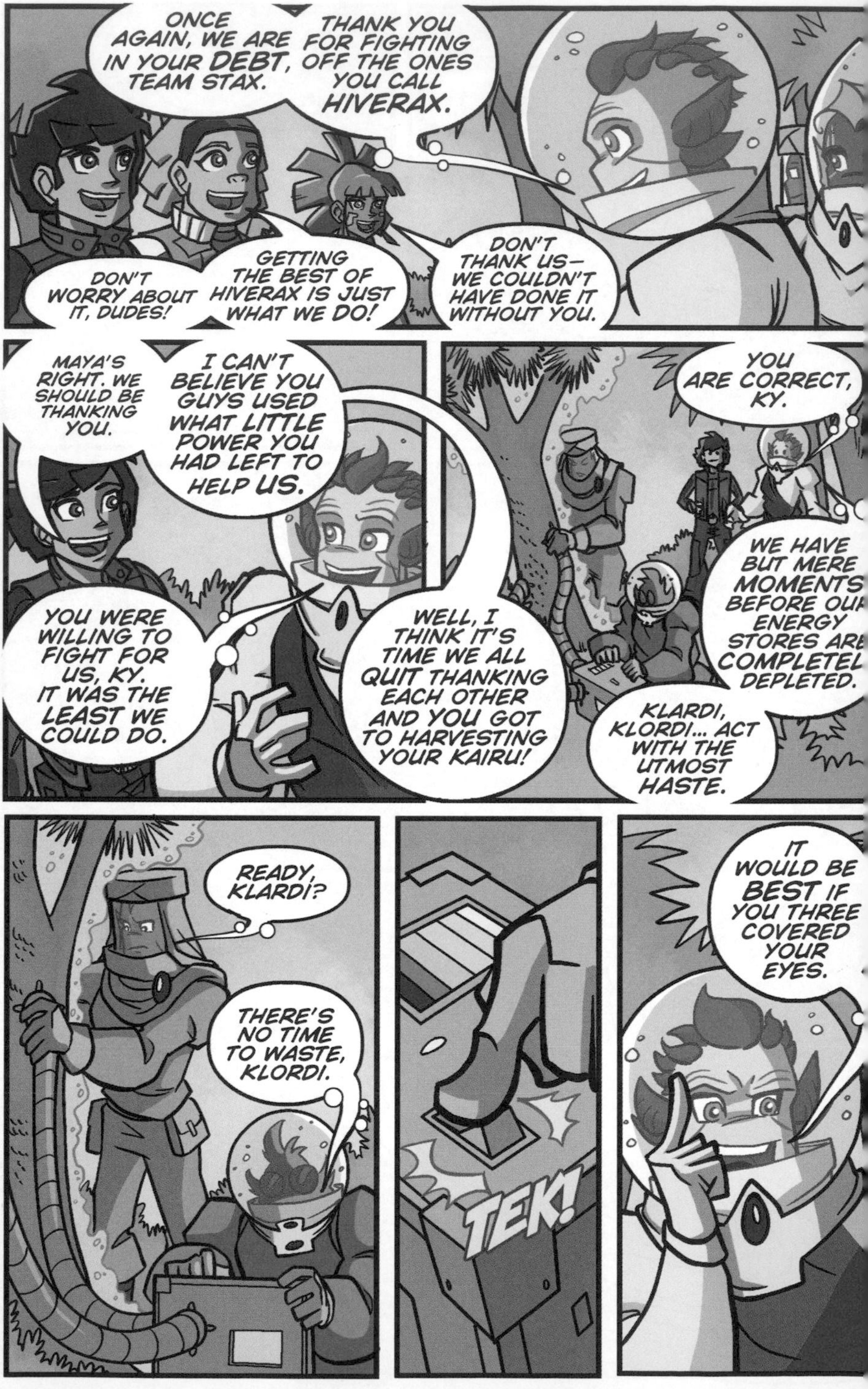
ONCE AGAIN, WE ARE IN YOUR DEBT, TEAM STAX.
THANK YOU FOR FIGHTING OFF THE ONES YOU CALL HIVERAX.
DON'T WORRY ABOUT IT, DUDES!
GETTING THE BEST OF HIVERAX IS JUST WHAT WE DO!
DON'T THANK US— WE COULDN'T HAVE DONE IT WITHOUT YOU.
MAYA'S RIGHT. WE SHOULD BE THANKING YOU.
I CAN'T BELIEVE YOU GUYS USED WHAT LITTLE POWER YOU HAD LEFT TO HELP US.
YOU WERE WILLING TO FIGHT FOR US, KY. IT WAS THE LEAST WE COULD DO.
WELL, I THINK IT'S TIME WE ALL QUIT THANKING EACH OTHER AND YOU GOT TO HARVESTING YOUR KAIRU!
YOU ARE CORRECT, KY.
WE HAVE BUT MERE MOMENTS BEFORE OUR ENERGY STORES ARE COMPLETEL DEPLETED.
KLARDI, KLORDI... ACT WITH THE UTMOST HASTE.
READY, KLARDI?
THERE'S NO TIME TO WASTE, KLORDI.
TEK!
IT WOULD BE BEST IF YOU THREE COVERED YOUR EYES.

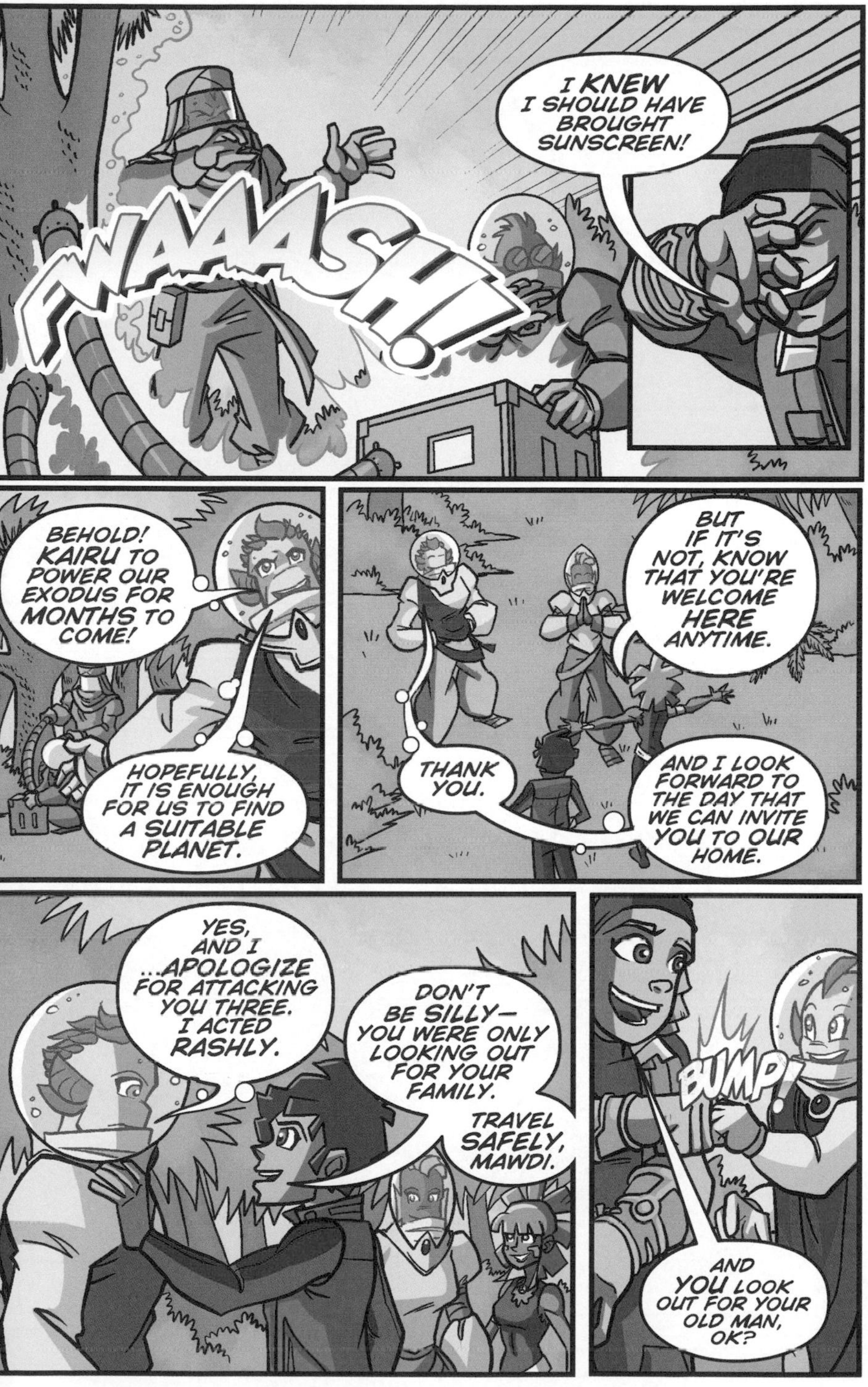
FWAAASH!
I KNEW I SHOULD HAVE BROUGHT SUNSCREEN!
BEHOLD! KAIRU TO POWER OUR EXODUS FOR MONTHS TO COME!
HOPEFULLY, IT IS ENOUGH FOR US TO FIND A SUITABLE PLANET.
BUT IF IT'S NOT, KNOW THAT YOU'RE WELCOME HERE ANYTIME.
THANK YOU.
AND I LOOK FORWARD TO THE DAY THAT WE CAN INVITE YOU TO OUR HOME.
YES, AND I ...APOLOGIZE FOR ATTACKING YOU THREE. I ACTED RASHLY.
DON'T BE SILLY— YOU WERE ONLY LOOKING OUT FOR YOUR FAMILY.
TRAVEL SAFELY, MAWDI.
BUMP!
AND YOU LOOK OUT FOR YOUR OLD MAN, OK?

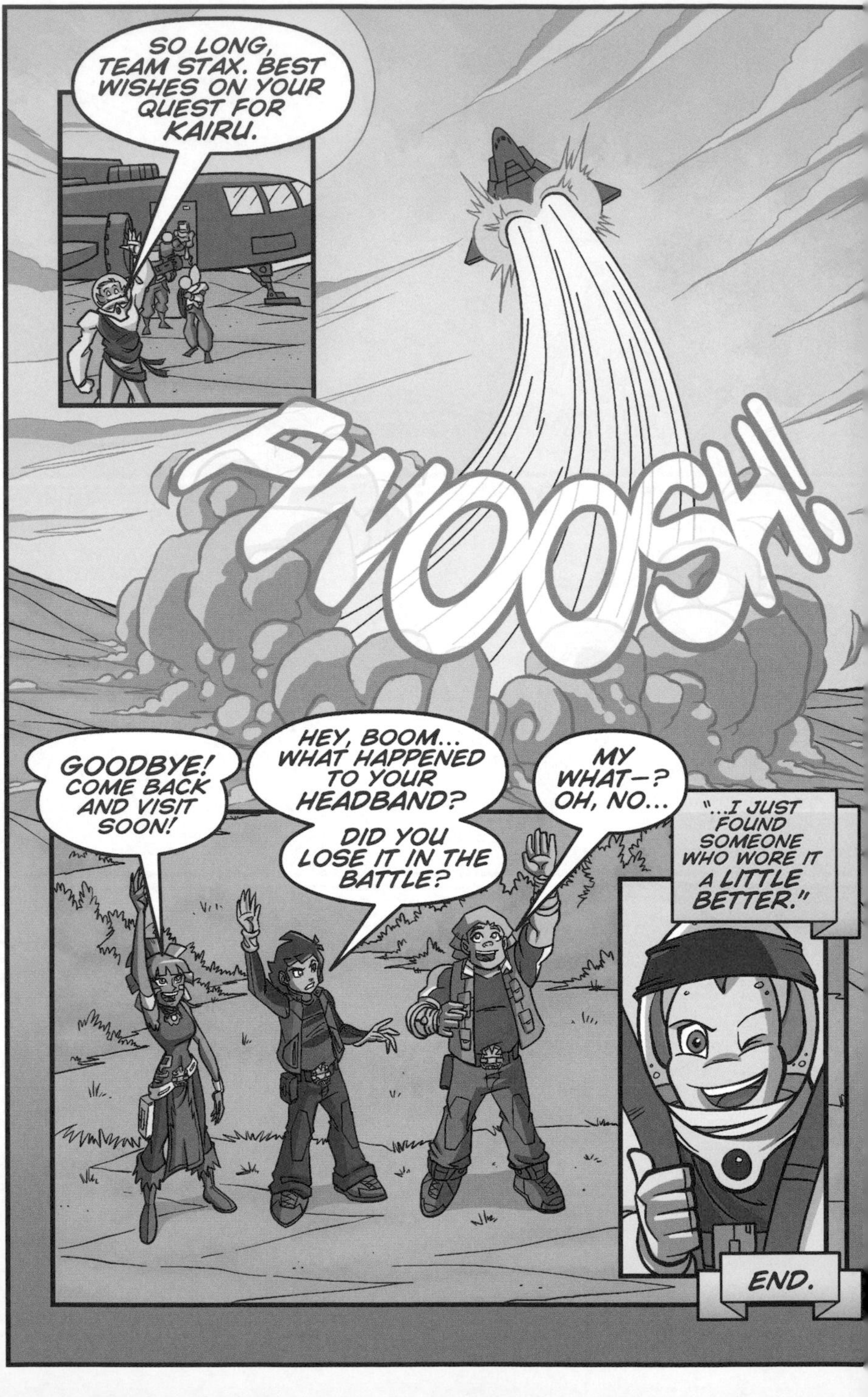
SO LONG, TEAM STAX. BEST WISHES ON YOUR QUEST FOR KAIRU.
FWOOSH!!
GOODBYE! COME BACK AND VISIT SOON!
HEY, BOOM... WHAT HAPPENED TO YOUR HEADBAND?
DID YOU LOSE IT IN THE BATTLE?
MY WHAT—? OH, NO...
"...I JUST FOUND SOMEONE WHO WORE IT A LITTLE BETTER."
END.

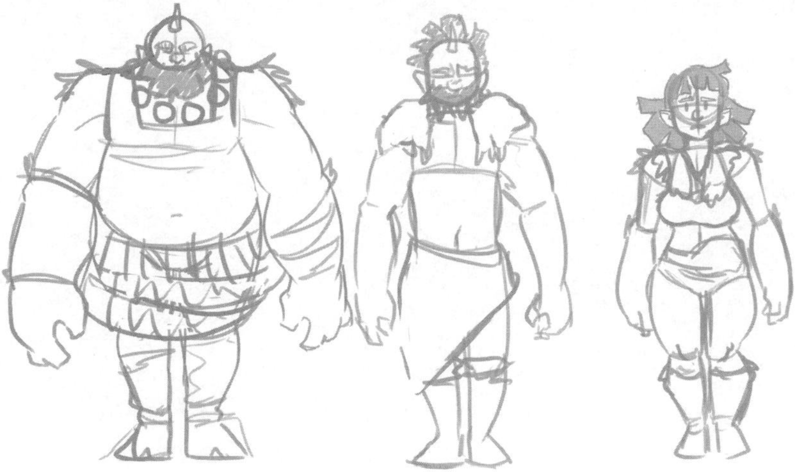

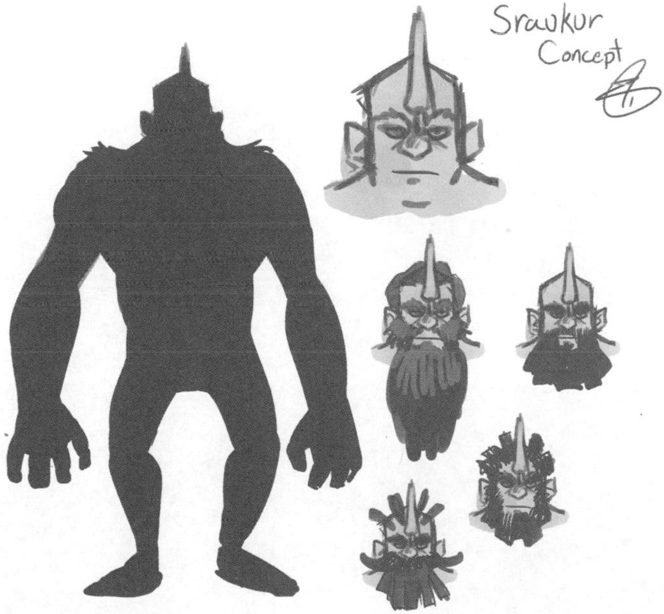
Sraukur
Concept

BONUS STORY
HOME, KAIRU, HOME

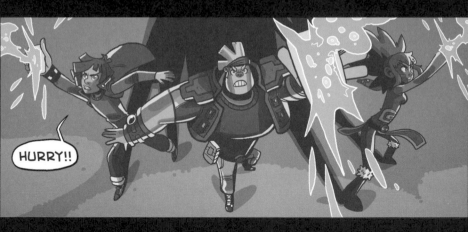

Story by **Mike Raicht**
Art by **Dan Ciurczak**
Colors by **Chad Walker**

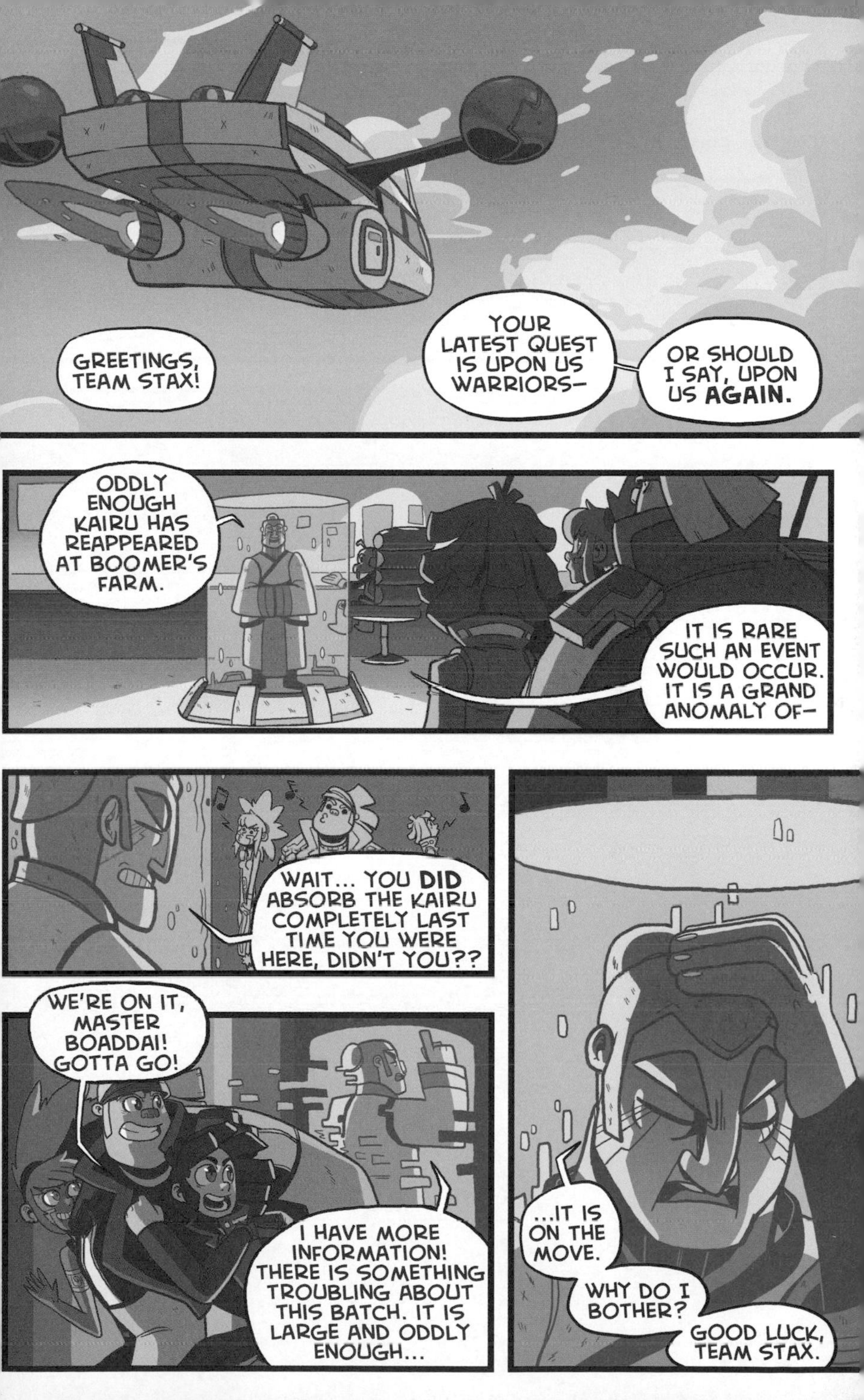
GREETINGS, TEAM STAX!
YOUR LATEST QUEST IS UPON US WARRIORS—
OR SHOULD I SAY, UPON US **AGAIN**.
ODDLY ENOUGH KAIRU HAS REAPPEARED AT BOOMER'S FARM.
IT IS RARE SUCH AN EVENT WOULD OCCUR. IT IS A GRAND ANOMALY OF—
WAIT... YOU **DID** ABSORB THE KAIRU COMPLETELY LAST TIME YOU WERE HERE, DIDN'T YOU??
WE'RE ON IT, MASTER BOADDAI! GOTTA GO!
I HAVE MORE INFORMATION! THERE IS SOMETHING TROUBLING ABOUT THIS BATCH. IT IS LARGE AND ODDLY ENOUGH...
...IT IS ON THE MOVE.
WHY DO I BOTHER?
GOOD LUCK, TEAM STAX.

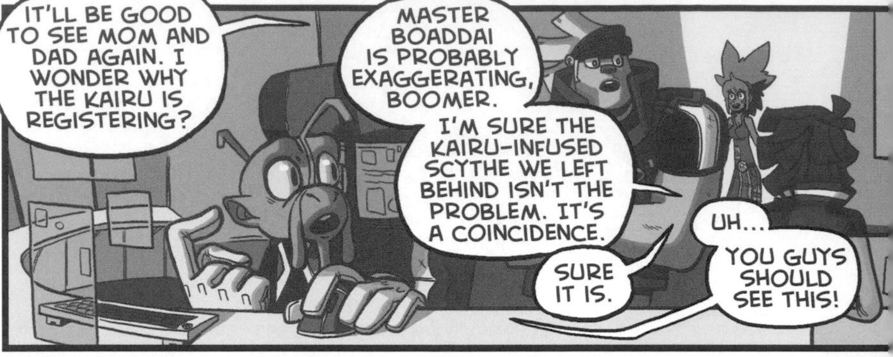
IT'LL BE GOOD TO SEE MOM AND DAD AGAIN. I WONDER WHY THE KAIRU IS REGISTERING?
MASTER BOADDAI IS PROBABLY EXAGGERATING, BOOMER.
I'M SURE THE KAIRU-INFUSED SCYTHE WE LEFT BEHIND ISN'T THE PROBLEM. IT'S A COINCIDENCE.
SURE IT IS.
UH...
YOU GUYS SHOULD SEE THIS!
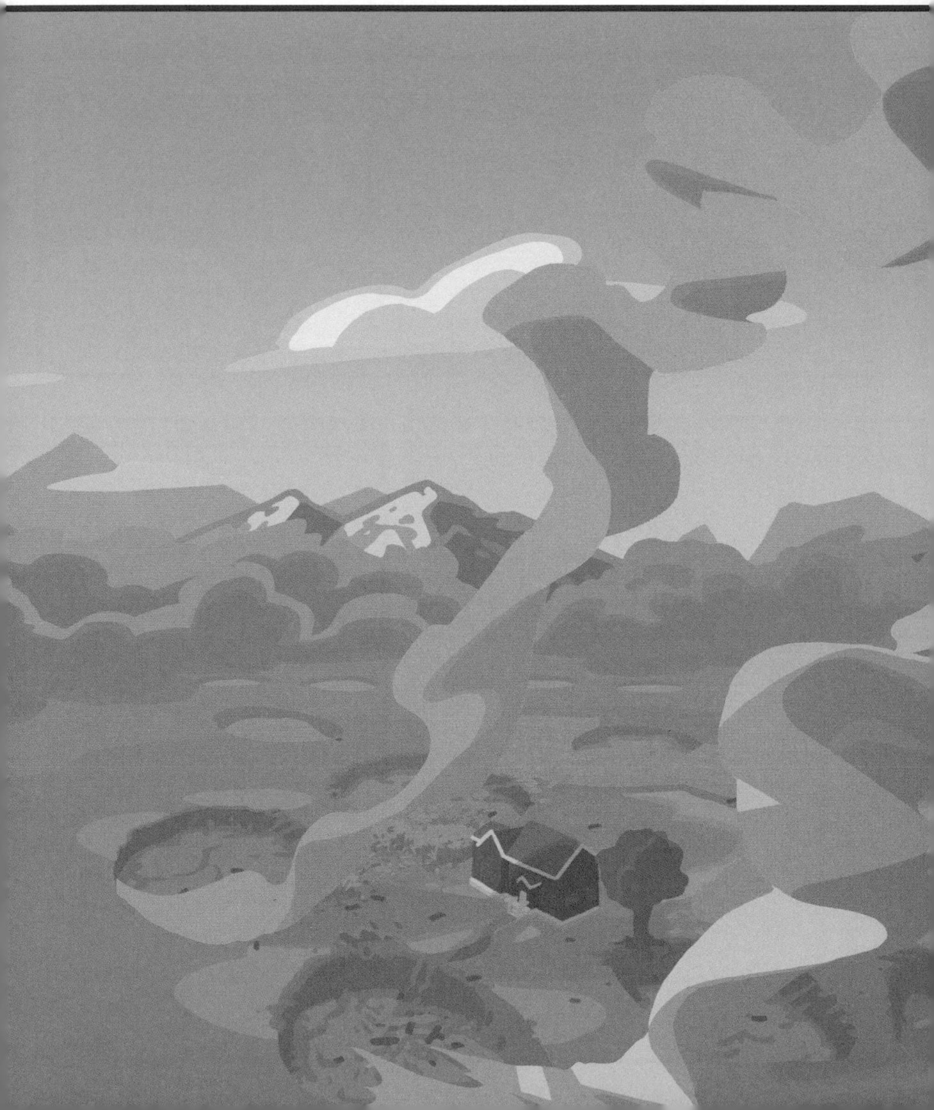

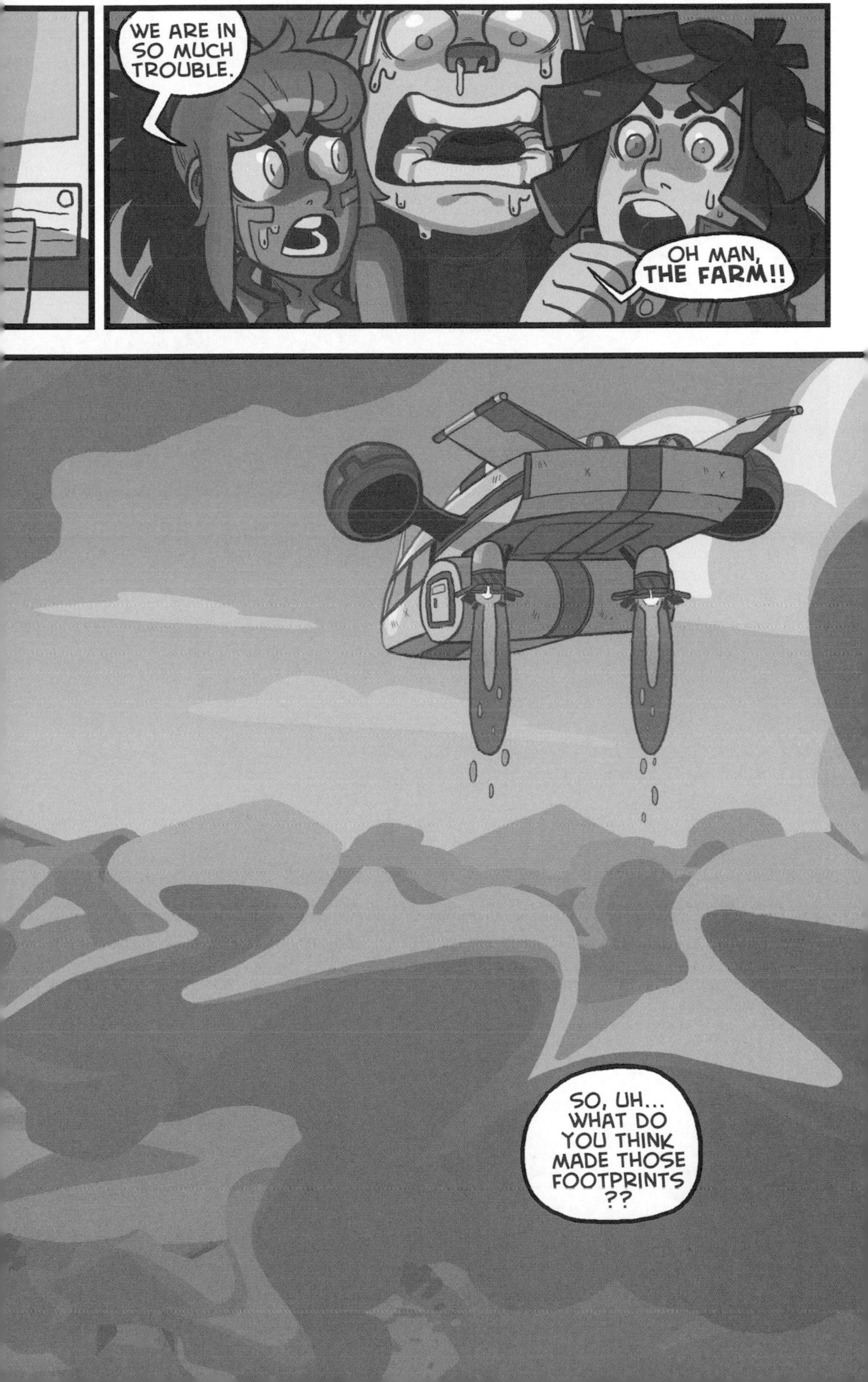
WE ARE IN SO MUCH TROUBLE.
OH MAN, THE FARM!!
SO, UH... WHAT DO YOU THINK MADE THOSE FOOTPRINTS ??

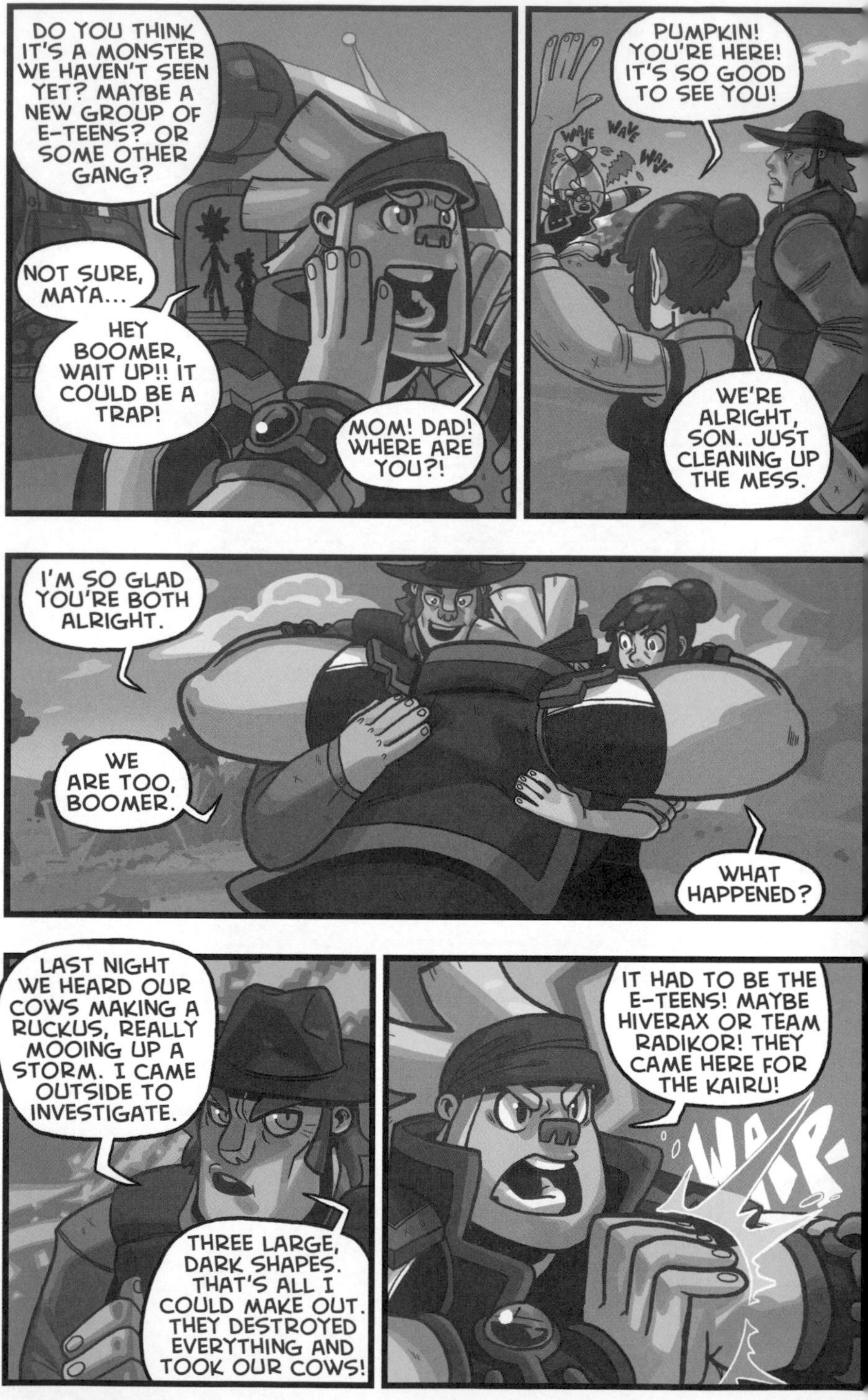
DO YOU THINK IT'S A MONSTER WE HAVEN'T SEEN YET? MAYBE A NEW GROUP OF E-TEENS? OR SOME OTHER GANG?
NOT SURE, MAYA...
HEY BOOMER, WAIT UP!! IT COULD BE A TRAP!
MOM! DAD! WHERE ARE YOU?!
PUMPKIN! YOU'RE HERE! IT'S SO GOOD TO SEE YOU!
WAVE WAVE WAVE
WE'RE ALRIGHT, SON. JUST CLEANING UP THE MESS.
I'M SO GLAD YOU'RE BOTH ALRIGHT.
WE ARE TOO, BOOMER.
WHAT HAPPENED?
LAST NIGHT WE HEARD OUR COWS MAKING A RUCKUS, REALLY MOOING UP A STORM. I CAME OUTSIDE TO INVESTIGATE.
THREE LARGE, DARK SHAPES. THAT'S ALL I COULD MAKE OUT. THEY DESTROYED EVERYTHING AND TOOK OUR COWS!
IT HAD TO BE THE E-TEENS! MAYBE HIVERAX OR TEAM RADIKOR! THEY CAME HERE FOR THE KAIRU!
WAP-

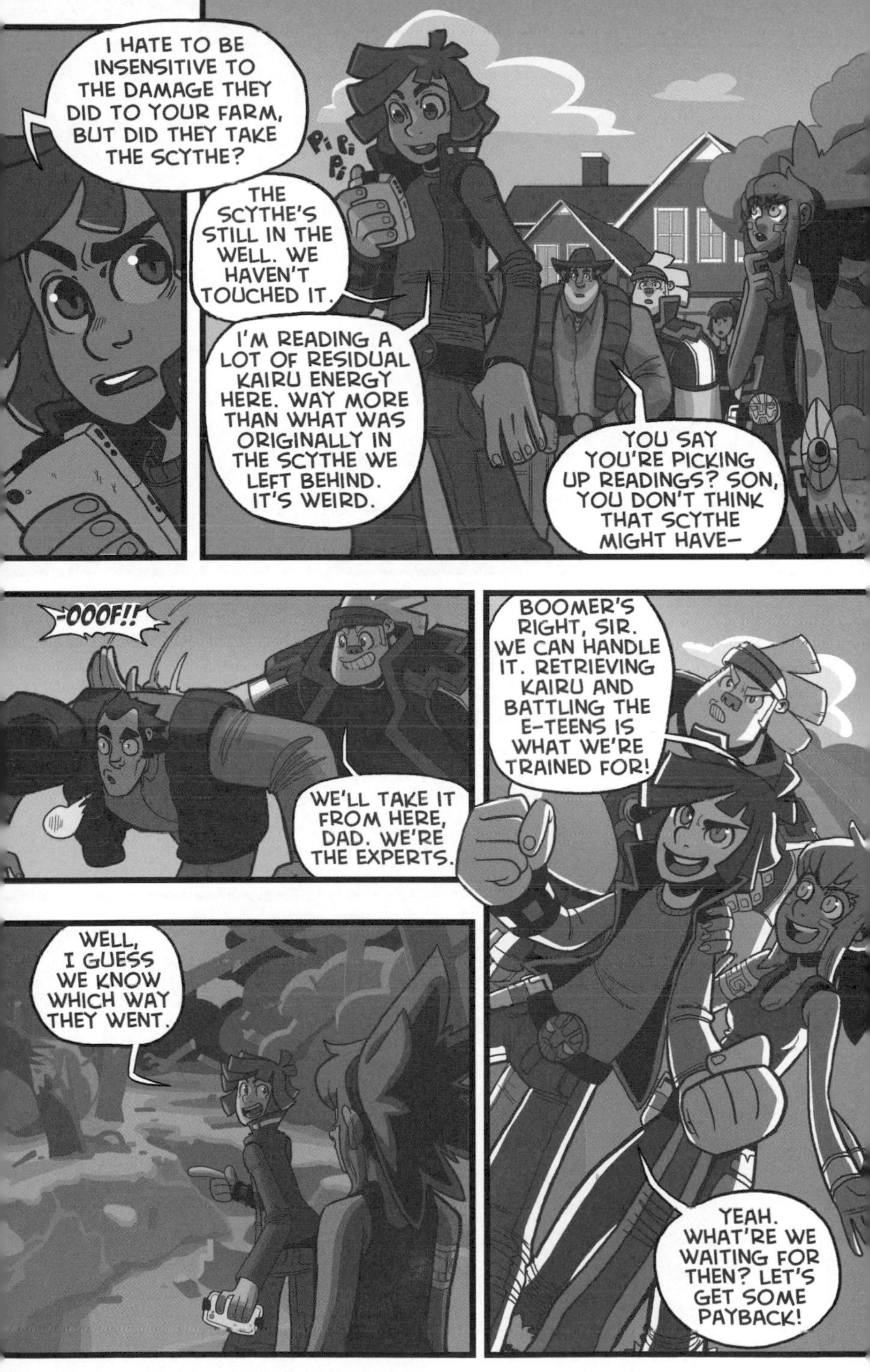
I HATE TO BE INSENSITIVE TO THE DAMAGE THEY DID TO YOUR FARM, BUT DID THEY TAKE THE SCYTHE?
Pi Pi Pi
THE SCYTHE'S STILL IN THE WELL. WE HAVEN'T TOUCHED IT.
I'M READING A LOT OF RESIDUAL KAIRU ENERGY HERE. WAY MORE THAN WHAT WAS ORIGINALLY IN THE SCYTHE WE LEFT BEHIND. IT'S WEIRD.
YOU SAY YOU'RE PICKING UP READINGS? SON, YOU DON'T THINK THAT SCYTHE MIGHT HAVE–
-OOOF!!
WE'LL TAKE IT FROM HERE, DAD. WE'RE THE EXPERTS.
BOOMER'S RIGHT, SIR. WE CAN HANDLE IT. RETRIEVING KAIRU AND BATTLING THE E-TEENS IS WHAT WE'RE TRAINED FOR!
WELL, I GUESS WE KNOW WHICH WAY THEY WENT.
YEAH. WHAT'RE WE WAITING FOR THEN? LET'S GET SOME PAYBACK!

GUYS, RELAX. YOU'RE NOT BEING VERY STEALTHY...

NO TIME. WE NEED TO FIND WHO TOOK THE KAIRU— FAST.

RIGHT. WELL, DOESN'T IT SEEM WEIRD WHOEVER ATTACKED WOULD USE THEIR MONSTER FORMS TO WREAK SO MUCH HAVOC?

WHY? BECAUSE THE E-TEENS ARE SUCH GOOD PEOPLE MOST OF THE TIME?

I'M NOT SAYING THAT, BOOMER. IT'S JUST...

WHY WASTE THE KAIRU TO RUN AWAY? THEY COULD HAVE JUST TAKEN WHAT THEY WANTED AND LEFT.

WHICH LEADS TO MY NEXT QUESTION. WHERE WAS THE OTHER KAIRU COMING FROM IF NOT THE SCYTHE?

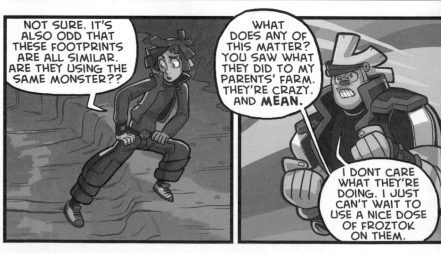

NOT SURE. IT'S ALSO ODD THAT THESE FOOTPRINTS ARE ALL SIMILAR. ARE THEY USING THE SAME MONSTER??

WHAT DOES ANY OF THIS MATTER? YOU SAW WHAT THEY DID TO MY PARENTS' FARM. THEY'RE CRAZY. AND **MEAN**.

I DONT CARE WHAT THEY'RE DOING. I JUST CAN'T WAIT TO USE A NICE DOSE OF FROZTOK ON THEM.

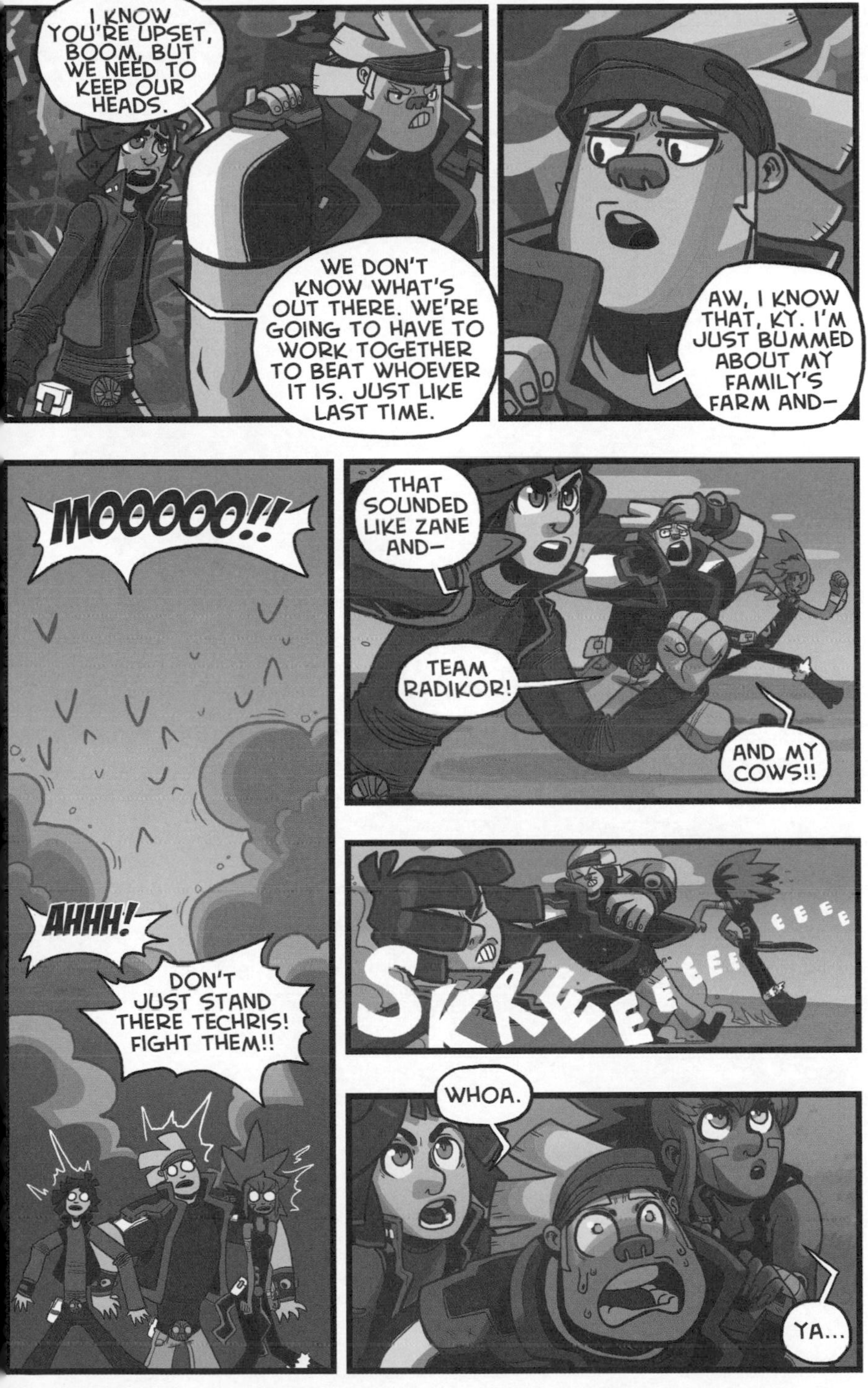
I KNOW YOU'RE UPSET, BOOM, BUT WE NEED TO KEEP OUR HEADS.
WE DON'T KNOW WHAT'S OUT THERE. WE'RE GOING TO HAVE TO WORK TOGETHER TO BEAT WHOEVER IT IS. JUST LIKE LAST TIME.
AW, I KNOW THAT, KY. I'M JUST BUMMED ABOUT MY FAMILY'S FARM AND—
MOOOOO!!
AHHH!
DON'T JUST STAND THERE TECHRIS! FIGHT THEM!!
THAT SOUNDED LIKE ZANE AND—
TEAM RADIKOR!
AND MY COWS!!
SKREEEEEEEEEEE
WHOA.
YA...

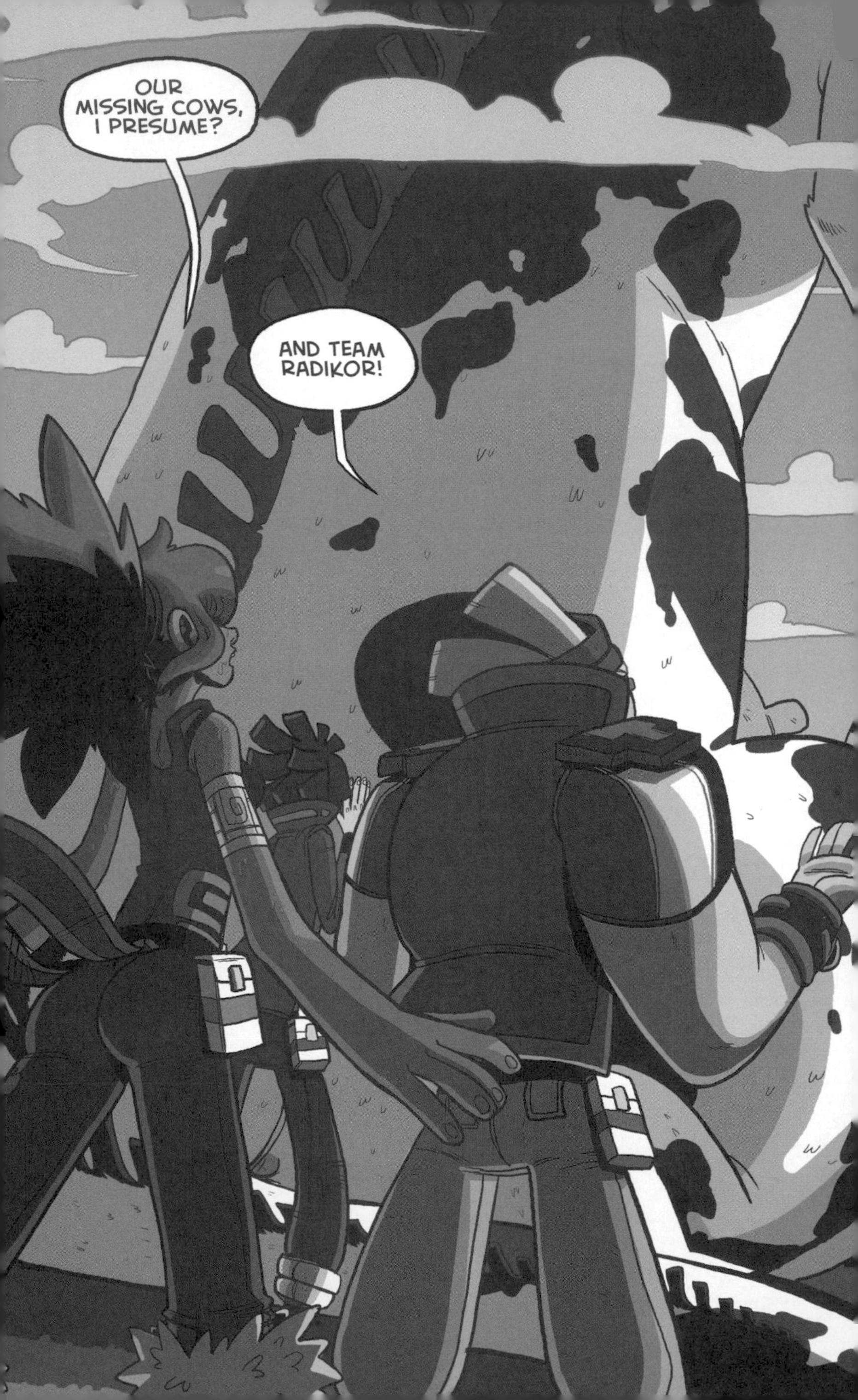
OUR MISSING COWS, I PRESUME?
AND TEAM RADIKOR!

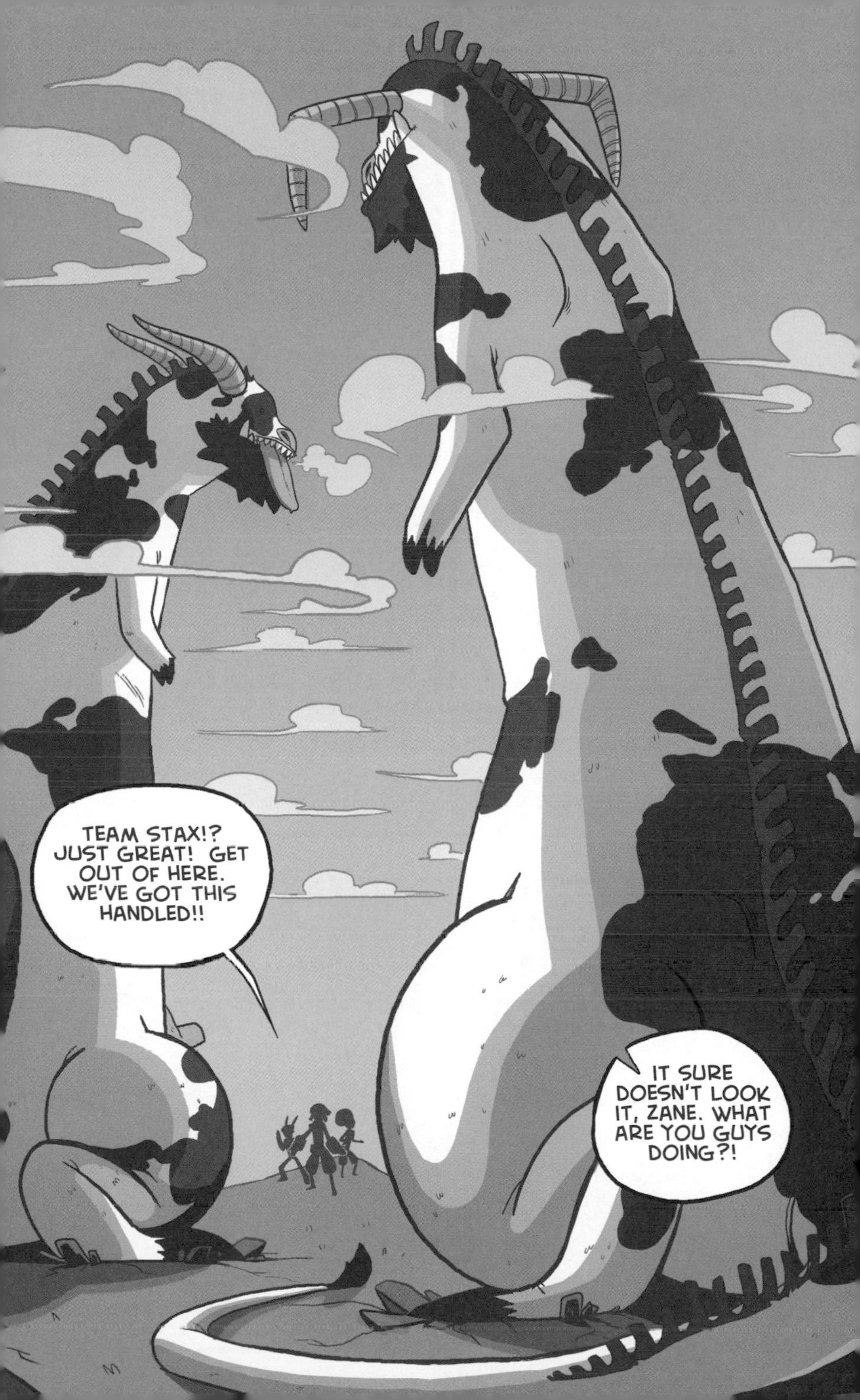
TEAM STAX!? JUST GREAT! GET OUT OF HERE. WE'VE GOT THIS HANDLED!!
IT SURE DOESN'T LOOK IT, ZANE. WHAT ARE YOU GUYS DOING?!

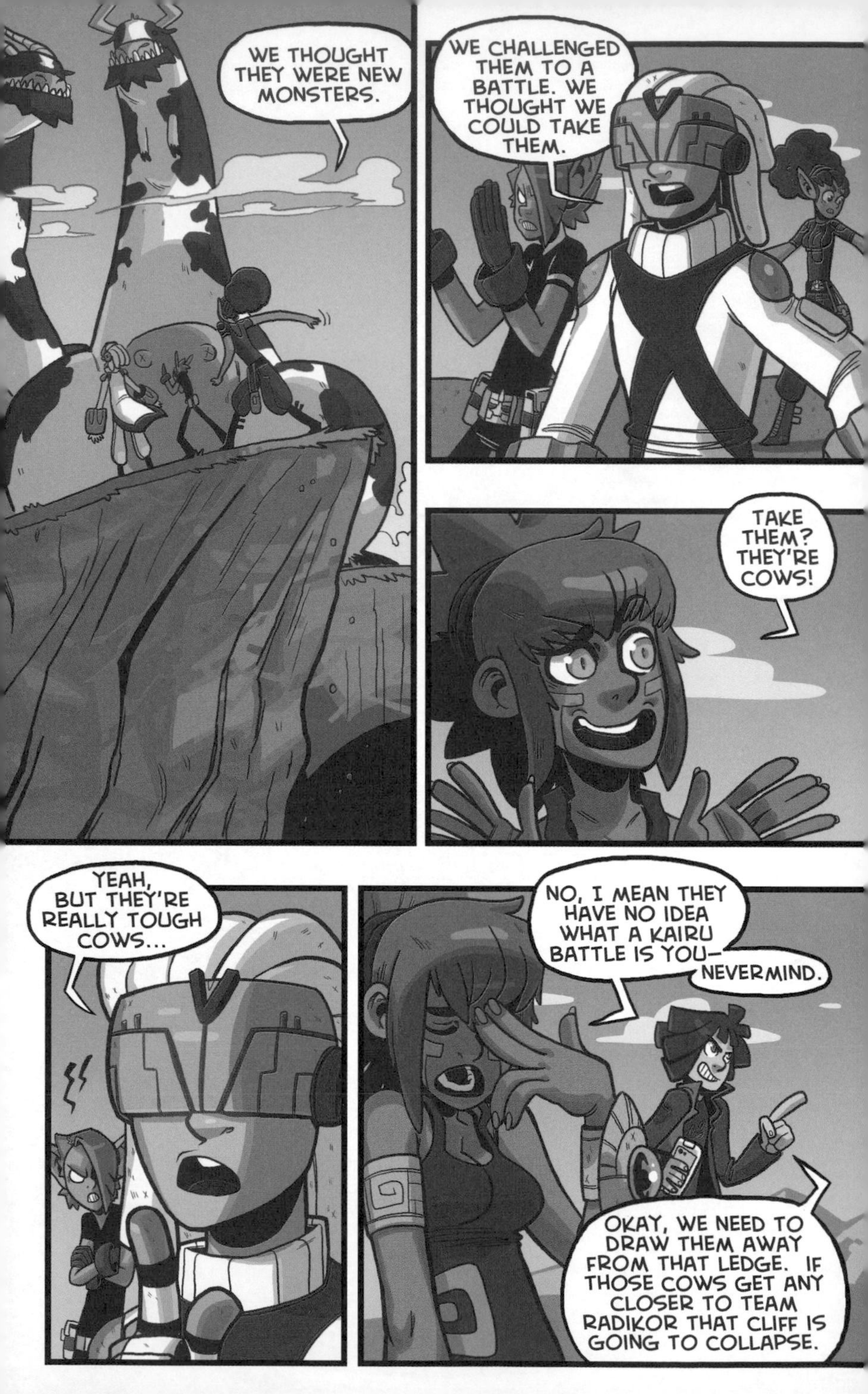
WE THOUGHT THEY WERE NEW MONSTERS.
WE CHALLENGED THEM TO A BATTLE. WE THOUGHT WE COULD TAKE THEM.
TAKE THEM? THEY'RE COWS!
YEAH, BUT THEY'RE REALLY TOUGH COWS...
NO, I MEAN THEY HAVE NO IDEA WHAT A KAIRU BATTLE IS YOU—
NEVERMIND.
OKAY, WE NEED TO DRAW THEM AWAY FROM THAT LEDGE. IF THOSE COWS GET ANY CLOSER TO TEAM RADIKOR THAT CLIFF IS GOING TO COLLAPSE.

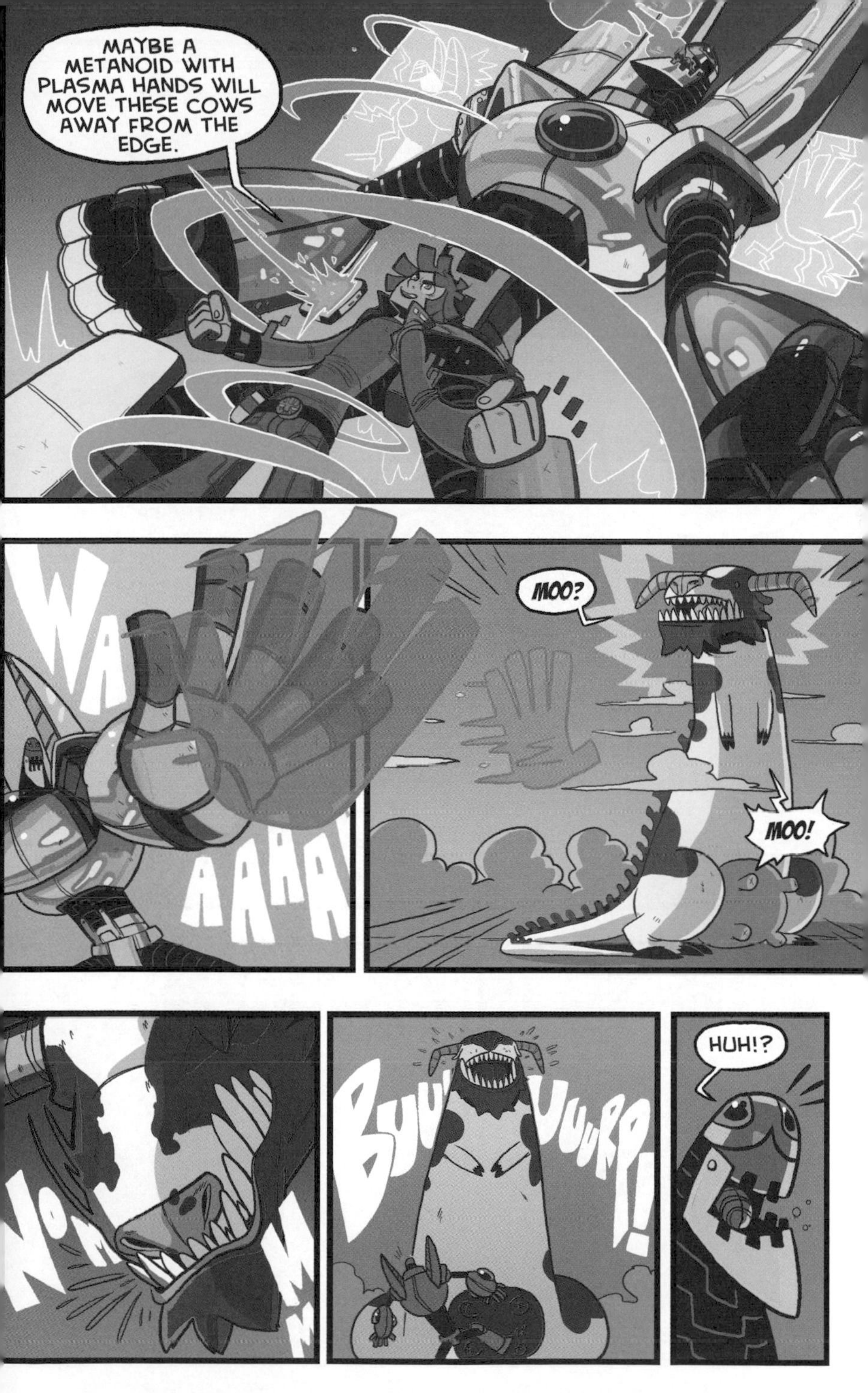
MAYBE A METANOID WITH PLASMA HANDS WILL MOVE THESE COWS AWAY FROM THE EDGE.
WAAAAA
MOO?
MOO!
NOM
BUUUUURP!
HUH!?

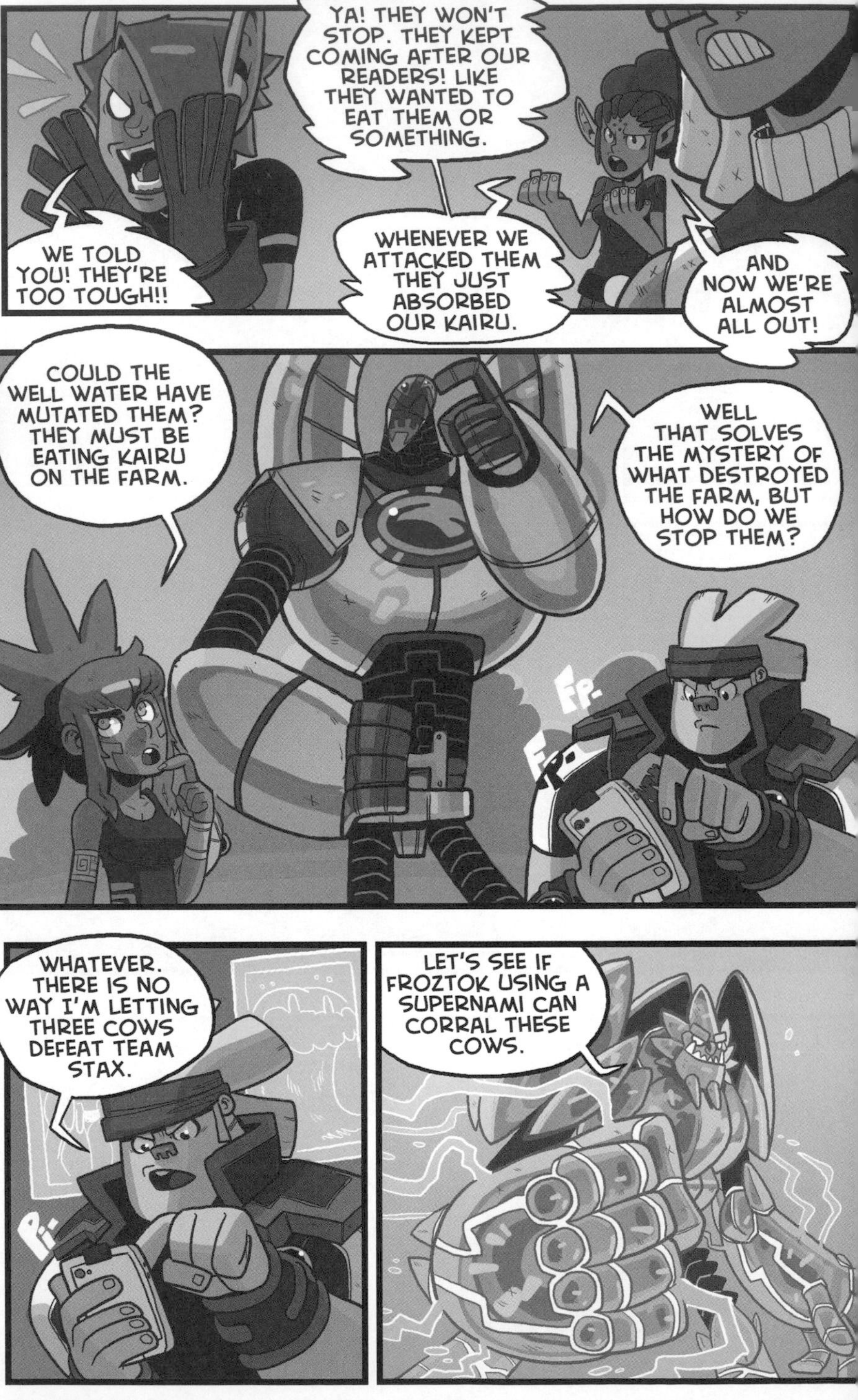

YA! THEY WON'T STOP. THEY KEPT COMING AFTER OUR READERS! LIKE THEY WANTED TO EAT THEM OR SOMETHING.
WE TOLD YOU! THEY'RE TOO TOUGH!!
WHENEVER WE ATTACKED THEM THEY JUST ABSORBED OUR KAIRU.
AND NOW WE'RE ALMOST ALL OUT!
COULD THE WELL WATER HAVE MUTATED THEM? THEY MUST BE EATING KAIRU ON THE FARM.
WELL THAT SOLVES THE MYSTERY OF WHAT DESTROYED THE FARM, BUT HOW DO WE STOP THEM?
FP-
FP-
WHATEVER. THERE IS NO WAY I'M LETTING THREE COWS DEFEAT TEAM STAX.
PI-
LET'S SEE IF FROZTOK USING A SUPERNAMI CAN CORRAL THESE COWS.

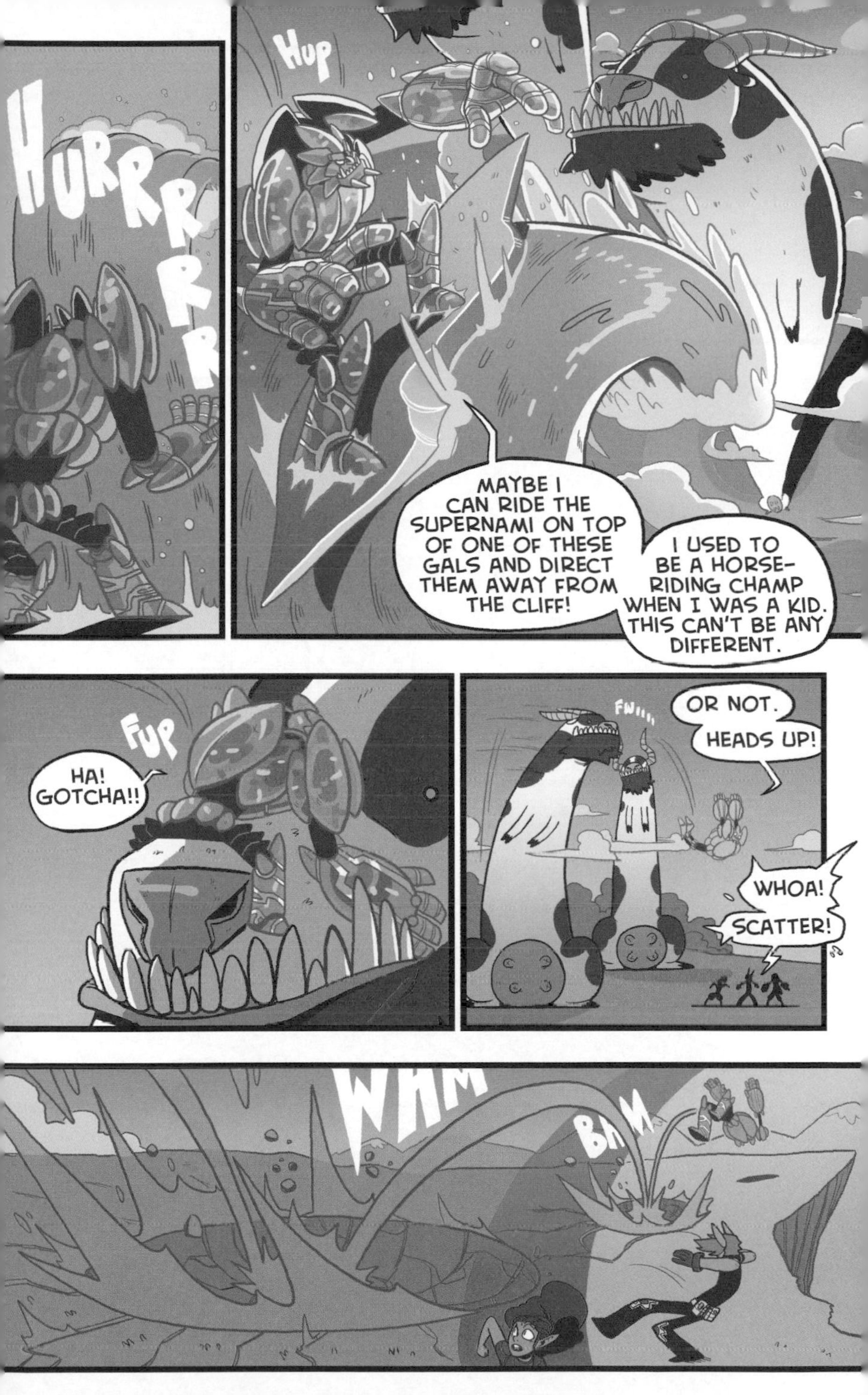
HURRRRR
HUP
MAYBE I CAN RIDE THE SUPERNAMI ON TOP OF ONE OF THESE GALS AND DIRECT THEM AWAY FROM THE CLIFF!
I USED TO BE A HORSE-RIDING CHAMP WHEN I WAS A KID. THIS CAN'T BE ANY DIFFERENT.
FUP
HA! GOTCHA!!
FWIII
OR NOT.
HEADS UP!
WHOA!
SCATTER!
WHAM
BAM

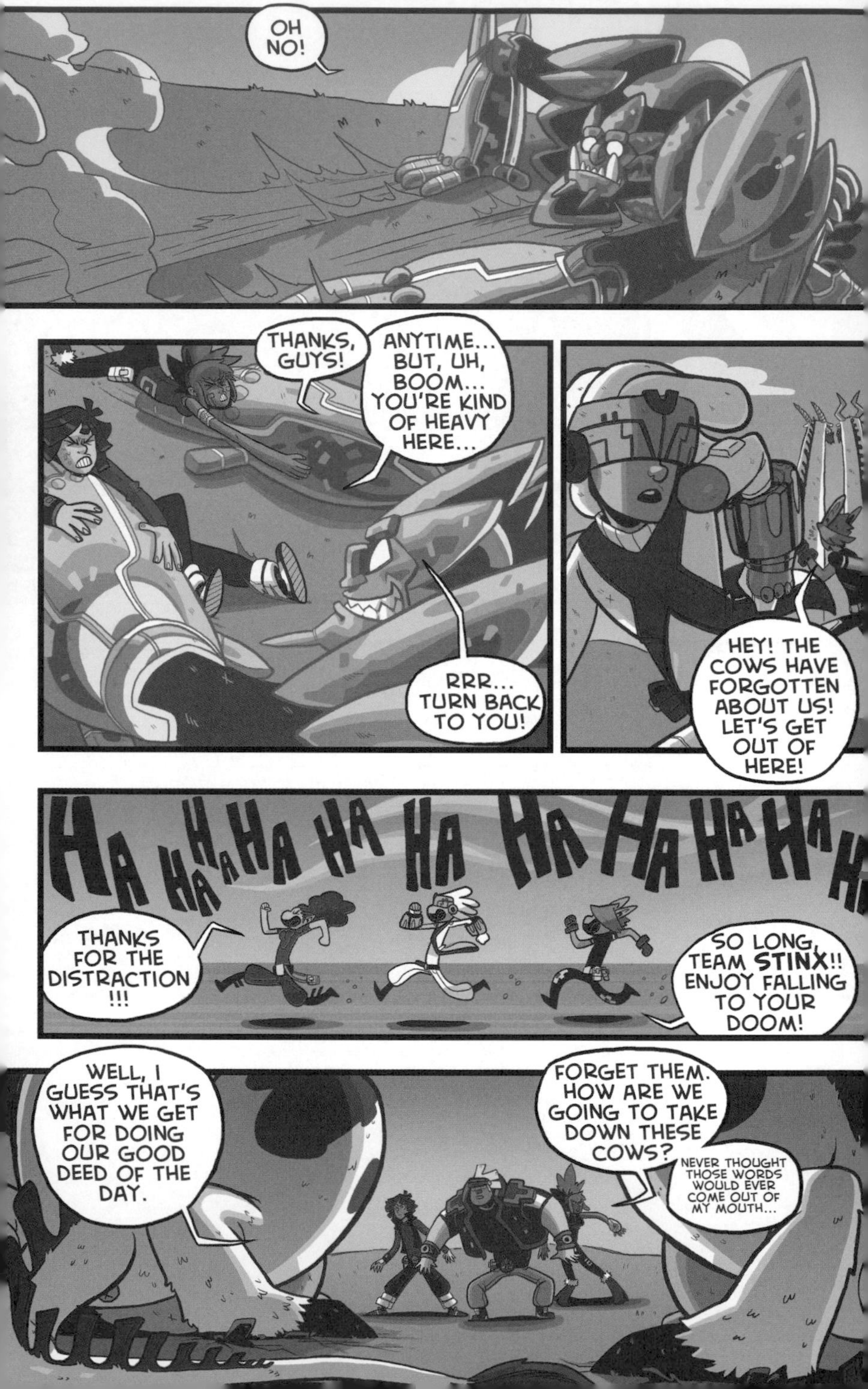
OH NO!
THANKS, GUYS!
ANYTIME... BUT, UH, BOOM... YOU'RE KIND OF HEAVY HERE...
RRR... TURN BACK TO YOU!
HEY! THE COWS HAVE FORGOTTEN ABOUT US! LET'S GET OUT OF HERE!
HA HA HA HA HA HA HA HA HA HA HA HA HA
THANKS FOR THE DISTRACTION !!!
SO LONG, TEAM STINX!! ENJOY FALLING TO YOUR DOOM!
WELL, I GUESS THAT'S WHAT WE GET FOR DOING OUR GOOD DEED OF THE DAY.
FORGET THEM. HOW ARE WE GOING TO TAKE DOWN THESE COWS?
NEVER THOUGHT THOSE WORDS WOULD EVER COME OUT OF MY MOUTH...

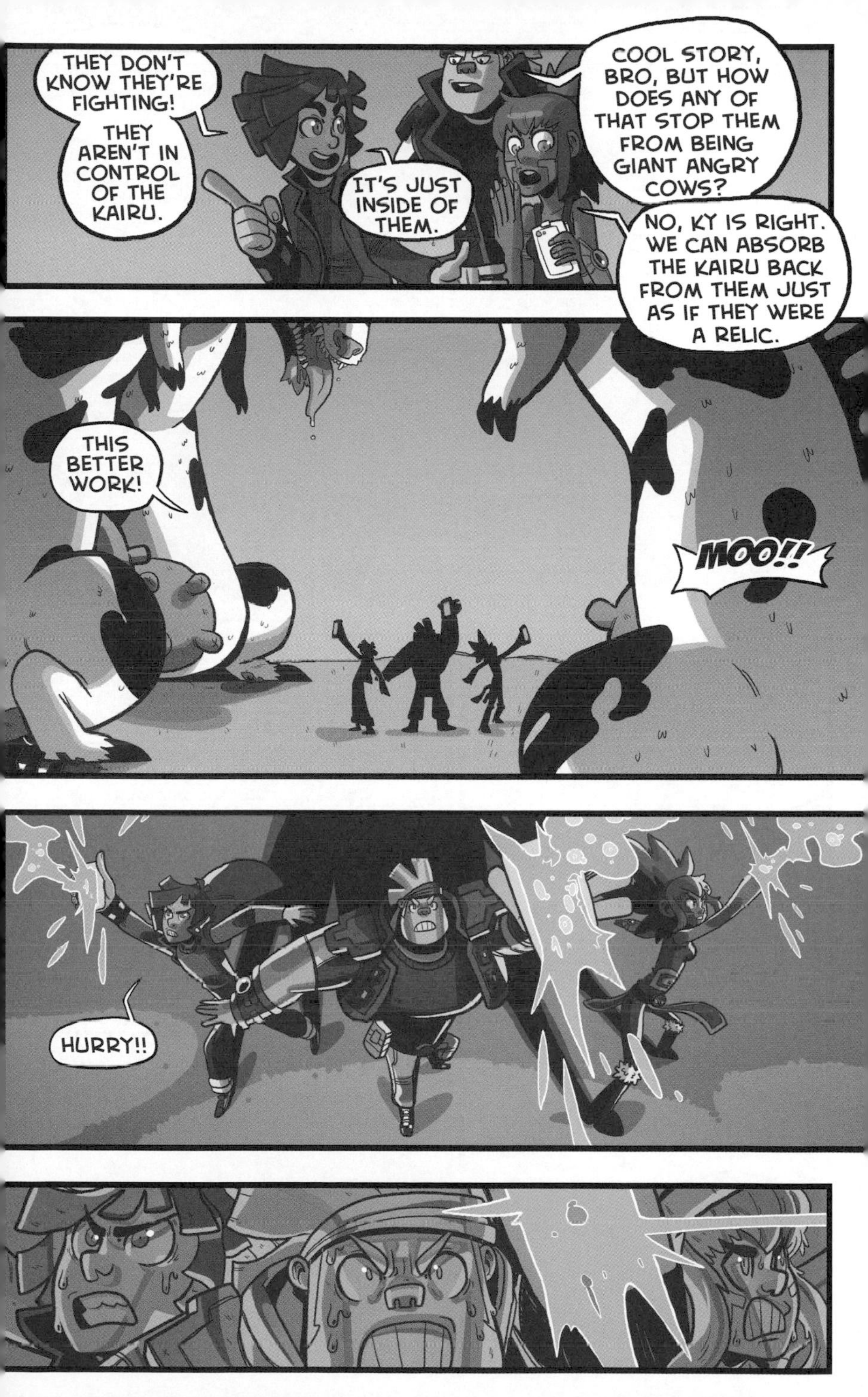
THEY DON'T KNOW THEY'RE FIGHTING!
THEY AREN'T IN CONTROL OF THE KAIRU.
IT'S JUST INSIDE OF THEM.
COOL STORY, BRO, BUT HOW DOES ANY OF THAT STOP THEM FROM BEING GIANT ANGRY COWS?
NO, KY IS RIGHT. WE CAN ABSORB THE KAIRU BACK FROM THEM JUST AS IF THEY WERE A RELIC.
THIS BETTER WORK!
MOO!!
HURRY!!

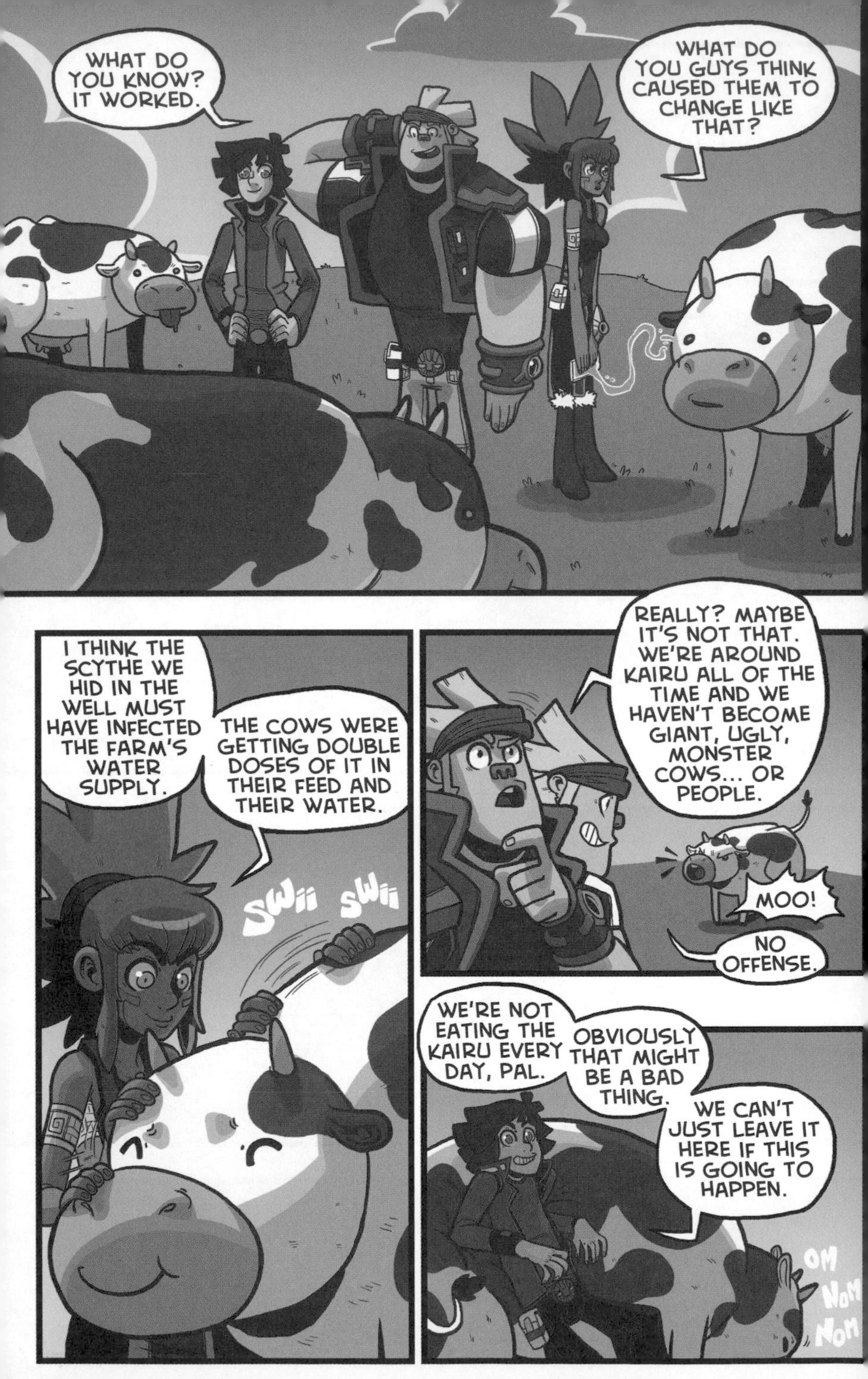
WHAT DO YOU KNOW? IT WORKED.
WHAT DO YOU GUYS THINK CAUSED THEM TO CHANGE LIKE THAT?
I THINK THE SCYTHE WE HID IN THE WELL MUST HAVE INFECTED THE FARM'S WATER SUPPLY.
THE COWS WERE GETTING DOUBLE DOSES OF IT IN THEIR FEED AND THEIR WATER.
SWII SWII
REALLY? MAYBE IT'S NOT THAT. WE'RE AROUND KAIRU ALL OF THE TIME AND WE HAVEN'T BECOME GIANT, UGLY, MONSTER COWS... OR PEOPLE.
MOO!
NO OFFENSE.
WE'RE NOT EATING THE KAIRU EVERY DAY, PAL.
OBVIOUSLY THAT MIGHT BE A BAD THING.
WE CAN'T JUST LEAVE IT HERE IF THIS IS GOING TO HAPPEN.
OM NOM NOM

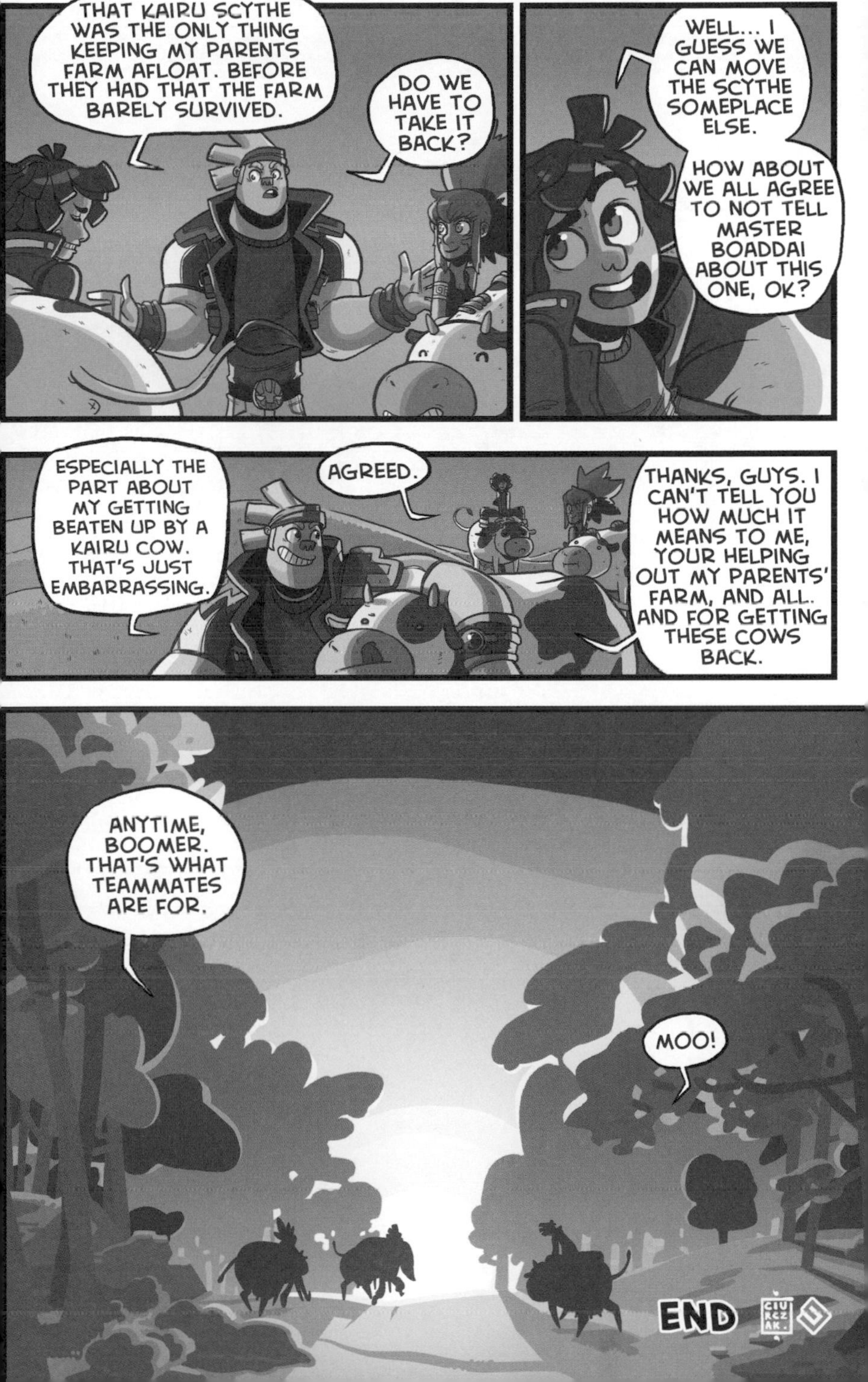
THAT KAIRU SCYTHE WAS THE ONLY THING KEEPING MY PARENTS FARM AFLOAT. BEFORE THEY HAD THAT THE FARM BARELY SURVIVED.
DO WE HAVE TO TAKE IT BACK?
WELL... I GUESS WE CAN MOVE THE SCYTHE SOMEPLACE ELSE.
HOW ABOUT WE ALL AGREE TO NOT TELL MASTER BOADDAI ABOUT THIS ONE, OK?
ESPECIALLY THE PART ABOUT MY GETTING BEATEN UP BY A KAIRU COW. THAT'S JUST EMBARRASSING.
AGREED.
THANKS, GUYS. I CAN'T TELL YOU HOW MUCH IT MEANS TO ME, YOUR HELPING OUT MY PARENTS' FARM, AND ALL. AND FOR GETTING THESE COWS BACK.
ANYTIME, BOOMER. THAT'S WHAT TEAMMATES ARE FOR.
MOO!
END
CIURCZAK

BONUS SKETCHES

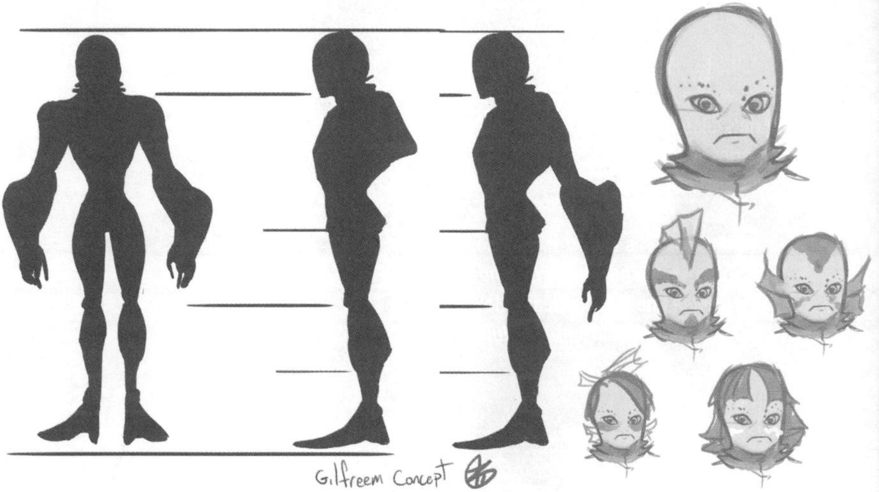
Gilfreem Concept

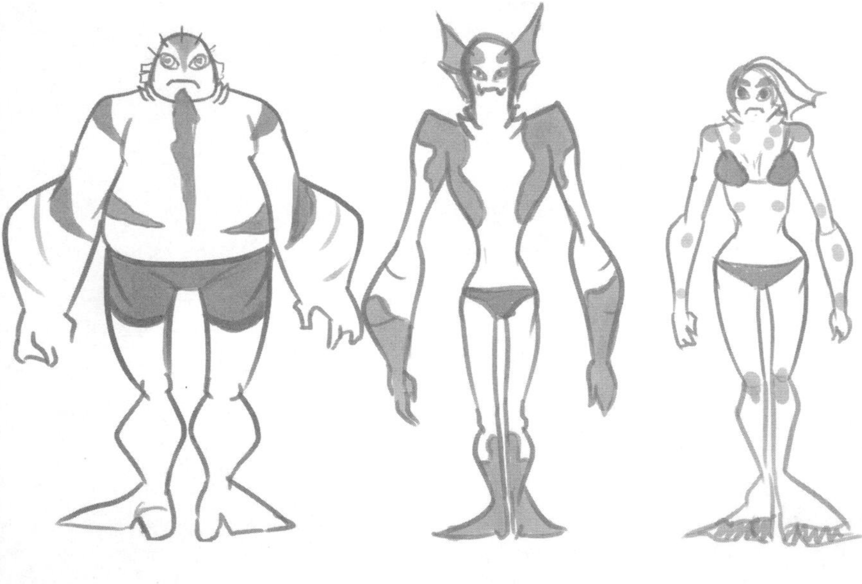

🦕 WRITERS

AUBREY SITTERSON began his comic book career at Marvel Comics, where he worked on many top-selling series including *New Avengers* and *Wolverine*. He's also written *Superboy* for DC Comics' *Superman 80-Page Giant* and a series of *Tech Jacket* stories in the pages of Robert Kirkman's *Invincible*, a series Aubrey also edited, for Image.

MIKE RAICHT is co-writer and co-creator of the *New York Times* best-selling graphic novel *The Stuff of Legend*. He worked as an editor at Marvel Comics on the *X-Men* line for four years. He's written both *Batman* and *Superman* for DC Comics, *Spider-Man* and *The Hulk* for Marvel and *GI Joe* and *Godzilla* for IDW.

🦕 ARTISTS

WRITE HEIGHT MEDIA is a creative team that includes Ray-Anthony Height, who has penciled for *Spider-Man* and *Teenage Mutant Ninja Turtles* for Marvel; artist Nate Lovett, who has worked with Hasbro properties including *GI Joe*, *Star Wars* and *Mr. Potato Head*; Matthew Wieman, who has inked for *Spider-Man* for Marvel and lettered for Bluewater; and Mickcy Clausen, who has done colors for *Toy Story* for Pixar and Boom; plus Paul Little on colors and Dwayne Biddix on pencils.

ZACK TURNER is a freelance artist working in comics and illustration. He has worked on several independent books as well as his own projects. He started out in the comics industry as a colorist on *Unimaginable* for Arcana and several projects for Bluewater and more recently has been working on full art duties.

DAN CIURCZAK is an independent comic book artist recently published in the Satellite Soda Anthology and is currently working on a new series for Oni Press.

CHAD "gammon" WALKER is a freelance artist and colorist living in Savannah, Georgia.

THERE'S MORE REDAKAI TO READ!

COMING SOON!
Volume 2: THE TIGER TERROR

Team Stax brings home a strange new energy source, a tiger idol infused with kairu and something else that attacks...*Master Boaddai*! Now Ky, Maya and Boomer are going to have to use all their training to save their teacher!

Plus, a bonus story, "Four's a Crowd." Is Connor trying to join Team Stax? That can't be anything but trouble!